Tracy Quan lives in New Y
Her writing has appear
Salon.com, *The Globe &*
Post, as well as other publ
been acquired by Revolu
picture, to be produced by Darren Star, creator of the TV
series *Sex and the City*. She is currently finishing her second
novel.

For automatic updates on Tracy Quan visit
harperperennial.co.uk and register for AuthorTracker.

'Chock-full of bad-girl secrets … tantalizing' *Cosmopolitan*

'Bridget Jones with attitude'   *Guardian*

'A page-turner'   *New York Daily News*

'Nothing's quite as refreshing as a novel that rings true, and
few recent novels have rung truer than *Diary of a Manhattan
Call Girl*. Long on humor and intriguing, utterly believable
scenarios, this book is rated R – for real'   *New York Post*

'Hilarious'   *New York Times*

'Wise, observant and – best of all – fun' *Los Angeles Times*

TRACY QUAN

Diary of a Manhattan Call Girl

HARPER PERENNIAL

London, New York, Toronto and Sydney

Harper Perennial
An imprint of HarperCollins*Publishers*
77–85 Fulham Palace Road, Hammersmith, London W6 8JB

www.harperperennial.co.uk

This edition published by Harper Perennial 2005
3

First published by Three Rivers Press, New York, 2001

A catalogue record for this book is available from the British Library

This novel is entirely a work of fiction. The names, characters and incidents
portrayed in it are the work of the author's imagination. Any resemblance to
actual persons, living or dead, events or localities is entirely coincidental.

ISBN 0 00 720439 6

Grateful acknowledgement is made to the following for permission to reprint
their copyrighted material appearing on pages 170 and 188–89:

Noonday Press: From 'High Windows' from *Philip Larkin: Collected Poems*
by Philip Larkin. Copyright © 1998 by the Estate of Philip Larkin. Used by
permission of Farrar, Straus & Giroux, Inc., and Faber and Faber (UK).

MCA Universal Music Publishing Group: From 'The Folks Who Live on the Hill'.
Words by Oscar Hammerstein II, music by Jerome Kern. Copyright © 1937 T.B.
Harms & Company Incorporated, USA. Universal Music Publishing Limited.
All rights reserved. International copyright secured.

Author photograph © Hamilton

Set in Simoncini Garamond

Printed and bound in Great Britain by Clays Ltd, St Ives plc

for
Mike Godwin

Acknowledgments

I'd like to thank David Talbot, Carol Lloyd, and Chris Colin of Salon.com, where Nancy's diary first appeared; my agents, John Brockman, Katinka Matson, and Peter Benedek; and my editor at Crown, Doug Pepper, for his guidance and constant support.

My special thanks to Mike Godwin for being an excellent editor and so much more—my first reader and dear friend whose vision and input made this book, and the Nancy Chan series in Salon, possible.

Bonnie Thompson, Charles Peck, Linda Jacobs (nee Nostradamus), and Dana Friedman (Dragonfly Technologies) rescued me from real and imaginary perils with practical solutions.

Steven Richardson-Ross, Hugh Loebner, Emma Hurley, Cynthia Connors, Joe Lavezzo, Jo Weldon, Melissa Hope, Steph Wilcock, Ellis Henican, Jerry Labush, Julian aka Boytoy, Ralph Martin, Synn Stern, Ben Burch, Ian Williams, Cheryl Overs, Dana Tierney, Giovanna, Andrew Sorfleet, Stan Bernstein, Jim Geffert, Vic St. Blaise, Sam Silver, Toisan Craigg, Will Crutchfield, Patricia Flynn, Mari Aldin, Paul Shields, Wendy-Joy Robertson, Adrian, David Andrew, Bruce Lambert, Desmond Mervyn, and Frances: thank you for your feedback, advice, and support.

For the special talents of Susan Schwartzman, Alex Lencicki, Stephen Lee, Jason Gordon, Juleyka Lantigua, Karen Minster, and Mary Schuck, I am immensely grateful.

Contents

All
professions
are
conspiracies
against
the
laity.
—GEORGE BERNARD SHAW

Everything
is more
glamorous
when
you
do it
in bed. . . .
—ANDY WARHOL

1 Ménage à Quoi?

Dear Diary,

Today I had the most embarrassing experience—with one
of my regulars. Howard was flat on his back enjoying our
threesome with Allison when I decided to straddle him
backward—something I've done hundreds of times. So I
carefully lowered my body, confident that my acrobatics looked
like zero effort.

Howard stood firm inside of me, but I threw in a just-in-case moan
for good measure. With my shoulder blades resting against his chest, all he
could see was the back of my neck. Lying still in that position is more work
than bouncing up and down, but it's usually the perfect strategy when
you're doing a session with another girl. Howard can't check to see whether
her tongue is really where it's supposed to be. And besides, it's his favorite
position.

I felt serene. Supple. At the top of my game. Allie slithered down to the
edge of my bed, placing her head somewhere between my legs—and his. I
felt her long blond hair tickling my thighs. My cue to start moaning louder:
"She's *soooo good* at that . . . she's licking my clit! Tell her not to stop! Oh,
please don't stop . . ."

Unfortunately, when I thought Allison was pretending to do *me,* she
was really doing Howard.

"Hey!" she whispered, when he had disappeared into the shower.
"When you were telling him all that stuff, I was tickling his balls with
my tongue!"

"You were?" I was indignant. "We're supposed to pretend you're eating my pussy! If you're going to change the routine, you have to tell me," I hissed. "You know I can't see what you're doing from that angle!"

"*He* seemed to like what I was doing!"

"Well," I was forced to concede, "I suppose that's what really matters." But still. How annoying.

Turning my attention to the bedroom phone, I quickly checked my voice mail. Jasmine's crisp clarity—"Thursday. Don't be late. Harry at five P.M.!"—was a welcome distraction. Then voice mail from Eileen: "I gave your number to Steven G. He's dying to meet another Oriental. But he's kind of kinky, so call me first. It's for today!" Eileen Wong's clients tend to be impulse buyers with a hundred strange quirks. And a message from Steven himself, sounding bashful but eager: "Hi, uh, well, I'll have to call you back. Hello? Are you there? I'm on my way to an ATM. I'll call back in ten minutes." There was street noise in the background. Car phone? Pay phone? Hard to tell. He sounds like the type of guy who's cautious enough to use a pay phone when he calls a working girl. Probably married. Or maybe just self-conscious and paranoid about whatever it is that turns him on.

Allison mumbled apologetically into her cashmere sweater as she pulled it over her face: "Honestly, I thought you could see me, Nancy! I didn't know . . ." As her pale shoulders disappeared into the sweater, her silly ingratiating grimace *almost* made me back down.

"How can I possibly see you if I'm staring at the ceiling?" I retorted crossly.

Howard returned, a towel wrapped around his soft damp middle, smirking with satisfaction. I was furious with myself for revealing a trade secret. To a john I've been seeing for more than five years! But I brazened it out with professional blitheness. As I bade him farewell, he winked and said, "See you next Monday—I'll bring two Oscars. You both earned them!" I flashed him a cool smile.

Allison followed me into the bathroom, pondering her latest dilemma out loud. "Guess who called? Jack! He's trying to make an appointment with me!"

This is so typical. Whenever I'm annoyed with Allison, she tries to distract me with her problems.

Jack can still find new girls through the back pages of *New York* magazine, but he's barred from the beds of girls like us who trade customers privately. Shouldn't Allie know better than to contemplate seeing Jack?

From behind the shower door, I reminded her, "We blacklisted him! Nobody wants to see Jack after what he did. And neither do you."

"Well, maybe I *do*," she said petulantly. "He misses me and he's offering me a lot of money. Maybe I should reconsider this—this blacklist thing."

We blacklisted him because of what he did last year—and Allie was the *first* girl to experience the terrible fallout of Jack's behavior. How can she forget? Much less forgive?

I pointed the handheld showerhead between my thighs, then aimed it cautiously at my breasts, to avoid splattering my hair. It's an occupational hazard, showering four times a day: My hair has to look great for work, yet I'm constantly in danger of wrecking it . . . Catch-22!

"He offered me a thousand!" Allie was saying. "Just to see me for—you know, the usual."

His normal rate is three hundred dollars. A grand for half an hour! That's hard to turn down. But Allison doesn't need to hear that. She needs to learn how to say no and mean it.

"After what he did to us, I think it would be a major betrayal for *any* girl to make an exception," I told her.

"But I have—I mean, Jack and I *had*—a different kind of . . ." Her voice grew squeaky and faint. "Well, anyway, I'd like to hear his side of the story."

Yeah, I'll *bet* she would! For a thousand dollars, who wouldn't? But the point is, your word's not worth much if you say yes to everything that looks financially appealing. Or easy.

"His *side*? He has no side. I don't care how much he pays, dealing with him is just too risky."

"He's so easy," Allie pointed out. "And he wears a condom for *everything*."

"We're not talking about *that* kind of risk! And you have to stop thinking in the short term! He gives you a grand today and that's great. What happens later? What if you lose all your contacts with the other girls? Jack's generosity won't make up for that. Ever."

As I slid the shower door open, Allison handed me a towel. That childish pleading look again! Even though we're the same size—we can trade bras—I suddenly felt like the huge clumsy playmate of a delicate fine-boned little girl. I stared into the bathroom mirror and saw, reflected back, a surprisingly graceful neck. Not the awkward galumphing outcast—a ghost from early puberty—that I sometimes imagine myself to be. And my hair had kept its shape.

Like me, Allie looks easily ten years younger than she really is. If we were aging at different rates, would we have stayed friends for so long? In fact, I wonder sometimes if looks are the basis for *most* female friendships: the looker who takes up with a lesser looker because it bolsters her ego; the attractive girl who (having learned *that* lesson) seeks out pretty friends so she won't have to deal with another woman's jealousy raging out of control—it's easier to manage your own insecurities, after all. Those of another girl can be hard to read, impossible to quell, and therefore highly dangerous. Allie and I have our problems—I know in my heart that it's not the healthiest friendship—but where looks are concerned, ours is a bond between equals. And that's important.

"I didn't agree to *do* anything with him," Allison was insisting. "We're just talking about it."

"You shouldn't even be talking to him," I warned her.

If I wasn't as pretty, she'd suspect me of sabotaging her out of jealousy. And if *she* wasn't as pretty, she'd hate me for being so dismissive of male admiration. Allie appeared to be listening respectfully, but she became distracted and started glancing at her watch. I gave up.

Before she left, Allison begged me not to mention Jack's phone calls to Jasmine. "You know how she jumps to conclusions!" she simpered. "Jasmine's so judgmental. And she might tell everyone." She tucked four hundreds into a shiny pink Louis Vuitton backpack and zipped it shut.

Maybe I *should* take the cut from Allie, instead of relying on her to send me back a date, but her parting words killed that possibility: "Oh, good! I can pay my rent now. Thanks! I'll send you someone soon. Okay?" Catching the look on my face, she added, "February's rent! It's due *tomorrow.* I have to get to the bank."

"You're seeing guys to pay the rent *the day before it's due*—?" Before I could finish, the phone interrupted me. Allie headed for the elevator as I grabbed the ringing phone.

"I think I missed Steven's call," I told Eileen. "I have to go out now. I can see him around seven."

"Oh. *Bummer.*" Eileen sighed. "You have to get this guy while he's hot. He'll call next week. Do you have sheer stockings? They have to be sheer, not stretch. And *please* don't wear platforms—he likes real heels."

"Platforms? Why would I wear platforms with a john?"

"You wouldn't believe what the last girl wore. These new girls! Listen, I know he'll call. He wants to see an Oriental—badly. Don't let him make an appointment for the next day, though.

He'll screw it up. If he calls when you're not busy, that's the best way to see him. He's very fast. Three fifty. Be cold and bitchy but don't order him around. He's not a slave. But he wants to worship you . . ."

What kind of guy knows the difference between sheer and stretch stockings? For $350, I'm quite intrigued. Eileen and I trade a lot of business—we both have clients who go for the petite Asian look, though I think my guys are less fixated on it. (A lot of my clients enjoy Allison, too—maybe it's the blond contrast.) Funny how every call girl I know ends up with a certain *type* of regular. Eileen's customers are fetishistic, Jasmine's are among the quickest. I'm not sure how to define a typical Allison client . . . not sure I *want* to.

"Hey, by the way. I've been getting these calls," Eileen said. "Hang-ups! And voice mail with lots of stupid breathing. Ever since I heard from you-know-who."

"Oh god. Jack?"

"Yeah. The nerve! He acts like nothing happened, you know? Like we don't *know*."

"Well, don't let on!" I said, alarmed. "Just tell him you're busy and get off the phone—*politely*."

When you blacklist a client, he's not supposed to know about it.

"Look, I don't have to humor him—not after what he did to *me!* Blabbing to that—"

"If he finds out he's being blacklisted, he might take it out on you in some way! What's more important? Being right? Or being happy? And safe?"

"Well, I hung up on him, okay? I told him to leave me alone. And now I'm getting these calls. I bet it's Jack! He has no right to do this."

Between Allison wanting to make up with him, and Eileen self-righteously provoking him, I really don't know what to do.

The whole idea was to turn the volume *down* on this guy in the hopes that he would just go away and stay out of our circle. Ever since he—

Yikes—almost 3:30. All the cabs are changing shifts! It will be a nightmare getting across town. Must log off *NOW, SOON,* five minutes ago, if I really plan to be on time for therapy.

MONDAY NIGHT

Despite the traffic, I actually snagged a taxi quickly, by offering an off-duty cabby twenty dollars. Stuck in Central Park traffic during the crosstown pilgrimage to Dr. Kessel's funky West Side office, I couldn't stop thinking about Allison and Jack. She still has a soft spot for the guy. Her taste in men has always been appalling. And yet she has a natural talent for this business. Strange. . . . And Eileen will be pissed if she hears that Allison has been talking to him. As will Jasmine. And everyone else. Oh god. And they'll be furious with me if they find out that I knew and didn't tell them. Why does Allie put me in these impossible binds? Why do I tolerate it?

As I emerged from the park, I spotted a big picture of Tony Soprano's shrink on the side of a bus shelter. This week, the Sopranos are everywhere—magazines, bus shelters, you name it—and everyone seems to identify with Tony for some reason. But my shrink's much hipper than Dr. Melfi; for one thing, she's on a first-name basis with her patients. And, unlike Tony, I'm a savvy veteran of self-absorption, as unembarrassed about seeing a shrink as I am about getting a monthly haircut. And yet. Just like Tony, I must take this radical leap of faith! In my case, it's about leaving my cozy East Side cocoon for the shopless tree-lined wasteland that is Riverside Drive.

I may be one of Manhattan's therapized elite, but I'm still coming to terms with some aspects of the process—like having my recently blown-out hair savagely *re*blown by the punishing wind off the Hudson. Examining my hair—again—in the lobby mirror of Dr. Kessel's solid prewar building, I was struck by the hugeness of her lobby. It's like being in a cathedral. The West Side, whether indoors or out, is so disorienting. Leaving the East Seventies is like getting squeezed out of a grid-shaped womb into wide-avenued *anarchy*.

I sat patiently in Dr. Wendy's waiting room, taking in the unchanged ethnic pottery, the Arts and Crafts furniture, while another patient went overtime. I've never told Wendy how simple it is to eavesdrop in that second chair to the left of the bookshelves.

"I can't stand it!" a female voice was saying. "I don't want to be confined or constrained in any way . . . I don't like it when he asks for a date on *Wednesday* . . ." The voice became muffled and my listening spree ended. Minutes later, a mousy girl—unaware that the acoustics had been working against her—strolled past, carrying a Coach briefcase. I was impressed. Some guy is trying to constrain *her?* Maybe she's more interesting than she looks. . . . My turn.

After ranting—not too audibly—about Allison for a few minutes, I noticed a bemused expression on Dr. Wendy's face.

"I feel betrayed," I grumbled, but I didn't go into the Howard mix-up. It would take half my session just to explain the physical mechanics, let alone the irritating dynamics, of my three-way with Allison. Instead, I sputtered on as best I could about Allison and Jack, trying to get the feelings accurate without discussing the money or the other girls or any of the classified details. I wanted to tell her about Eileen, but I stopped myself.

Finally, I said, "I guess I'm stuck with Allison. With her lousy judgment and her silly narcissism. And the fallout."

"Is this why you came back?" Wendy interrupted. "Because of your relationship with Allison?"

"No." I fell silent. It's been over a year and there's quite a lot Wendy doesn't know. And not *just* because I have to withhold so much business info in our sessions. "It's a relationship with a guy. I'm—we're—in love. We got involved last spring."

"Well, perhaps we should get caught up on that. Is he a client?"

"No, a straight guy."

"When you say he's a straight guy, you mean . . . ?"

I held up my left hand as if it were a shield and spun my ring around. I told her: "He works on Wall Street. His boss is Pamela Knight. She was on *Moneyline* last week. He's one of her bright young rising stars." Wendy's dark lashes flickered, but I couldn't tell whether she recognized Pam's name. "He wouldn't understand my business. He's always had a straight job. His entire life he's been so—so normal that he doesn't even know how normal he is. The other night, we were watching *The Sopranos* and he started telling me how corporate life is just like a Mafia hierarchy. Where does he get these ideas? The most unusual job he ever had was a stint as a golf caddie in college! He would never understand how his girlfriend could have a job that's—well, not exactly legal." To say the least. "And all the guys I've been with."

"But most of your clients are, essentially, straight guys and *they* understand. Don't they?"

"Y-yes. Pretty much."

"Obviously, it's not his work that sets your boyfriend apart from your clients."

"Okay," I said. "It's not him. It's me! He doesn't know I'm a hooker. I'm pretending to be a straight chick. And it's working! And that makes him a straight guy. It's . . . I feel like Dr. Frankenhooker."

Wendy smiled. "Well, it's how he perceives you rather than who he might actually be. If you feel like you're shaping his reality, it's a heady but onerous responsibility—"

"And his sister's an assistant D.A.!" I interrupted. "And my cousin Miranda introduced us. So if Matt finds out what I really do, he could freak out and say something to her. To my family! To *his* family."

"Hang on," she said. "Just refresh me on Miranda. She's older than you? A sort of big sister?"

If I can keep track of my clients' stories, why can't my shrink keep track of mine?

"No. Miranda's almost ten years *younger* than me," I seethed. "After college she moved to New York and bought a co-op loft. Uncle Gregory pays all her bills. That's her dad. *He's* older. I mean, he's my mother's eldest brother."

"Yes." Dr. Wendy looked alert. "I remember now." She did not apologize for the oversight, and I wasn't sure she understood how irked I was. Wendy adjusted her glasses. The red frames, unfashionably large, make her look a bit like an office manager. Her frizzy hair always looks like it needs a good cut. But she's got these sexy almond-shaped eyes—and a worked-out body—that save her from looking frumpy.

I suppressed my irritation and added, "Miranda has no idea what I do for a living. She doesn't think about how other people make ends meet. You know the type."

"Yes. I remember. And I know the type."

Miranda's downtown existence is entirely subsidized by Uncle Gregory, and she's blissfully unaware of our parents' income disparities—which is quite handy. She never asks how I get by because she's never had to get by. Miranda fancies herself a class traitor and sees me as the chic fogy. When she discovered Matt at a gallery opening, she deemed him "too East Side" for her downtown sensibilities but perfect for me. She takes real pride in our resulting courtship, but I wonder what she would say if she knew about my very East Side profession.

"It's not that my family is so refined," I added. "It's just that we don't talk openly about money. Miranda probably thinks I get money from my parents, too. If she thinks of it at all."

I glanced at my engagement ring again, then looked up at Wendy.

"It's a lovely ring," Wendy said. "So . . ." The inevitable question: "How do you feel about it?"

"Like a fraud." There was more silence, as our time ran out. "Not entirely like a fraud," I added, quietly. "More like . . . a successful fraud. My girlfriends in the business see this as a victory. And my regulars are delighted for me. It's like being an athlete who's just won a trophy and everyone expects you to make an effective speech and maybe win more trophies and endorse a breakfast cereal—except that I could lose the endorsement if my corporate sponsor finds out who I really am. I'm terrified!"

"So. If your corporate sponsor finds out who you really are?" She echoed my words back. "What then?"

I stared at her, defeated by the enormity of her mental exercise.

"Maybe," she proposed, "your 'corporate sponsor' appreciates a side of you that *is* real, but it's not the complete you. That's not the same thing as being a fraud."

"Maybe," I said, unable to look away from my substantial-yet-tasteful diamond.

"Are you still keeping a journal? It might be helpful at a time like this."

"Sort of. But I lost a whole month! Trying to encrypt it in Word! Don't ask."

Wendy nodded sympathetically. "You should consider getting an iBook." My shrink, the Mac hugger. I guess it goes with all that ethnic pottery.

On my way home, I popped into what looked like a reputable lingerie shop on Broadway. I requested sheer stockings—supplies for Steven, Eileen's client. A tattooed salesgirl with eyebrow rings and a vacant smile—was she also on Ecstasy, perhaps?—tried to sell me fishnet thigh-highs. Then, sensing my dismay, she steered me toward a rack of sheer black pantyhose with virtual lace "garters" built into the sides. Interesting, and rather pretty, but not what this new client is looking for. I was about to demand the manager—was there a responsible adult in the shop who understands "garter belt"?—when my cell phone rang. Steven, the cause of this maddening culture clash.

"I was just thinking about you," I chirped. Suddenly I remembered Steven's specs: bitchy, not chirpy. "No, tomorrow looks uncertain. . . . Confirm with me in the morning. I can't talk," I added in a firmer voice. "I'm shopping." For him, actually. But I didn't say that because, well, it's like telling a john you're at the drugstore picking up some more K-Y.

Sheer stockings, like a girl's lubrication, should simply materialize, out of the erotic ether. *Do not let daylight in upon magic.*

The salesgirl drifted away, in search of easier customers. Unable to resist a bargain, I snatched up three pairs of half-price thong panties—cute little animal prints. Perfect for Ted P., who likes to watch me changing my underwear in his office, and the more panties per minute the better. Some fetishists are so easy to shop for. Others must wait.

WEDNESDAY, 2/2/00

Every girl has a favorite customer. Plus, a john whom she barely tolerates in order to meet her weekly quota. In between the two extremes are bread-and-butter guys—the mainstay of a call girl's business. You plan for bread-and-butter guys, cultivate them, seek them out. But you never plan to have a favorite john.

Allison's favorite was Jack.

Last summer, he practically went into mourning when she decided (for the umpteenth time) to quit the business. Jack didn't want Allison to know he was seeing other girls, and he mostly saw her friends so he could mope about how much he missed her. To have a regular who's so easy—a quick blow-job-with-a-condom—and so devoted! We all sort of envied her. Who wouldn't? Jack seemed like the perfect client.

Until he got a call from Tom Winters, a twisted IRS agent who was auditing Allison and calling everyone she knew. Winters wanted to prove that she had vast reserves of hidden wealth; he couldn't believe that she simply had no savings or real assets after more than five years in the Life. Winters was curious about Allison's lifestyle—her apartment, her prices, even her body. (He asked one girl if Allison had had a lot of expensive plastic surgery. Yes, paying cash for major cosmetic work leaves a major trail, if you're being audited for undeclared income.)

Jack told the IRS how much he paid Allie and how often. He described the furniture in her living room. Never mind that these antiques came from her grandmother. Winters was convinced he could "prove" that Allie spent gobs of undeclared income at big-ticket antique shops. Auditing call girls was more than a job for Tom Winters: it was a hobby, an obsession, a calling.

And Jack didn't just tell him about Allison. He told the IRS how they had been introduced—about the other girls she worked with, like me and Eileen, and he ended up providing Tom Winters with a list of private call girls on the East Side. Allison lost many of her best clients—along with the best part of her mind—all because of Jack, the weak link. Winters decided to LUD her, as they say. He got a printout of her Local Usage Dialing records and started checking up on everyone she had ever called. He used her phone records to connect the dots and came up with some alarmingly accurate theories. He threatened her clients with professional and marital embarrassment—i.e., the tax audit from hell, meaning lots of loaded questions aimed at surprised wives, prickly bosses, and gossipy junior associates. Allison's clients were terrified of being linked with a "known tax evader."

One night last fall, Allison woke me with a drunken hysterical call: "You're the only person who had this information! I should have known!"

"Allison?" I whispered, trying not to wake my exhausted boyfriend.

"How else could the IRS know all these things? How else could they know that Fred came over to my place on Tuesday, May the fourth? Or the name of the girl who sent him?" she wailed in a high-pitched voice.

I sat up fast and moved away from Matt, hoping he couldn't hear her.

"What are you talking about?" I asked in a horrified whisper.

"I'm talking about that IRS agent—who I never should have seen today!" She stopped suddenly and I heard a deep raw sob. "*He knew everything!* My clients, my prices, he even knows I charge extra for—for—" There was a humiliated whimper that made me cringe. "So, when did you turn me in?"

"Please calm down," I begged as her accusations grew clearer.

"I'm not as stupid as you think!" she cried. "You won't get away with this. I've got stuff on you, too!"

When I hung up, I was shaking.

"What time is it?" Matt demanded angrily. "Who *was* that? Why are all your friends either *in* trouble or causing trouble?" he railed. "What is wrong with you? Do you have even one normal girlfriend?"

The weeks that followed were harrowing. I did not speak to Allison and barely spoke to my boyfriend, for fear of saying something incriminating. Matt started quizzing me.

"What's going on in your life? Was Allison threatening you?" When I tried to brush the whole thing off as girlish hysteria, he refused to believe me. "You were trying to hide your conversation the other night! Why?" My distress made him angry. "What have you *done?*" he demanded.

For the first time, I was forced to consider just what Allison, in fact, had on me. We've been trading customers for five, maybe six, years. She knows my boyfriend. We've had dinner with each other's families. She's the only working girl I've ever introduced to my mom or my cousin, and yet she's the most unstable. What was I thinking when I allowed her into my personal life? Allison even knows where I hide my cash—whatever I don't spend, that is. I hired a lawyer, the notorious Barry Horowitz, who normally defends rich sociopaths—like those Dalton kids who hacked off that homeless man's hand in Central Park. I hired him to defend myself against my best friend! And against Tom Winters, the IRS agent, who was also asking people about *my* furniture and *my* clients and looking for a weak link in *my* life.

Tom Winters was neutralized before he could get to my boyfriend. By mid-November he was a front-page story in the *Post,* a public embarrassment for the U.S. Treasury Department. He had been caught—on tape—doing the very thing he accused every call girl in New York of doing: pocketing undeclared income. Winters had used his government job to extort cash from terrified shopaholic hookers who were caught spending far more than the income they declared on their tax returns. A small Barneys shopping bag filled with hundreds did him in. (It's amazing how much cash you can fit into a bag that was designed to carry a bottle of foundation.)

When Allison came to her senses, I felt like I was waking from a bad dream. You know, that moment when you're not sure it *was* a dream and you're not sure you're awake yet?

Jasmine had cautioned me last fall about making up with Allie. "If a girl ever threatened *me* like that—you don't get to do that in this business! Not without consequences. And if it wasn't for that silly bitch, your boyfriend wouldn't have been asking you all those questions."

Yes, Allie got me into trouble with my boyfriend, but I managed to get myself out of it. I've kept his mind off "all those questions" by keeping Allie at arm's length. I never converse with her when he's around, always turn my cell off when I'm with him, and, to date, he's none the wiser. Yes, I am always looking over my shoulder and sometimes I need to be alone just to decompress from my own shadow, but that's the cost of making friends with the girls you work with. (Some hookers refuse to socialize with the other girls—and who can blame them?)

I persuaded Jasmine not to tell anyone about Allison's insane threats. Allison needed to get back on her feet and replace the business she had lost. If the other girls knew she had threatened to turn someone in, they'd be shocked—and she would never get any business from them again. Eileen, for example, is angry enough at Jack; I can just imagine how she'd take it if she knew about Allie's recent conversations with him.

Allie has never been the sharpest eyebrow pencil at the makeup counter. Her reputation as the natural blonde with the wonderful voice—too-dim-to-hurt-a-flea—has been her meal ticket. And not just with men! Allie's the kind of girl madams adore because she's too disorganized to steal their customers. During the last seven years, she has decided to quit the business at least four times. Professional call girls regard her as harmless competition. Fortunately for Allie, nobody knows about her angry threats. Well, nobody but me. And Jasmine.

Today, Jasmine remarked, "That girl owes you big-time. You protected her reputation." We were walking back from the nail salon, after an emergency pedicure (for Jasmine, due to a stubbed toe) and a routine manicure (for me). I still haven't said anything to Jasmine about Allison and Jack.

"If I were a bitch," she continued. "I'd blackmail Allison and she'd be paying *me* to keep your secret. How much do you think it's worth? Three hundred a week? If it's any more than that, it's not worth it, she might as well quit the business. But I think she could come up with a couple of hundred. The logic of black-mail—"

"Don't even *think* that way!" I said in horror.

"Please, Allison's so kinky she'd fucking *love* it, having to turn tricks to pay off some evil blackmailer. Wasn't she claiming to be a sex addict last summer? This is right up her alley!"

"Stop it," I moaned.

"Oh, come on. She's lucky I'm *not* a bitch. Therefore I won't do all those things—which, by the way, I know she would love to have done to her. That girl loves attention, and if there's one thing a blackmailer gives you, it's attention."

I suppressed a spiteful giggle. "Blackmail is *not* something to joke about," I said primly.

Jasmine became eerily calm. "No," she agreed. "It's not." We were standing at the corner of York and Seventy-ninth, waiting for the light to change.

"And not being a bitch is not some sort of unique accomplishment that you get a great big medal for," I added.

"Maybe not," Jasmine allowed, heading into the crosswalk, "but it should be."

Uh-oh. Five o'clock. Time to rinse off my camphor mask, rewind the video, change the sheets. Milton's due to arrive any minute now!

THURSDAY, 2/3/00

This morning, an emergency rendezvous with Allie at the health club. I was climbing backward on the StairMaster when she appeared, flushed and damp, in flower-print running shorts and a cropped T-shirt.

"I have to talk to you," she panted. "I need your advice. You're the only person I can talk to. . . . Why—uh—are you doing it like *that?*"

"It's supposed to work the glutes," I said through clenched teeth. "Can you just broadcast our problems a little louder?"

When I got to the women's locker room, Allie had already showered. She was standing in front of a full-length mirror, sprinkling talc-free powder on her breasts. The nine-to-fivers had cleared out and the moms had gone off to Power Yoga, leaving the room empty.

"It's about Jack," Allie began. Then, frowning at her image in the mirror, she added, "Does my tummy look sort of . . . huge today? I feel so puffy."

"Your abs look fine," I reassured her. "What's going on with Jack?"

She patted the thin strip of blond hair between her legs with a powder puff, then stood on the scale—carefully setting the powder puff aside before she dared look at the number settings. She stepped off the scale, began pulling her panties on, then confessed, "I—um—ran into him last night."

"Ran into him?" I squinted at her furiously. "You *saw* him, didn't you."

"No! I mean, yes, but not the way you mean. I ran into him because—" She blushed. "He surprised me. I was coming home from a call, and Jack was standing outside my building holding a huge bouquet of lilies! You know I love lilies."

"Allie. A john who shows up without an appointment is a *stalker*. Even if—*especially if*—he's carrying your favorite flowers. You could have been walking home with a straight friend—with a boyfriend or something—and then what? Sneaking up on a hooker is pathological and disrespectful," I told her. "Not to mention ungentlemanly."

"Well, I *was* nervous when I saw him standing there," she

admitted. "But he was very polite and he just gave me the flowers, said good night, and walked away."

"God, how creepy."

But at least he didn't make a scene in front of her doorman.

"And when I got upstairs there was a note. Do you want to see it?" She pulled a small envelope out of her gym bag.

> *I know why you're holding back from seeing me. I'm truly sorry about what happened, and you'll always be special to me. I think about you constantly. I miss everything about you. Please give me a chance.*
> *All my love, J.*

"Then he called this morning! I think I should see him. He's being very generous. He's offering me a lot of money, and you've always said I should treat this more like a business. Well, this is a business decision for me."

"You should set some sort of weekly quota for yourself. But that doesn't mean you can't have standards. Some things are not for sale," I pointed out. "While he's thinking about you constantly, he's making breather calls to Eileen. He's a loose cannon."

"She doesn't *know* it's him. Eileen doesn't even have Caller ID! How can she say that?" A towel attendant entered the changing room, and we both clammed up. "Welllll," Allie mumbled. "Don't tell Jasmine. Or any of the other girls. Promise me you won't say a word. But I asked him for *two* thousand. And he agreed." Despite wanting to elude everyone's disdain, she looked rather pleased with herself. "Soooo," she said, with a hint of smugness. "What would *you* do?"

Every girl has a favorite john, and who this guy is tells you a lot about the girl. Jasmine's favorite is Harry from Darien, who keeps a black Town Car waiting while he's getting a blow job upstairs in his socks and wing tips. Because he's her steadiest customer and a quickie, she hasn't raised his price in two years. In my case, there's Milton. Unlike Harry, Milt is no quickie. Sometimes, he's a lot of work. But he spends far more than my other regulars, and he's willing to help if I get myself into a financial pickle. How could I *not* like him? He's *financially* faithful. And the bottom line with a favorite john is that deep down you like it when he's faithful. Allison's favorite? A spineless weasel who married into a real estate family, who ratted on us all to the IRS because he was afraid his rich wife would find out about his midday excursions to call girls. Though he likes a bit of variety, he's really obsessed with Allie. And who else would be flattered to hear that a john "thinks about her constantly"? Most professionals would run for the hills if a client said that.

"When you have a business," I told Allie, "you have to set your own standards. Weed out the undesirables. Being a call girl is like being responsible for a really hot restaurant. Some people get a little dessert on the house, and some don't even get in the door. Jack shouldn't be able to get a reservation. He's been tainted by this IRS mess, and we can't afford to have him around."

"You're blaming the victim. That IRS agent threatened to ruin his life! You're not being fair to him."

"That IRS guy threatened to ruin *my* life, too. But I didn't become an informant, did I?"

"But you don't have children! Jack has a family, a marriage, people who depend on him."

"Jack's 'children' are grown! It's not as if Jack's wife was going to get custody of two people in their late twenties!"

"No," she agreed. "But he didn't want to hurt her. He was trying to protect his family. You shouldn't condemn him for that."

"He blabbed to the IRS about us—and now they have every reason to think they can come back for *more*. What kind of man 'protects his family' by turning himself into a sitting duck?" I asked. "Even if what he did was justifiable, we can't afford to deal with him. What if he gets subpoenaed? Every conversation, every transaction you have increases the risk."

Allison appeared to be listening, so I pressed on.

"Look," I said very patiently. "Your girlfriends have been sticking together and *we're* not seeing this guy—"

"That's why he keeps calling me!" she said brightly. "And offering me so much money! None of the other girls will see him. Maybe I should ask for *three* thousand."

I shrank back in horror.

2 Through the Hooking Glass

Last night, after our appointment with Harry, Jasmine dragged me to the Mark for a martini. Not wanting to show up blotto for dinner with my fiancé, I opted for a ladylike Kir Royale—"just one." Jasmine ordered her usual: Absolut, straight up, with an olive.

"I'm worried about Allison," I confided.

"Stop the fucking presses!" Jasmine sputtered. "When have you *not* worried about Allison? What sort of problem might Her Blondness be causing—I mean, having—this week?"

I told her about Jack's showing up at her building without an appointment and Allison's latest bright idea, the $3,000 question. "Don't discuss this with Allie," I added. "Promise you won't say a word about what I've told you!"

Jasmine gave me a searing look that unnerved me.

"Allie might say something about us to Jack," I explained. "Do you want him as an enemy? Who knows when he might get interviewed again by the IRS? Or if she might tell him that we turned her against him . . . not that we did exactly . . ."

My sheepish voice trailed off into a maze of denial. I tried not to think about the sin I was committing. Spilling one best friend's secret (against her specific wishes) to another best friend! Is there a special place in hell? I hope there's a waiting list.

"That girl . . ." Jasmine was muttering darkly. "That girl's soul is composed of cotton candy." (I see what Allie means about Jasmine being judgmental.) "She's a moral idiot!"

And if Jasmine knew that Allison had asked me to keep a secret?

Would she trust me not to blab *her* business around? But I would never tell Jasmine's secrets to Allie. That's the difference. I swallowed the rest of my apéritif. The sweet alcoholic potion was doing its job, morphing into a weird elixir of self-justification, smoothing out my wrinkled conscience.

"And Eileen's been getting creepy phone calls from him," I went on. "She slammed the phone down. He retaliated by calling her *back*. And now Eileen's telling everyone who will listen how she stood up to this jerk! What should we do?"

Jasmine frowned into her empty glass. "We should get another drink. And keep Jack in perpetual limbo—if we can. Eileen's too confrontational for her own good." As she signaled to the waiter, her wrist glittered winningly. (That guy on Forty-seventh Street who does those Bulgari knockoffs. I *must* remember to ask for his number.)

Jasmine sighed and shook her head. "Eileen reminds me of those big dumb guys from my old neighborhood who were always getting into bar fights!" she said. Eileen's about five feet tall, but Jasmine has a point. "They never went anywhere in life, and they're probably still getting into brawls and getting kicked out of bars. But Eileen should know better! How long has she been around? Eight years? What is her problem? Why is she provoking a *phone fight?*"

Suddenly, Jasmine's attention shifted. "Did you pay retail for that?" She was eyeing my pony-skin Baguette with harsh curiosity.

"Of course not!" I lied.

"It really works with the sweater," she acknowledged, "but you spend money as fast as you make it. That's gotta stop!"

Who does she think she is? My mother?

"Hey, look." She pulled an envelope out of her black crocodile tote (a sleek find at 70 percent off, last summer) and waved an invitation in my face. A benefit for the S_____ Foundation.

"Two Benefactor-level tickets courtesy of Harry. He's got a conflict that night. This is a great way to find new guys. Maybe we can pick up some *Super*-Benefactors. Their tickets are in the megadigits."

"They're not spending that kind of money to sit with mere Benefactors," I pointed out. "They'll be at their own tables—miles from ours."

Jasmine doesn't usually venture beyond our private circle for new customers. The girls we work with operate strictly from their books. There are very few acceptable methods for getting new business: You can trade dates with another girl or pay a cut for each new client. Work for a reputable madam and risk her extreme displeasure if she catches you "stealing." When a girl is leaving town or retiring, you might buy her book. But how often does a good book become available? It's rare. Sometimes an established customer refers a new client, but that's also rare. Most of my regulars would be a little turned off if I had sex with their pals.

Of course, other kinds of girls—through advertising on websites or working for escort services—can afford to eschew these niceties. They have an endless supply of new guys (obtained at great risk), but private girls and reputable madams don't work with them. Very few "escorts" have the patience to cross over. A small number will try to make a go of working privately, but the minute things get slow, a hard-core escort goes right back to the escort agency, or to advertising. And if she gets arrested? All the private girls in her address book are at risk.

A private girl braves the slow months to preserve the quality of her book, her contacts—her way of life. I should know. I crossed over a long time ago. And stayed here. I'll never go back. No matter how slow it gets.

"Look," Jasmine was saying, "this isn't like advertising. It's a totally cool way to enhance your client book."

"Soliciting at a social event?" I was appalled.

"Noooo," she said disdainfully. "We'll work these guys as sugar daddies, do a little research on them, make sure they're legit—and find out how rich they are. And then . . . say you have a monthly expense. Like, you're taking some lessons at the French Institute. That's five hundred dollars a month right there! So you hit the guy up for your French lessons. Or a summer share in Sag Harbor. You get the idea."

"Or your ailing mother's hospital bills?" I suggested, rolling my eyes. "I'm a professional. And so are you. That stuff's for *lite-hooks*." (Girls who kind of sort of sometimes maybe in a way get paid for sex. More often than they admit, but not often enough to make a living at it.)

"You're missing the point! If you're *pretending* to litehook, then it's different—you're not really a litehook! You're the ulti-mate pro. *Passing* for a litehook."

"Surely you're not that desperate for new business."

"Desperate? Please. You should always be building your book. Never take your existing customers for granted. Cultivate your john book as if it were a vegetable garden." Jasmine was twisting the stem of her martini glass between her fingertips. "Water it, plant new seeds. Grow potatoes in the fall, tomatoes in summer. Learn about new farming technologies." Her eyes shone as she warmed to her theme: the hooker in the dell.

"Potatoes?" I said. "How glamorous." I studied the invitation. "I can't," I said, sipping my second Kir Royale carefully. "I prom-ised Allison I would go to a meeting with her that night."

"A meeting? With Allison? You're not going to join that crazy hookers' union!" Jasmine exploded. "Do you know what will happen to the price of pussy if those airheads succeed in chang-ing the fucking laws?"

"For god's sake, lower your voice!" I warned her. "Do you want everyone to hear? You'd better order some carbs before you get too drunk. Anyway, I'm not joining," I explained. "I'm just being supportive. Of Allison."

Narrowing her green eyes, Jasmine interrupted, in a half-slurred half whisper: "Do you know why they want to make it legal?"

I shook my head and moved closer. A middle-aged guy in a pin-striped suit with a graying ponytail was eyeing Jasmine from a love seat near the entrance.

Her voice turned steely. "If those girls ever get their way, girls like us will be doing it for ninety-nine dollars and ninety-nine cents—just like them! Have you seen those ads for tantric hand jobs? They're all over the *Village Voice*! That's the element you're going to encounter at whatchamacallit—the trollops' council or whatever they call themselves."

The ponytailed fellow stood up to greet a tall angular blonde; she was wearing Harry Potter eyeglasses, dark red lipstick, and a bright blue boa around her neck. She was also lugging an incongruously boxy red North Face backpack. He offered her the love seat and perched on one of the muffin-shaped stools, which gave him a great view of her long legs, her massive Mary Jane wedgies, and her tiny miniskirt.

Jasmine, by comparison, was a picture of sanity, in low-heeled ankle boots, well-cut trousers, light brown lip gloss, her face a more angular version of Gayfryd Steinberg's circa 1986. A reasonable voyeur might see a streamlined brunette debating hairdressers or nursery schools with her school chum. But Jasmine was off on a tangent. And we're not school chums—in any traditional sense of the term.

"It's sexual socialism," she was saying. "A redistribution of resources. Terrible. Like the minimum wage." She took another sip. "Ayn Rand had a name for these types. Secondhanders!"

"What's in it for Allison?" I asked, rolling my eyes. "Professionally speaking, she's not one of those girls. She's one of us."

"In my opinion? It all comes down to those pink handbags!" Jasmine said. "Her taste in handbags is so juvenile, it's excruciating. Last year, she was calling herself a *sex addict* and carrying around that Kate Spade number—in pink, remember? This year it's pink Louis Vuitton! And now she's calling herself a sex *worker*. It's too predictable for words. Infantile! A hooker's accessories should radiate discretion. Power. Sexual maturity." She reached into the grande-dame-ish alligator tote sitting at her knee and took out a black nylon wallet. "Now, this," she said, opening it, "I got on the street from one of those African guys. You *have* to invest in an expensive bag, but a wallet's something else entirely. Everybody sees your bag, but almost no one sees your wallet."

A waiter arrived with our bill. I opened my own wallet— speckled pony skin accented with a matte plastic trim. Only Jasmine could succeed in making me feel uneasy about this chic new addition to my extended family of mostly Italian accessories.

"Let's split it," I said.

"Christ. Having all hundreds is almost as devastating as having no cash at all!" she muttered crossly. "Get the next one. I have to break a bill."

*

At Demarchelier, Matt was waiting impatiently, fiddling with his cell phone. "Where were you?" he demanded. "You're twenty minutes late!"

"I had a drink with Jasmine, and I tried to call you," I riffed in a snippy voice. "Is your ringer off again? Your voice mail's not working, you know!" My irritation was so authentic that my white lie felt completely real. Besides, Matt just upgraded his phone and hasn't had time to learn the new features. His compulsive upgrading is a godsend, providing endless new excuses for any failure to communicate. I wonder how many other relationships rely on technology for this very reason.

"Well, you should have invited her to dinner," he said.

"Jasmine," I began. *Jasmine was too exercised over the hypothetical price of pussy to pass for a normal person tonight?* I don't think so! "She had other plans," I told him. "Take us out for dinner next week, if you like."

Matt was absentmindedly stroking the underside of my wrist: a minitruce in the war on lateness. "I've never had a *date* date with two girls," he replied, clearly enticed.

I looked vaguely past his shoulder and acted as if I hadn't really caught the innuendo. For a second, I wondered if Matt could guess that Jasmine and I, just hours before, were . . . doing another kind of date together. He couldn't possibly. Could he?

Compared to some of the men I routinely bed, Matt seems so young and healthy. Sure, he's turned on by the idea of two girls, like any other guy. But he doesn't *require* two girls just to get a hard-on; some of my clients are so jaded that nothing normal turns them on anymore. And, though I hardly qualify as being Into Girls, I've probably been in bed with more women than he has. It boggles the mind. Even my mind.

But that's one thing I treasure about Matt. A relationship with a guy who hasn't turned into a raving decadent. I smiled softly across the table and gazed into his eyes. Never change! I wanted to say out loud. We looked at each other for a while, and I wondered what *he* was thinking.

Over dessert—virtuous strawberries for me, sinful crème brûlée for Matt—I contemplated my session with Dr. Wendy: *Maybe he knows one side of you. It's not the complete you, but that's not the same thing as being a fraud.* Is it?

"My sister thinks we should come up with a date," Matt was saying.

"Why?" I asked. "Elspeth's not the one who's getting married."

"I know, but she wants to plan her year—"

"Can't she plan her year without planning our wedding?" I shot back. "Why is she always interfering?"

As an older sister myself, with two brothers, I know that a younger brother must put his foot down in order to gain a big sister's respect.

He changed his tack. "Well, anyway, I was thinking, if you aren't ready to set a date, why don't we move in together?"

"Move in?" I was floored. "Where?"

"Wherever you want. I mean, we could move into your place or my place and see how we like living together."

I couldn't hide my dismay. We've only just *begun* discussing the engagement, my shrink and I. And Matt wants us to move in together! How will I keep seeing my clients? Oh, what was I thinking when I said yes? And what now? Can a girl march down the aisle and just say "Whatever!" instead of "I do"?

"Why do you look so surprised?" he asked playfully. "We'll be living together when we're married, you know."

"I know that," I snapped. "But—but—my place is too small for a couple. My bedroom's *tiny*. Where will you put all your suits?"

"Okay. Mine's bigger," he offered.

"This—is very sudden," I stammered. "We—we just got engaged!"

"We've been engaged for a while, honey, almost three months. You're upset. What's wrong?"

"I'm fine," I insisted, though I had the urge to bolt from the table. "Was this Elspeth's idea? I wish you wouldn't discuss our relationship with—"

"Calm down, okay?" He wasn't playful anymore. "This has nothing to do with my sister." And turning this into a fight about his sister was not going to be an easy way out.

I silently recalled the time Matt almost found out about my

second phone number: One weekend, last summer, I stupidly forgot to unplug my business phone. When it rang, I was so startled that I almost gave the entire game away, dashing madly from one end of the apartment to the other! And what if both phone lines had started ringing at once? I made up some story about buying a new phone because the old one was broken. The memory of that day made my stomach tense up. I smiled stiffly.

In a more patient voice, he said, "Just think about it. You don't have to decide this minute." He paused. "God, you look . . . are you okay?"

My palms were sticky. *If we broke up now . . .* I thought, it would all be so simple. I stared at my ring.

"I'm sorry," I said, picking up a strawberry with my spoon. "You deserve someone more stable. Less neurotic." My fingers trembled. The strawberry tumbled onto the tablecloth.

"Don't be silly," he told me. "It doesn't matter what I deserve. That's not how love works."

"How love *works?* You're an expert? Is that something they covered in business school?" My eyes filled with tears and I rushed off to the ladies' room where I calmed my nerves by checking the voice mail on my cell phone.

A tongue-in-cheek message from Milton: "Put those dirty videos back in the deep freeze, kiddo—I'll be in Tokyo for the next three weeks." He promised to call after his business trip. Milton's bottomless appetite for porn videos, awkward positions, and oversize sex toys doesn't turn me on. But the sound of his voice is always so reassuring. I closed my eyes and replayed the message.

Then I dabbed some powder under my eyes and returned to my boyfriend, emotionally refreshed—much to his relief and mine. You see, the thing is, I really think Matt *benefits* from me being in the business, even though it has to be kept a secret. I'm a much better girlfriend when I'm feeling secure about my clients,

my bargaining power—when I'm having a good week. W
seeing other guys—for money—I'm better in bed, too. I kn

Later, helping me into my coat, Matt brushed his lips against n
left ear. I felt his teeth nipping discreetly at my lobe. "I must really
be in love with you," he whispered. "You're so fucking impossible!"

A shiver of pleasure ran through me as he steered me toward
the sidewalk. I smiled up at him, brought back to safety by his
desire for something more immediate—something I knew I could
deliver.

As we proceeded to my apartment, I went over my mental
checklist: Is the ringer on my business phone off? Did I put my
excessively diverse condom assortment in the special drawer?
Hide that incriminating dildo? Stash all my cash? Lock up the
videos? A working girl can't be too careful.

My body was responding to his unambiguous grip—his hand
circling my arm—and the nervous feeling in my chest was migrat-
ing through me, toward my panties. Toward *him*.

MONDAY AFTERNOON, 2/7/00

This morning, I got one of those calls. "It's Bob! Remember
me?"

"Of course!" I trilled.

Oh, dear. Which Bob? As I made small talk with the familiar
voice, I ran through my Bobs: Bobby M., the lawyer in his forties
from Short Hills; Bob, no last name, in the insurance business,
who wears glasses; a "snowbird" called Bob in his sixties who
hangs out in Boca Raton, needs a large-size Trojan; a Bob from
Greenwich who—

"Is this still Sabrina's number?" Bob asked, thrown off by my
voice.

Ah. The snowbird! Taking a break from his sun-drenched
winter.

"It's me!" I assured him in a softer voice; this Bob thinks I'm twenty-six.

Jasmine regards multiple naming of the working self with impatience: "Who can keep up with all your names?" Jasmine doesn't use a work name, she calls herself Jasmine at all times. "Suppose some guy runs into you at a gallery opening, calls you Boopsie or Cupcake or whatever, and screws everything up for you? Hide it in plain sight," she insists. "Besides, they think it's tacky when a girl has too many names."

Different names are handy because so many clients have the *same* name. Bobby the lawyer calls me Suzy, Insurance Bob calls me Lisa, and Bob the Snowbird knows me as the kittenish "Sabrina." I can identify nine out of ten johns (or Bobs) by cross-checking a guy's voice with the name he calls me. This is like having Caller ID software implanted in your forehead. Unlike some girls, I never have to crassly inquire "Which Bob are you?" to a man I've had sex with. In other words, it might actually be classier to have a few working names. Despite what Jasmine thinks.

Two years ago, I bought a small list of guys from Daria, who left the business . . . to get married. Neither she nor I had an inkling, then, that I, too, would contract the marriage virus. Half-Persian, half-German, from somewhere vaguely south of L.A., Daria was confident that I would do well with her clients because, as she put it, "You're exotic like me. You're not as busty, but that's okay because you're Asian." (Like so many Californian hookers, Daria had pretty much assimilated after five years on the East Coast. But her D-cup breasts were undeniably *West* Coast and so was her assessment of my figure. By local standards, I'm almost busty. Really.)

I gave myself a new name, making myself years younger and much newer to the business. Daria's former clients think "Sabrina" has been working for two years at the most.

As a child, I used to harangue my mother: "Why was I called Nancy? Why can't I be a Suzy or a Barbara? Why wasn't I named *Felicity?*" Not having the faintest idea what she was foretelling, Mother replied, in that prim tone (which remains her parental hallmark), "When you grow up, you will have the freedom to choose any name you wish. Until then you will be called Nancy."

So what would Matt think if he knew how I've realized my earliest ambitions? He'd be ... appalled. I'm sure he has no idea how much fun it is to rename yourself at will. And how do you explain a thing like that to a guy like Matt, anyway?

You don't.

TUESDAY, 2/8/00

When Bob showed up, I was wearing a short pleated skirt with high narrow heels. My red toenails glistened against strappy golden Pradas—a confectionery bare-legged look that I could never wear to a john's office or a good hotel. Wouldn't dream of wearing outside of my apartment, actually.

"Look who's here!" I cooed.

I fluttered around the living room, bending forward to adjust the VCR—and to grant a quick peek up my skirt. Easy to do, in heels. If I were traveling through the halls of the Peninsula or the Four Seasons, these shoes might throw me off. But within the radius of my bed, I'm gliding; I belong in them.

I'm a better twenty-six-year-old today, at thirty-something, than I was at twenty-six. And I enjoy being a "new" girl—more than I ever enjoyed it when I really *was* new. So when Bob mentioned the Stanhope, a hotel I've been to many times, I feigned ignorance.

"Sabrina," he chuckled. "Didn't Daria teach you anything?"

"Only the important things." I giggled and pulled my skirt down to hide my transparent white panties.

"Don't do that," he protested. "Daria wouldn't want you to cover up your pussy like that, would she?"

"Daria taught me how to eat pussy," I remarked in a friendly voice. "She teaches by example."

His eyes twinkled as I slipped into his crude routine.

"Does she?" he replied gamely. "So she did teach you something. Daria likes to have her snatch licked, doesn't she?"

"Only if you know what you're doing," I told him. "And she tells me you have a well-trained tongue."

(Daria and I didn't know each other *that* well. In fact, we worked together just a few times before I bought her book. But her clients like to think we were lovers. Before she moved on, Daria planted this cute idea in their minds—and called during her honeymoon to remind me. She was a conscientious call girl, even in retirement.)

Soon I was standing in front of Bob in my panties and heels, bent over with my skirt at my feet and my smooth rump in his face.

"What a gorgeous ass," he sighed. I could hear him unzipping his pants.

"Are you playing with your cock?" I murmured, pulling my panties clearly to one side. I tilted my pussy to give him a better view.

There was a hungry moan as he held back from coming too fast.

"Let's go in the bedroom," he suggested.

"Good idea," I agreed, glancing at the clock on the VCR. "Where we can relax . . . and I can try out your tongue."

This wouldn't work if Bob knew how long I've been in the business. He needs me to be Sabrina: naive, dirty-mouthed, willing to do all the work, very much in control, excited by my "new" career. A tall, complicated order. Especially when you're really new.

I teased him and sat over his face, demanding that he lick my ass.

"Your tongue . . ." I was cooing again. "I could get addicted to that tongue!"

I changed positions and slipped a condom onto his erection. "Are you going to fuck me today?" I was kneeling on the bed, poised to suck his cock. I ran a fingertip over his dark chest, flicking the gold chain to one side; Bob's generation still believes you can't be too rich or too tan.

"Oh, my god. Sabrina—you're such a hot little girl!" His erection was impressive. I placed it in my mouth and gave some attention to the head, then worked my way toward the base. "Not yet, not yet," he moaned, pressing his cock upward. Only with a condom could I give him the following treat; I felt an unexpected throb as I pulled him into my throat. He exhaled loudly, turning rapidly to jelly—my signal to pull away, grab a tissue, and shift gears.

As I tidied up, I turned off my slutty act but continued to play bubbly Sabrina. My boyfriend never sees this part of me. Guys like Matt don't mate with bubbly chicks. It's true, I do seem unambitious, compared to the women in Matt's daily life—his boss, his up-and-coming female colleagues. But unambitious is permissible (in a girl) if you're not too bubbly, and if you're respectable. My fake job isn't a power gig—nor is it glamorous—but it has nothing to do with my looks. And Matt wouldn't want to be seen as a guy who marries a girl for her looks! (Though of course he wouldn't have fallen for a girl who *wasn't* pretty.) That stack of volumes on my bedroom floor by dead white novelists from Thackeray to Mrs. Gaskell to Henry James, interspersed with stuff by live brown ones implies that I'm serious at the core. Matt never reads fiction that was written before 1960 but wants to marry a girl who does.

Whereas Matt finds my reading tastes respectable, Bob's

impressed that I read anything at all. Bob's the kind of self-made guy who could marry a woman who doesn't even read. He made all his money in real estate speculation.

"You're a very nice girl," Bob assured me in a deliberate, fatherly tone. "A wonderful young lady." He was sliding some hundreds under the tissue box on my bedside table.

I was touched by his desire to validate the fluffy dirty-mouthed girl he sees three times a year. I suddenly wondered if Matt, upon meeting such a bimbette, would bother to say something corny, something kind. Would he know that it makes a difference? Would he care? I don't want to go there, I guess; anyway, Matt belongs to a different part of my life.

As I closed the door I could hear Bob stepping into the elevator, and I wondered: What happens to the bubbly "Sabrina" when Nancy marries Matt? Must I burn the bimbette to save the woman?

FRIDAY AFTERNOON, 2/11/00

Etienne is back from a short trip to Paris. "Realizing this is intolerably short notice," he began in a wheedling voice. "I hope you still remember who I am? What a week! Could we perhaps . . . this evening? Allow me to forget this gruesome week . . ."

After almost ten years—he's one of my oldest customers, by which I mean longest—he still employs these coy icebreakers.

"Be here no later than six!" I cautioned him.

I have to meet Matt at seven, but didn't tell him that, of course. Never let a guy feel he's being rushed. And never let him know why! Just in case he *does* feel rushed.

"Bien sûr," he purred agreeably. Etienne has lived on East Sixty-seventh Street for more than three decades, but his accent remains strangely intact. One of his many style decisions.

Etienne arrived last night, carrying a chocolate-brown umbrella with an engraved brass handle in the shape of a swan's head.

"Very handsome," I told him. "Did you find it in Paris?"

"It keeps me dry," he said with a humorous shrug. "My children gave it to me for Christmas."

Etienne's son is an eye surgeon, and his two daughters are teachers. I think he once told me that the oldest daughter is married to a guy at Salomon.

Lying on the couch with my bare feet nestled in Etienne's lap, I smiled as he traced gentle lines on my calves with his fingertips. "Do you know what your most interesting feature is?" he asked dreamily. "I am always curious to know what a woman will designate as her most important feature. Women are so often at odds with their paramours."

I gazed down at my legs. Sometimes, when I'm with Matt, I get paranoid about my thighs. But never when I'm with a customer. At work, a pragmatic self-appreciation kicks in: I instantly feel, oh, 10 to 30 percent more attractive as soon as I have an appointment lined up. It's an engine that switches on by itself. You answer the phone, make the appointment, look in the mirror, and you see what the client will be getting. It's hard to be so objective with a boyfriend. And lovely to be appreciated by a succession of men over fifty.

I was wearing my new zebra-print thong and nothing else— so I couldn't hide the effect this was having on my nipples. A familiar tingle caused my thighs to turn in slightly. Etienne ran a considerate fingertip over my right breast and smiled. Now, I thought, smiling back, here he comes, as predictable as a clock. Sensing my body's pliant mood, he moved closer. His lips made a dangerous beeline for mine, but I dodged him gracefully and I slid away from his kiss.

"Let's continue this biology lesson in the bedroom!" I giggled, grabbing his hand.

"You are a foul-tempered devil," he muttered. "Why do you welcome my kisses here," he said, tapping the front of my panties, "but not here?" He touched a finger to the corner of my mouth.

"One of life's mysteries," I murmured, slipping out of my panties.

"You never answered," he said, placing his mouth against one breast. His tongue was warm, not too demanding, and my nipple couldn't help but encourage him. "If you had to choose just one important feature?"

"I'd pick two," I said, knowing how much my vanity pleases Etienne. "My face and my breasts." I couldn't exactly repeat my secret answer: "If only I didn't rely on them so much! My face has made me rather lazy about exercise, and my tummy always threatens to betray me. I should go to the gym more often, but I seem to be getting away with it because you keep calling."

He smiled and cupped one breast, then ran his hand over my abdomen. "No quarrel with your assessment—but for me, it's your skin."

"Really?" How, after a decade of seeing me, does this man come up with such charming new material? He's a born flirt, the genuine article.

"The texture is what I find so . . . compelling." And then, as my flattered smile registered on Etienne, his intrusive mouth sought another off-limits kiss.

"Darling," I breathed, maneuvering my neck to evade him, "my pussy is getting so impatient . . ." I tactfully directed his face toward my open thighs. Almost six-thirty. How time flies when you're being hustled by a veteran john!

When I emerged from my building—just a few moments after Etienne's departure—Matt was waiting in a cab, delighted that, for once, I was ready on time.

*

Elspeth's buffet was in full swing when we arrived at her apartment. My cousin Miranda was standing next to a giant brioche, halfheartedly fending off a sandy-haired, somewhat beefy-looking guy I've seen many times before. He's at all of Elspeth's parties and I think he must be one of her junior lawyers, but I can never remember his name. Miranda has a permanent tan from growing up in Trinidad, and her mother, like my dad, is half-Indian.

"Fascinating," the sandy-haired guy was saying. "I had no idea such a unique mixture of beauty was actually possible. Your *father's* Chinese?"

Miranda smiled oddly and pulled me toward her.

"Meet my cousin Nancy," she told him. "This is . . . um . . . Christopher. I'll be back!" she added, pulling me in yet another direction. "Let's get Nancy a drink."

"Well, I guess Matt can keep him busy," I said. "How's everything?"

"Oh, fine, now that you're here! All these men keep hitting on me!" she complained. "I thought you'd never arrive. And that . . . Christopher. He keeps talking about how exotic I am. You know, I feel like an object," she said in a low bitter voice.

The terrible twenties! She really believes she doesn't *want* all this attention. Even though she's wearing a cropped cashmere sweater and the tightest Dolce & Gabbana pants I've seen in weeks.

"Your outfit's kind of sexy," I pointed out, as she steered me toward the champagne. "And your belly-button ring is a definite draw."

"Not that kind of object!" she said. "He keeps harping on how *exotic* I look just because—just because I'm half-Chinese." And she still has that trace of a Trinidad accent, which suburban New

Yorkers like Christopher don't expect a Chinese-looking girl to have. I don't have that accent, because I left at the age of two.

"He meant it as a compliment," I said. "Be nice to him, he's trying to be poetic and charming. And don't take it so personally! To him, you *are* exotic."

"Well, I'm sick of everyone asking me where I'm *from,*" she told me. "Especially men."

"Then go back to Trinidad where everybody will know *exactly* where you're from. And you won't be exotic anymore. But you'd *hate* having to deal with Trinidadian men. Can you imagine?"

In this, we're viscerally united. Neither of us has ever had a boyfriend from the islands. Though she still has the accent, she really can't go back. Miranda clinked her champagne glass against mine and gave me a rueful smile.

"I suppose that's right. Look, here he comes. Mr. Exotic himself."

"You just resent him because he's not wearing one of those strange little goatees. He's a nice guy! Let him take you out to dinner sometime."

"Oh, he's not my type," she sighed, rolling her eyes at me as if I were one of our great-aunts. Except that she would never actually roll her eyes in that way at any of our great-aunts. It would have to be done on the sly.

Christopher and Matt were heading toward us, led by Elspeth, who was dressed in party Manolos, black satin capris, and a transparent silk T-shirt. Elspeth is one of those A-cup gals who can maintain her respectability in a see-through blouse. Her short auburn hair topped off a smooth, pretty line that ended at her pointy toes. An audible "Nancy!" startled a few guests. That brittle voice takes some getting used to—it doesn't really go with her pixielike features. "Miranda!" Much air-kissing. "Being engaged to my little brother really agrees with her!" she exclaimed. "You look different tonight. Isn't she radiant!" she said to Matt and Miranda. "I swear to god, you're glowing, Nancy."

That's because, while rushing Etienne through his session, I felt obliged to throw in a real orgasm. A man won't think of you as a pleasure-pinching hooker if you take a little time out for an orgasm. If, just minutes ago, he felt the tremors of your clitoris against his tongue, it's a cinch to get him off, then send him out early, feeling pleased with himself.

I glanced around at all the high-heeled guests and felt a twinge of ambivalence. Should I have worn sluttish stilts instead of flats? Nobody would guess that less than one hour ago I was lying in bed with my thighs wrapped around the face of a gray-haired man, conjuring up degrading fantasies (with Matt in the lead role) so I could get my orgasm *over with, already*. Not with all these women gliding around on their party stilts while I stand here in my shiny good-girl flats. Deep cover.

"Men are dogs," Elspeth was saying. "Jason promised to be here no later than six! To help! Yeah, right. He's stuck in a meeting and he totally forgot. Did you get my e-mail?" she asked. "About the fabric dyes?"

"I haven't had a chance to log on all day," I explained. "I was, um, trying to get this project finished and I got sort of caught up—overwhelmed by it."

"And listen, there's this website that—don't knock it till you try it—helps you organize your wedding. I wish this had been around five years ago, when *I* got married. Take it from me, the Day will go more smoothly if you break it down into components. They have a private chat list for anxious brides. Lucy, my colorist, says they discuss *everything*." She cast a meaningful glance at Matt, to indicate the Girls Only quality of the list.

"Really? Like, first-night jitters?" Matt said, with a mischievous smirk.

"No." Elspeth pretended to be annoyed. "Lingerie and bouquets. So, Nancy: this project that keeps you so busy. What's the latest? Are you almost done?"

Miranda turned away from Christopher and leaned in to hear more. I felt a quiver of insecurity in my solar plexus, which I tried to quell with champagne, then managed to make a few nonremarks about my fake job. Matt, Elspeth, my family, his family—they all think of me as a part-time slacker who does copyediting for extra money. Miranda is so clearly a girl with an allowance that any relative of hers can be tarred with the same brush, so Matt assumes that my work supplements a modest income from my parents.

Fortunately, most people think the doings of a copy editor are pretty boring. It's easy to get them distracted from my supposed job: Just talk about it! The subject usually changes, quite rapidly, when I explain that my current "project" is a massive treatise on Eastern medicine that the author hopes to translate into German. It's important to mention a language that is totally unsexy.

"How did you *meet* this guy?" Elspeth asked. "This—what is he, an acupuncturist? *And* a chiropractor? From where?" She wasn't letting go of the subject as easily as I had hoped.

"Oh, ah, he's a family friend of the translator," I explained. "She's going to translate the whole thing when I'm finished, and we're having this terrible problem because a file got corrupted and he only made one backup."

Christopher was trying to look interested and Matt was examining the wine bottles as Elspeth went on.

"And where did he train?" she said, looking directly at me.

I was stumped. Where did this fictional chiropractor learn how to be an acupuncturist? She was waiting for an answer.

"Uh, you mean his *computer* training or his medical training?" I did my best to appear confused. "His computer skills are negligible," I added.

Elspeth glanced at Matt and began to say something. Then she stopped. I turned to the bar for another glass of champagne, horrified by my questionable performance. When I came back, Elspeth was having a rather quiet tête-à-tête with her brother. Matt looked up and came closer, to put his arm around my waist while Elspeth gave us both a long, thoughtful stare.

"So, what's the publication date?" Elspeth demanded, in a cheery yet ominous voice.

"Well, I . . ." Leaning into Matt's light embrace, I cleared my throat pensively. "The thing is, I made an agreement. I've signed a contract not to discuss—I'm not really allowed to disclose any of the details. I know it's a bit silly—with a book like this—but it's part of my arrangement with the translator."

"Really? Is that a common practice?" Elspeth wanted to know.

Jesus Christ.

"I thought it was, but I really don't know. Why?"

It bothered me that she had stopped asking where the chiropractor trained and was now on a new line of questioning altogether—just when I thought I might have a suitable answer for the *last* question. And this was all supposed to be so boring!

"I wonder if a contract of this sort is enforceable," she said. "What are the limits? Did you show it to a lawyer? If you did, you'd have to tell your lawyer about the book. What if you told your doctor? Or your psychiatrist? Could a publisher call them to testify about what you leaked? What if there was a crime involved?"

"Elspeth had too much coffee this morning," Matt sighed.

"Well, a contract like that raises important privilege issues that Nancy might not have considered." She looked at me quizzically. "Not that you're the kind of girl with any secrets to keep. Or are you?" she asked with a sharp, mischievous smile.

A tall blonde in a red scoop-necked blouse and a leather skirt caused Elspeth to break away. "Karen! You look great! I'd like you to meet my future sister-in-law, Nancy."

I wondered if Karen was one of Elspeth's law school buddies, a fellow prosecutor, perhaps. Increasingly, I find that the more provocative the outfit, the straighter the job. I almost wonder if a display of cleavage and flesh will make me blend in more.

"My brother's a player," Elspeth said proudly. She grabbed my hand to show Karen my three-carat diamond. "When he does something, he really does it."

"It's gorgeous," Karen gushed. "We have to talk! I just heard about a fabulous two-bedroom—would you consider moving downtown? Tribeca?"

"Karen's a real estate genius," Elspeth chimed in. "Give them your card—I was telling Matt the other day, 'You can't expect Nancy to start a new life with you in that bachelor pad!'"

Elspeth's husband appeared in the doorway carrying a huge briefcase. Jason's the money in that marriage—an M&A lawyer. Elspeth, the assistant D.A., sees herself as the integrity. Naturally, he's the polite one and she's the loudmouth.

"Better late than never!" she rasped cheerfully. "Where *were* you?"

As he leaned forward for our perfunctory kiss on the cheek, we exchanged a brief look, that "Eye Contract" entered into by two people who might never have met if two *other* people weren't related to each other. Restrained sympathy. A curious desire to understand the other person. Followed by relief because you don't really have to.

When I turned around, Karen and Matt were trading business cards, and I could feel the walls of an unseen apartment closing in on me.

"Matt says you have a new e-mail address? Here's mine. You're going to love this place—it's perfect for a young couple," Karen told me.

"Oh, I'd love it if you two moved downtown," Miranda said. "There's so much happening! We can meet for lunch, Nancy, near the museum." Miranda works at the New Museum of Contemporary Art, which is smack-dab in the middle of thronging hell! But she loves it because she has no memory of what SoHo was like when it was just a budding restaurant scene with a few nice shops.

"And it's closer to work," Matt said. "Definitely. Can we see it this weekend?"

What did I get myself into here? Tribeca? Oh god. Overpriced, inconvenient, miles from my hairdresser and my bikini waxing . . . not to mention my shrink. But my geographic horror gave way to relief. Thanks to Karen and Miranda and Matt, all singing the praises of an overrated neighborhood, Elspeth was now focusing on us as a couple and seemed to be less curious about *me*. Thank god.

SUNDAY, 2/13/00

Update on the Tribeca 2BR. According to Karen's bubbly e-mail, it's got a breakfast nook and a balcony. The current occupants bought in '92, before the market started going haywire, and the husband has persuaded his wife to relocate to East End Avenue so their daughter can walk to school. Karen has a special rapport with the co-op board, which insists on vetting all prospective renters—in the flesh. "I'll get you in, no problem," she threatened—I mean, promised.

This morning, while Matt was in the shower, I snuck in a quick call to Liane. "I can't talk long," I warned her. "My boyfriend and I are going to look at a rental on Franklin Street. I just have a minute."

Like every madam I've known, Liane is exceedingly generous with her wisdom. At seventy-something, tall, slender, and

Dioresque, she is still the epitome of 1950s elegance. And fifties ethics, too.

"Under no circumstances should a girl like you 'live with' a man," she said. "These trial marriages are a big mistake."

Trial marriage? Wow. If I tell Liane that I'm responsible for putting off the wedding date, I'll never hear the end of it.

"Well, I'm not going to tell you how to conduct your life, dear. Don't you know *anyone* who's available tomorrow night?" she asked, changing the subject.

February fourteenth. A great night to be a call girl *without* a valentine and a terrible night for madams, because too many girls have relationships that tie them up (so to speak) for the evening.

"You, of course, have a good reason to take tomorrow night off," Liane remarked. "Your fellow has made a commitment, and he's a catch. Though you'll soon see that commitment evaporating if you move in with him! What is your fiancé planning for Valentine's Day?"

"We're going to a chamber-music recital." Liane indicated her approval. "Avoiding the crowds," I said. "Don't you think Valentine's Day can be a bit—"

"Of a nuisance? Frankly, dear, yes. I have a lovely gentleman from Buenos Aires flying in. He'll be in meetings all day tomorrow and he wants a brunette with real breasts to arrive at eight, leave at midnight. He's at the Four Seasons. Dinner in his room, pleasant conversation, garter belt, stockings, two thousand." She sighed. "He's so easy, too! Or so I've heard. You'd be perfect."

I felt a twinge of regret, despite the fact that 40 percent would go to Liane if I were to see him.

"How about Jasmine?"

"She's too businesslike," Liane objected. "And he prefers someone petite. Well, I suppose, in her little Chanel ballet flats, Jasmine really *looks* petite and she's trim and pretty, so he's not going to send her away . . ." Jasmine's five feet five, but I held my tongue as Liane tried to sell herself on the idea. "She has a nice bust—not too big. She hasn't had her breasts done, has she?"

"No way!" I assured her. "I'll call you later."

I quickly dialed my hairdresser's number, allowed it to ring once, and quietly hung up. Just in case Matt happened to hit the redial button.

We've all heard the horror stories—innocent boyfriends accidentally hitting redial, stumbling across numbers and clients and . . . welcome to Hooker Hell. If that isn't every call girl's worst nightmare, it certainly should be!

MONDAY, 2/14/00

Today I showed Wendy the keys to Matt's . . . bachelor pad, as Elspeth calls it. (What *do* you call the apartment of a man who wants to forsake bachelorhood for you and you alone?)

"So you have the keys to your 'corporate sponsor's' headquarters?" my shrink asked, cocking her head to one side.

The keys were sitting on the small table between us, next to her tissue box.

"I never use them. Only to lock up when I'm leaving—if he's not there."

"Never?"

"Well, he might be inspired to ask for a set of mine. I couldn't possibly let Matt have keys to my place! And I'm always afraid he'll bring that up. This morning . . ." I scowled unhappily. "I resolved to throw them into the Hudson."

"Really. What's going on?"

I crossed my arms uncomfortably. "His sister's pushing me to set a wedding date, and she introduced us to this real estate broker." I told Wendy about the two-bedroom on Franklin Street. "Matt thinks it's wonderful and he just assumes I do, too. He has this idea that we'll become some kind of downtown couple, but his whole idea of what downtown is really about is just silly! And false! *Moving* downtown isn't what makes you a downtown person. It's so naive! He's not really a New Yorker," I explained, "and it's becoming more obvious. How can I live in Tribeca with some guy who doesn't even know that he's not *really* living downtown, that the whole area has become an overpriced travesty! He has zero sense of real estate irony."

"So you're angry at your boyfriend because he's still an out-of-towner."

Wendy blinked, betraying a hint of a smile, and I suddenly felt unfaithful. Boyfriend-bashing is fine if restricted to certain topics, but this was pushing the envelope. You're supposed to be able to say anything about anybody in therapy, but I felt guilty. Admitting that he's geographically unhip to the point of clueless! A good girlfriend doesn't speak derisively about a guy who is so . . . invested in her.

"Where is Matt from, if you don't mind my asking?"

"Connecticut."

"Irish-Catholic?"

"No, some kind of part-time Protestant. His mother came from one of those Hudson Valley Huguenot families. But he's not very interested in his ancestors. Or his religion. He's . . ." I smiled and blushed. "Very keen on the present and the future."

"Yes?" Wendy looked quizzical. "You had a pleasurable thought."

"Oh, nothing. He's so cute," I sighed. "Sometimes, I just want us to keep dating. I'd like to stop time and be old enough to know better and young enough to play the game and . . . be pursued by this up-and-coming guy for the rest of my life. I guess I'm like one of those clients—those men who keep holding back because they don't want to come. They don't want their session to end, and they just keep prolonging it."

"And how do you feel about those men?"

"I used to hate them! But now I'm used to it. I know how to pace myself, how to hurry them along—gently, of course. But nobody feels upbeat about getting a difficult customer."

"So if you're a difficult customer, what does this new apartment signify? The end of an 'exciting session'?"

"Look, any normal woman would be thrilled. It's really a very nice place. It's close to Wall Street, so it's perfect for Matt, but it's miles away from everything *I* do. Does he expect me to give up my home, my neighborhood, my entire life? Just like that?"

"To be fair, I don't think Matt has any idea what you'll be giving up if you move in with him."

"No kidding! If I move in with him, I'll—I'll be reduced to doing outcalls." (What else? Rent Jasmine's bedroom by the hour? The bulk of my business today is in my apartment.) "He doesn't understand how I support myself. I think he thinks I'm getting money from my family."

"Did you tell him that?"

"Um, no. I just sort of let him think it. I mean, there's no way I could dress the way I do and live where I live if I really made my entire living as a freelance copy editor."

"Interesting. Why *did* you get engaged?" Dr. Wendy asked in a quieter voice.

Tears of self-pity began to pour down my cheeks. Fortunately, Dr. Wendy's office and my bedroom are two places where you never have to hunt around for a tissue!

I blew my nose and explained, "It was totally unprofessional of me—I didn't think it through! I accepted his ring. I was too dazzled to think—disoriented, afraid—"

"What were you afraid of?"

"He came over to pick up his keys." I pointed to the keys on the table. "We had broken up a few days before, and he was acting strange. I started thinking he was going to assault me."

"Has he assaulted you before?" Wendy was alarmed.

"Of course not!" Matt smacking a girl—that's unthinkable. But you can't even joke about such matters these days. Everybody, even your shrink who has known you for half a decade, will suspect that you're protecting a social monster. "It was a misunderstanding," I assured her. "I was disoriented. I felt so distant from him at first, and he seemed like a stranger to me, and I didn't know why he was there. We weren't seeing each other anymore. But he said he needed his keys because he was locked out of his apartment. And then my mind flashed on this terrible thing that happened when I was sixteen!"

"Yes?"

"A john who waved a gun in my face. I was terrified. And when I started screaming my head off, the client got so scared of the racket I was making, he begged me to leave."

"He did?" Wendy sat up straighter. "You weren't afraid to express your feelings. Your emotions saved your life! I think that's something to be proud of. Especially at sixteen."

"Well," I sniffled, "I ran out of his apartment and I tripped on my own pants—I was wearing harem pants with those cords at the ankles, but they were loose—and when I tripped, I slid down the stairs on my back in my high heels."

Wendy was now gripping the arms of her chair. "My god. At sixteen?"

"Oh." I stopped crying. "I was fine. When I got to the bottom of the stairs, I was kind of shocked, but I wasn't hurt."

"You could have broken your neck! Or your back!"

"But I didn't. I got right up, buttoned my blouse, found a cab, and went back to the escort agency. I was so relieved that none of the neighbors saw me." I had just started working for Jeannie's Dream Dates, an outcall service owned by a madam named Mary. She ran it from a midtown studio apartment, advertised in the Yellow Pages (and some other publications I prefer not to think about), and felt that Mary was a terrible name for a madam. So she called herself Jeannie.

Wendy took a deep breath. "So this is what was going through your mind when Matt proposed? A narrow escape from a gun-toting john. Did that happen in New York?"

"Yes." I laughed briefly. "In a very nice town house right off Park Avenue in Murray Hill. Too much coke. The client was upset because I couldn't make him come and his hour was up."

Maybe my flexible teenaged body saved me when I tumbled down those stairs. But the point is, I've gotten away with so much—how much longer can it go on? I'm not a teenager any-more.

"And Matt's proposal—was it really a surprise?"

"God, yes. I never imagined . . ."

Wendy jutted her chin forward—her Listening Gesture.

"I had broken up with him and I was ready to devote myself to my business. I decided to swear off boyfriends. Then Matt called. He made up that story about the keys, which I believed.

Wendy nodded.

"When he grabbed my hand, I got nervous. He was so much stronger. And suddenly, I remembered that guy with the gun. I thought: I've come this far, I have my own clients, I don't have to work for some sleazy escort service, I'm well-connected and go to the best hotels. My clients are the movers and shakers of the uni-verse. They run Manhattan. But my own boyfriend turns out to be a random nutcase just like that guy! I've allowed a maniac into my home! At least, when I was sixteen, that guy didn't enter my life—I could leave his apartment! For a minute I wasn't really a success after all. Women who get killed by guys they don't under-stand are, by definition, failures. Right?"

There was a pause. Dr. Wendy doesn't like to call anyone a fail-ure. "And then what happened?"

"He pulled out this beautiful Lucida ring and he was so incredibly gentle and persuasive and passionate, and everything was okay again. I realized that I *was* a success. My nightmare was a delusion. I never dreamed, when I was a sixteen-year-old hooker, that a guy like Matt would propose to me—that I would even want him to! Don't you see? I was spellbound! By my own respectability!"

"That's a lot of material to be processing while your boyfriend's trying to propose to you."

"After all the stories I've told him, and all the lies he believed, that story about the keys—I really believed him!"

"You fell for *his* ruse."

"Yes. I took it as a sign! It made me feel that we belonged together after all. He used his wits—he figured out a scheme to get back into my apartment and into my life. I was so . . ." My heart still skips a beat when I remember the confusion, the fear, and the sudden realization that I had been romantically snared— by this guy who didn't know exactly who or what I was but could still get the better of me. "It made me, you know, respect him as a guy. We had . . ." I paused and remembered the reckless lovemaking that had followed. "We had very good sex that night," I added primly.

"But when Matt came to collect his keys you were reminded of an unsatisfied sex partner from over a decade ago—a man who also wanted something more than you could give."

This certainly appealed to my therapeutic vanity. And my latent Sinderella Complex. The commercial nymphet in danger, saved by her scheming Galahad. But I fessed up.

"I *know* marriage is supposed to be the alternative to strange guys waving their weapons in your face. But the truth is, that's the only time anyone has ever threatened me with a gun. I'm not in that kind of danger. Most of my guys are regular clients. I was just so dazzled. My heart was pounding because he had captured me.

He proved that he wasn't just my mental toy—he surprised me totally."

"And now? In the cooler light of day?"

"Maybe girls like me aren't supposed to marry. Wasn't that the first thing Gigi's aunt taught her? *We don't marry.* Maybe those Old World courtesans had the right idea."

Wendy knows that *Gigi* is one of my favorite adult fairy tales. The book, the movie, even the corny songs. So does Matt. He, however, just thinks it's some kind of strange retro quirk.

"Gigi comes from a family of courtesans," Wendy began. "But the only successful courtesan in the story is her aunt, who also happens to be the head of the family. And she masterminds a marriage for Gigi, despite herself. So, *Gigi* is really a story about ambivalence in the demimonde."

I savored the phrase, the emotional geography. In the demimonde: ambivalence. A golden age of hooking when girls like me could retreat into their own social *country.* No wonder they could say, without regret, "We don't marry."

"But ambivalence about marriage is not unique to your profession," Wendy continued. "I meet hundreds of women in my practice—and a lot of men—who use their work to explain a romantic disappointment or a fractured relationship."

I nodded in agreement but felt rather wistful. So much for my Belle Epoque fantasy of a romantic caste system!

3 Mau-Mauing the Flatbackers

What with actresses wanting to be amateurs because
they think it's ladylike, and amateurs wanting to be
actresses because they think it's immoral, the theatre is
no place for an honest workman.

—George Bernard Shaw

TUESDAY, 2/15/00. The morning after the night off

In the cab on the way to Carnegie Hall last night, I felt my
temperature rising as I checked the clock on my cell phone. As
usual, I had not given myself enough time to find a taxi—a bad habit
that I mostly indulge in with boyfriends and rarely with clients. I closed
my eyes to block out the Valentine traffic jam on Second Avenue.

I opened my eyes at Park Avenue and Fifty-seventh. Two girls in smart
black suits got out of a limo in front of the Four Seasons Hotel—where I
would be tonight if I were working. Maybe I could somehow escape from
this Sinderella Spiral and become, like Jasmine, a sexually active spinster—
a woman with a past, a future, and no serious boyfriend. A woman without
nosy future in-laws who ask awkward questions. A woman with less to lose!
All the pieces of my life can't possibly fit together for much longer. Something's got to give—but what?

When I got to my destination, Matt was waiting in the lobby, looking
a little shy—and rather adorable in the tie I gave him for Christmas, the
one with small yellow giraffes on a bright red background. He's mine!
I thought, with a sudden surge of confidence. His face lit up when I
approached.

"Each time I see you," he murmured affectionately, "it's a kind of revelation to me."

I melted against the arm of his jacket and my regrets faded. The pieces *do* fit, I thought. With Matt, I have a future. My body, still tingling with anxiety about its checkered past, now felt safe, desirable, mysteriously protected.

My doubts drifted out of me during the recital. Later, in his bed, I closed my eyes while he—quite happily—did all the work. I reveled in my laziness and encouraged him to take his time.

WEDNESDAY, 2/16/00

A phone call this morning from Jack! "Suzy? Are you available today?"

"I'm sorry," I said carefully. "I, um, have an exercise class in five minutes—can't talk." You should never tell a john you've blacklisted him. He'll want to have a long conversation with you, attempting to *explain* himself, pledging to reform—or trying to convince you that he's innocent. Or he'll try to find out who spread the word of his misdeeds, if he's vengeful. So I'm accidentally unavailable when Jack calls. Unlike Eileen, who feels the need to confront her foes, I'm very clear about not wanting to have enemies in this business. "Can I call you back?" I suggested, as a stall.

"No, don't call me at work," he said nervously. "My son's in the office. Okay, fine, call, but if he answers, just act like you have a wrong number. Call me before five—I want to see you," he added abruptly. "I'll come right over."

My other phone started ringing, and I quickly hung up.

"It's me!" Allie announced. "I just saw Jack!"

"But he just— When? Where? What's going on? Where are you?"

"I just got home. We had lunch at La Côte Basque." She gig-gled and added, "He gave me an envelope. You'll be proud of me. I stood my ground! I told him we couldn't have sex. He said I should keep the envelope anyway. There's enough in here for . . . oh, wow. I think I made the right decision."

"Well, he just called me."

"He called *you?*" Allie sounded incredulous. "When?"

"Just now!"

There was silence. So Allie met with him, took his money, and left him with an unrequited hard-on.

"And what did he want?" she asked. "Did he talk about *me?*"

"What do you *think* he wanted? Look, if you insist on playing head games with Jack, he's going to look for satisfaction else-where. And no, he didn't say anything about you. The man is not a eunuch. Even if he agrees to act like one when he's having lunch with you."

"Well, I'm not possessive! I don't care who he sees." There was a pause in which I said nothing. Doesn't care who he sees? Nobody asked her! But I didn't want to be the one to point this out. "And don't forget the NYCOT meeting," she reminded me. "You promised to come! See you tomorrow?"

That meeting. Ever since Allison got involved with "the sex workers' community," I've noticed a definite loosening of stan-dards. I think I preferred it when she was a Recovering Hooker, trying to kick the habit.

"Allie, you're playing a dangerous game," I started to warn her. "You're not being professional about this—" But she had already hung up.

LATER

Amazing news from Karen about Franklin Street. The owners are staying put. Apparently, the wife suddenly panicked at the prospect of moving to the Upper East Side. She broke out in hives! Canceled the deal on their new condo. Had to forfeit a mortgage broker's fee. Turns out this is the second time hubby has tried to pry his wife away from her cultural roots. And lost a mortgage broker's fee.

"They've got all this money," Karen sighed. "And the husband's a partner at _____." She named some white-shoe-sounding law firm. "But *she* gets a hysterical illness whenever she has to go above Fourteenth Street! And now that she has this child, well, she's never going to let him tell her where to live."

"Oh, dear," I sighed back, trying not to sound too relieved.

Saved by a bourgeois bohemian's worst hang-ups! I ♥ Manhattan and its many varied neuroses. The neighborhood caste system is alive, and all's right with the world. Or at least with the borough.

THURSDAY, 2/17/00. Pumpkin time—home at last

Tonight, as I was leaving for the NYCOT meeting, I suddenly realized I had no idea where I was going. With my keys dangling in the door, I dashed back inside and had to boot up my laptop just to retrieve the address; I've been careful not to print out any of Allison's recent e-mail. I cringed as I reread her message:

> *The New York Council of Trollops (NYCOT) wants YOU. As sex workers, we have been penalized for daring to transcend patriarchal concepts of sexual virtue that have kept all human beings in a state of sex-negative paralysis for millennia. Be we prostitutes, be we strippers, pro-dommes, or phone-sex workers, we are all sexual and social healers. As we enter a new millennium, we honor the history of all whores, take responsibility for healing the sex-negativity in our*

lives and in the penal code, celebrate the contribu-
tions of sex workers everywhere . . .

When I saw the location, I groaned; my outfit was all wrong. Wear a casual fur on Avenue C and you'll be totally misinterpreted, maybe even assaulted—what was I thinking? Suddenly, my lunaraine mink sweater looked less jaunty, less casual, and more controversial.

As the cab pulled up in front of a run-down redbrick walk-up, I was glad I had changed into my quilted black jacket, the perfect transitional outfit for traveling below Fourteenth and back. A coat for all zip codes. You can't tell what it costs unless you look carefully—at the inside.

On the second floor, I was overwhelmed by an aroma of burning sage, and by Allison's latest role model. Roxana Blair is New York's most politically correct ex-hooker. When she isn't organizing NYCOT meetings, she facilitates VagInal Empowerment Workshops, coyly referred to as Group VIEWs. Roxana also believes that intimate relationships interfere with our sexual empowerment by discouraging women from perfecting their masturbation skills. Whatever!

So far, I've resisted her efforts to recruit my, er, body for a weekend VIEWing. Roxana and I have reached what I would call a vaginal detente: you don't show me yours, and I won't show you mine. But I did agree to attend the NYCOT meeting for Allison's sake, on the strict understanding that this was *not,* repeat not, one of Roxy's vaginal encounter groups.

"Nancy's here!" Roxana mooed to the room. "Welcome!" She was dressed in an oversize tie-dyed T-shirt, which rode up when she hugged me. At the sight of Roxana's unkempt pubic hair, I froze. *Have I been tricked into joining one of her G-spot search parties? And why doesn't she wax?*

"I haven't seen you in *months,*" Roxana continued, completely ignoring my alarmed expression. "Not since our lunch at Zen Palate." (That's when Roxana tried to befriend me by ordering twenty different kinds of wheat gluten followed by tofu for dessert. She was under the mistaken impression that because I look Chinese, I must be a vegan Buddhist. I haven't had the heart to tell her that, where I come from, Chinese people are Catholic or Anglican—and carnivorous.)

I glanced around the room and saw a skinny girl in her twenties with short spiky hair and a U-shaped nose ring. Her black bra was peeking out of a half-open leather vest, but she, unlike Roxana, was wearing pants. Her jeans had holes in the knees, but, mercifully, not at the crotch. An overweight woman with chin-length gray hair, wearing a long flowered dress and black sneakers, handed me a sign-in sheet.

"For the NYCOT mailing list," she explained cheerfully.

"I don't want to be on any mailing list!" I said, unable to control my shrillness. "Where's Allison?" And where were all the other members?

Nobody else seemed to care—much less notice—that Roxana was chairing this meeting without her panties. Allison appeared, carrying some paper cups and a large pitcher of red liquid.

"Oh, Nancy's here—good. Everybody help yourselves to cranberry juice!"

"This needs sugar," the skinny girl with the nose ring complained.

"It's made with Hain's unsweetened concentrate, and it's very good for the bladder," Roxana told her. "This is a sugar-free dwelling, Gretchen."

"Well, we're going to discuss inclusiveness," the girl replied. "If we want to do outreach to the entire sex industry, we have to acknowledge different kinds of cultural norms."

Allison scribbled dutifully in her Kate Spade organizer and looked up. "What else is on the agenda?" she asked brightly.

"We have two new members," Roxana announced. "Gretchen and Nancy."

Members? When did I say I was becoming a member? I guess there are no free vegan lunches. Gretchen and I regarded each other from across the room with wary expression-free eyes.

"So, why don't we all introduce ourselves," Roxana continued. "Please tell the room who you are, what kind of sex work you do, and why you're here." As members began to introduce themselves, Roxana jotted notes on a huge yellow pad, nodding emphatically.

"I'm Belinda," said the gray-haired woman. "I've been a dominatrix for twenty years. All my friends know I'm a pro-domme, I have an ad in *Corporal,* and I'm a proud bisexual volunteer at the Gay and Lesbian Anti-Violence Project, a member of the Lambda Independent Democrats, and a founder of the Lower East Side Coalition. And I'll be speaking at this year's Leather Leadership Conference in D.C. I joined NYCOT because I want to make the world a better place for the next generation of sex workers."

How does she find time to work?

"Also," Belinda continued, "I'm having a dispute with the billing department of *Screw* about an ad I was running. The patriarchal males who control the adult publications are threatened by pro-dommes because we're strong independent women who don't give blow jobs. Now I noticed that Nancy, here, says she doesn't want to be on the mailing list. I'd like to know why—"

"That's wonderful!" Roxana interrupted. "Can we limit the introductions to introducing ourselves and wait until Nancy has her turn before we start the actual discussion?"

I was not exactly looking forward to explaining myself to the downtown dominatrix who doesn't give blow jobs. (*Or* take care of her hair.) Fortunately, Allison gave me some breathing time.

"I've been a sex worker for eight challenging and fulfilling years," she began. It was bizarre to hear her lapsing into NYCOT-speak—"sex worker"? She beamed at Belinda, who beamed back. "I just want to say that lately I have been aware of the goddess within *every* sex worker. For example, my friend Nancy, whether she wants to be on the mailing list or not, has been—"

"I think we should limit ourselves to ourselves," Roxana interrupted again. "Wait until Nancy has spoken." Her gentle New Age manners were beginning to wear off.

The girl with the nose ring took the floor. "I'm Gretchen. Today I run a needle exchange program in Hunts Point and I have a master's in public health, but I worked on the street for eight years." When everyone sat up, she began to vent. "The hookers' movement is always talking about changing the laws, but what are you doing for IV-using street workers?" she asked. "Nothing! You're all just talking to yourselves! You can't go to Hunts Point and expect to reach women on the street by telling them how fulfilling your life is," she told Allie. "You're out of touch with reality. *I* was out there at the age of fifteen—whoring! And what were you? A fucking cheerleader?"

Allie went rigid—and looked rather startled. Like the proverbial creature caught in the headlights.

"If there's a *goddess,* why would she allow cops to lean on teenage girls for blow jobs? Without condoms!" Gretchen added.

Roxana cleared her throat but didn't scold Gretchen for veering off-topic. Or for impugning Allison's high school career. So much for limiting our introductions to ourselves! Do I detect a double standard? Unbridled, Gretchen began to berate Roxana's elitist attachment to sugar-free beverages.

"You can't have a policy like that at group meetings," Gretchen told her. "You're excluding people like *me.* You can't do outreach in Hunts Point with sugar-free beverages!"

Roxana and Belinda seemed to enjoy Gretchen's tongue-lashing.

"I want you to know that I feel *privileged* to be having this dialogue with you," Roxana mooed. "I wasn't aware of the classist assumptions I was making."

Belinda, the dominatrix, chimed in. "Heroin should be legalized," she said, in a rather submissive tone.

Heroin. So that's it. I was wondering how anyone with such a pronounced sweet tooth could be so skinny.

"Um—where is Hunts Point?" Allison humbly inquired.

"The Bronx," Gretchen said with a knowing sneer.

I managed to introduce myself as "Um, Nancy, I'm a working girl." That was all I wanted to say.

"Thank you so much for coming," Roxana said to me. "We want you to think about joining this committee."

"This committee?"

"This is the steering committee. We really feel the lack of your perspective around here."

My perspective? Does that mean I should have worn my mink sweater after all?

*

Later, as we searched Houston Street for a cab, I tried to give Allie moral support. "How can you be expected to know the geography of the Bronx? You have no reason to go there!" I carped. "Gretchen didn't have to be so snotty about it."

Ignoring my remarks, Allison gave me a curious look. "Why don't you talk to her about your past?" she asked. "Didn't *you* start working when you were fifteen?"

"That's none of Gretchen's business." (Besides, I was still, technically, fourteen when I started hooking.)

"But you share a common experience as sex workers!"

"Gretchen and I have nothing in common. I never had to give

a blow job to a cop, and I never worked on the street. And I'm beginning to wish I'd never told you anything about my life, because you obviously don't understand it. Don't you dare start talking to Gretchen about me! Do you hear?"

Allison blinked, hurt by my outburst, but not for long.

"You should reach out to her," she said firmly. "I see a lot of potential for a mutually healing dialogue!"

"With Gretchen? She's not interested in making friends with me. Or you, for that matter. Don't kid yourself," I snapped.

"NYCOT is committed to healing the divisions between sex workers. We Are All Bad Girls," Allie intoned. "Roxana says we have to expect—*embrace*—our growing pains. . . . The process of empowerment involves change, and change involves—" A vacant cab interrupted Allie's train of thought, and we got in.

As we headed up First Avenue, Allison continued to chatter. "Change—sometimes even for the sake of change—can reveal our hidden strengths as agents of social change . . ." At Fifty-ninth Street, she ran out of steam and changed the subject. "I'm going to be interviewed next week. Did I tell you? The producer called today. Roxana has to go out of town that night, and she says I'm ready to represent NYCOT publicly—"

"You can't go on TV! Have you lost your mind? Everybody in your building will recognize you! And nobody will ever work with you again! Do you think Liane would let you work for her if she saw you on—"

"Noooo, silly, I'm going to be on the *radio*—it's a call-in show!" Allison reassured me. "Besides, Roxana takes all the TV calls. She says I'm not ready for TV."

I breathed a sigh of relief. Roxana's grabby sense of turf should keep Allison off TV for quite some time.

"What was that Roxana was saying about 'my perspective'?" I asked. "I hope you haven't been telling *her* about my past."

"We don't have a woman of color on the steering committee. NYCOT is facing the challenge of diversity. We need a committee that looks like New York."

"Let's see: You've got a dominatrix who's a partisan Democrat. A heroin-addicted streetwalker with an attitude. And a blonde who's always late with the rent," I said. "If that isn't a committee that looks like New York, I don't know what is."

Allie frowned and opened a small compact. She dabbed her nose. "Jack showed up again—I wasn't expecting him! I was *seeing someone,* and my doorman buzzed. He said, 'A gentleman wants to bring a plant upstairs.' So I told him I would pick it up later. Then Jack started calling me"—she lowered her voice so the cabdriver wouldn't hear—"while I was trying to get this guy off! And the phone wouldn't stop ringing because Jack knew I was in the apartment. He left a bunch of messages, begging me to pick up the phone. Why do men say 'pick up the phone' when they know they're already in voice mail? It's crazy! My customer was really nervous. He took forever to come—all those interruptions!"

Recalling the interruptions, she looked flustered.

"He's acting like a lovesick teenager!" I said. "An adult *sends* flowers—or brings them when he's invited."

"You're right," she said, with an odd smile. "He is."

"And it's not amusing when"—I dropped my voice, too—"a client does that. It's a stalker thing. Completely unacceptable."

"Well, I do have a doorman to protect me from stuff like that."

"Great. Jack's making a spectacle of himself in front of your doorman. And screwing up your existing business! You're going to be sorry you took that money."

"I know what I'm doing," she proclaimed.

"That thing Gretchen said. *Were* you a cheerleader?"

In a stiff voice, she said, "That's completely irrelevant. It has nothing to do with *any* of this. I don't want to talk about it."

"Sorry! I didn't know it was such a sensitive subject."

She feels perfectly okay about barging into *my* past and bringing up my teen hooker years, yet she's hung up about . . . being a cheerleader? I guess she's embarrassed. Being a former cheerleader won't help her—or might even hurt her chances—in a popularity contest that puts so much store in a girl's street cred. She may have changed, but she hasn't exactly grown. In fact, she's still a cheerleader; Allie hopes I'll reveal my history to Gretchen because it will make *her* look better for having brought me to the meeting. Trying to use *me* to increase her own credibility as a hooker! You've gotta watch these cheerleaders—they're an exploitive breed. Even when they think they're being avant-garde, they're really trying to be popular.

Anyway, home sweet home—where I'm greeted by my boyfriend's amorous voice mail. He's working late at the office, he misses me, he'll be finished at . . . just about now. But I'm not in the mood for an impromptu sleepover! Being stuck in Roxana's living room for two hours, surrounded by the reek of incense and badly dressed girls, has completely turned me off to all forms of lovemaking, paid or unpaid. And besides, I'm saving myself. For an early-morning date at the Carlyle with Jasmine. Do I call him back? Pretend I'm not around to get the message? What is the etiquette when a working girl becomes engaged?

Lately, I'm paranoid about having him in my apartment. I worry about Matt finding things while I'm fast asleep. Like those over-the-top black crotchless panties I wear for Milton. With the red frilly opening. Yikes.

FRIDAY, 2/18/00

Well, I opted for an impromptu sleepover—at Matt's place—after hinting that I "just want to cuddle." In preparation for a night of sexless bonding, I showered and changed into a pair of white cotton panties. My Not Tonight Gear is actually more expensive than some of my workwear. Sexy understuff is as rare as bottled water these days. And there's always a special at Bloomingdale's or the local lingerie boutique. But you hardly ever see good seamless Swiss panties on sale. Good-girl undies, like the girls they were designed for, get harder to find every day. One of my millennium resolutions was to pamper my lower body in all its moods and phases, so I've invested in high-quality off-duty cotton panties. In white, of course. It's a mistake to stint. You don't spend a whole lot of time in your work panties—they're off before you know it—but your off-duty unders have to stay on, sometimes overnight. The sixty-dollar panties I wore last night are comfy and loose but properly fitted. With a demure embroidered flower on the right hip.

I arrived at my boyfriend's bachelor pad wearing my pristine waist-high armor. You know how they always say "Wear something risqué under your business suit—even if *you* are the only one who knows about it, *you* will feel like a sex kitten." Well, same thing here.

Having doped myself up with melatonin, I took to Matt's bed feeling very much like a neutered being. As I was drifting off in one of his T-shirts, I heard him showering, then setting the clock. Then I felt his hands making experimental advances. He slid the T-shirt up to my waist and ran his fingertip beneath one leg of my panties.

"So . . . where were you when I called?" he asked in a friendly voice. "What did you do tonight?"

How could I begin to explain my night? Roxana's incense-filled den of activism, a bitchy encounter with a former street kid, that aging dominatrix with her ad in *Screw,* and his girlfriend being asked to join the Council of Trollops steering committee because she's . . . a Call Girl of Color?

"I was hanging out with Allison," I said in a sleepy voice.

His hands delved deeper, and I pulled my lower body out of reach. As I drifted off into chaste slumber, or tried to, he whispered a dirty endearment into my ear. My response was lukewarm. Then I heard him saying, in that hushed reverent tone that boyfriends reserve for pastel-colored underwear: "You should wear these panties more often. They're . . . so soft."

Should I bite the bullet and invest in some *actively* unattractive panties? Stop discarding the old pairs? Life is so unfair! I can't bring myself to wear anything that makes me look bad. Even on nights like this.

This morning, I crawled out of an empty bed. Disoriented, I realized that my boyfriend had forgotten to reset the alarm. Could I have OD'd on melatonin? I dashed home in my hugest face-saving eight A.M. sunglasses so I could linger over freshly brewed aged Sumatra in my oxygen mask. Then I lost track of the time and was almost late for my ten-thirty at the Carlyle.

While Jasmine's client, Roberto, took a business call—naked—in the living room of his suite, we sprawled out on his bed, gossiping in our garter belts. It was a bit early for both of us, but more so for me, what with the melatonin hangover. Jasmine snickered with undisguised satisfaction when I told her about the NYCOT meeting.

"It was awful," I complained. "Between Roxana's pubic hair and the cheap incense, I was completely disoriented."

"No kidding!" she said in a low voice. "That feminazi doesn't bother to wax her muff, yet she has the nerve to pass herself off as a spokeswoman for hookers? What's *up* with that? You should have come to that benefit with me," Jasmine added. "The room was crawling with money. I picked up five business cards! And I met this dot-com grillionaire . . . *and* got a good night's sleep."

A night of drumming up new business would have put me in the mood for Matt, I suddenly realized. I looked up at Roberto. He was standing in the doorway, and the sight of him, fully erect, massaging his cock absentmindedly, made me touch the front of my panties. A conscientious-working-girl reflex; I was doing it because it was my job, the way some secretaries absentmindedly tidy up their desks. But a pleasant sensation ran through my body. Jasmine rose to her knees. She began fondling a nipple through my bra, telling Roberto how hot this made me. Of course, she was exaggerating wildly and, as far as she was concerned, we were pretending. But I quietly enjoyed the attention she gave my breasts and let her assume I was faking it. (Jasmine's one of those stalwart pros who never comes when she's working—"That's the customer's job!"—and gets irate if she suspects that a co-hooker is really getting into *her*.)

Warmed up by my colleague, I turned to face Roberto and wriggled closer, so he could rub his cock against my breasts. He stood at the edge of the sheets, entranced by Jasmine's hungry-sounding moans. I couldn't see her, but I knew she was fingering herself for his amusement, as he watched her watching us. Jasmine's climactic sound effects grew louder, and Roberto joined in. A white liquid arc collapsed into a small pool between my breasts. I smiled the satisfied smile of a girl who has made $400 before noon without even showing her pussy.

The scent of his fresh come disappeared under a pile of tissues. Roberto was summoned back to the living room by a ringing phone. When he returned to pay us, we were half-dressed, debating a late breakfast at the Mark (across the street) or at E.J.'s, closer to home. The Gallery, downstairs, would be lovely but, given all the business we do at the Carlyle, the public areas there are mostly off-limits. Can't afford to be conspicuous. And Roberto would be very turned off if he ran into us downstairs. It wouldn't look right.

This afternoon, a call from Eileen complaining about Jack's continuing harassment: "He's saying these weird *things*—about you, about Allison, about his blood pressure. When I told him to leave me alone, he called back and left a really insulting message on my voice mail."

"What did he say?"

"He called me—" She paused, caught her breath, then said, "You know what? I am not going to stoop to his level, repeating such a stupid disgusting thing." She was outraged. "That fucking creep! I might have to change my number if this keeps up! But you know what? I *can't* change my number, I've worked too hard to build this!"

"Of course you can't change your number. Nobody can—you'd lose half your guys. Don't do anything impulsive," I told her.

I called Allison's cell phone. "Where are you? Can you talk?"

"I'm at Duane Reade," she said cheerfully.

"We have to talk about Jack. He's becoming a problem, and I think you've made it worse by taking that money. You really shouldn't have done that."

"Oh, really!" Allie sighed impatiently. "I wish you'd stop! You are soooo paranoid, Nancy! He *wanted* to give it to me. He practically begged me to take it!"

"With what kind of understanding? What does he expect in return?"

"How would *I* know?" she squeaked. "Maybe nothing. Hold on. I have to pick up a prescription. . . . Di*flu*can," her voice rang out. (Why not just tell the whole store you have a yeast infection?) "Allison Rogers. R-O-G . . ."

"Listen, if you want to play dumb with Jack, that's one thing. But don't play dumb with me," I said. "When you take money from a guy, you should know what his expectations are. It's business. Even if you don't come through for him, you should know what you're depriving him of—what he expects and what you plan to do about it. You can't just wing it. And if a guy knows you're a working girl, you can't suddenly act like a dumb little party girl."

"These patriarchal categories—" Allie began.

"Shut up and listen!" I implored her. "Your phone's starting to break up! Guys don't like it when they feel they've been taken for a ride by a hooker." I thought of the cantankerous cokehead, many years ago, who was so affronted when his hour ended that he grabbed his gun. "And he's pestering Eileen, making ugly annoying phone calls, and she knows it's him. Do you know if he has a drinking problem?"

"I don't think so. I'm getting another call—I'll call you when I get home!"

I hung up and started to punch in Eileen's number. I was furious, ready to spill the beans on Allie, ready to *talk*—about the money, the stupid flowers, Allie's lunch with Jack. Then I stopped, slammed the phone down, and thought: Bad idea. Telling Eileen about Allison's behavior won't solve a thing. Eileen would tell the other girls about that brainless, destructive floozy—Allison—and it would certainly teach Allie a lesson. But it wouldn't make Jack go away. Then I started dialing Jasmine's number. Maybe she could come up with a game plan to— Oh, hell. I hung up after the first ring.

I ran myself a hot bath, into which I poured a liberal helping of lavender oil. It's the real thing, purchased in a teensy Provençal village the last time I was in France, and inhaling the intense yet soothing aroma, I could feel my frayed boundaries recovering. Immersed in the scented water with my hair tucked high on the rubber pillow, I heard the phone ringing at the other end of my apartment. Probably Allison. I let it ring.

Around eleven last night, I got a totally strange call from Jack—
he never calls girls at that hour! That's when he's supposed to be
contained—in the twenty-room cond-op with his rich wife and
their perpetually dependent adult son. But last night, he
sounded dangerously free. Perhaps his wife's out of town?
Sirens in the background made me think he could be roaming
the city streets. Or standing on the balcony in his slippers with a
cell phone. It was a cold night for either.

There was little hope of detecting Jack's whereabouts because
I don't have Caller ID on my landline. Caller ID is lethal. It leaves
a numeric trail for boyfriends and other visitors to decipher. Private clients dislike it. Caller ID is for girls who advertise, for
people who consort with the public. No one in our safe little circle has Caller ID at home. We all have our numbers blocked, as
do a number of clients. If a private girl tried to prevent blocked
numbers from coming through, her phone might simply stop
ringing. But Caller ID was starting to have some appeal last night.
Jack's phone calls are downright creepy.

"Listen," Jack said, in a pushy urgent voice. "I really have to
talk to you. It's about Allison. I'll make it worth your while! I
want to surprise her. Can you set it up?"

"Set *what* up?"

"The three of us, at your place. You can get her over there,
can't you? She says you're her best friend. And besides, she's—"
His voice lowered to a desperate lust-filled whisper. "She's really
hot for you. I know it. She likes it when you take control."

Good god, is he jerking off? I felt like blowing the whistle on
our feigned lesbianism, right then and there. Listening cautiously,
I tried to detect some telltale heavy breathing.

"Look," he said, rather testily. "If you're not interested, there are
plenty of other girls. But I'd rather do this with you. So would she!"

"Um, how do you know this?"

"She was telling me how much she likes partying with you."

"Really? When?"

"The other day. Come on. Help me out here. You're not being fair to me!"

Did Allie spin this two-girl tale while they were having lunch? That's really annoying, if true. She has no business using me as bait.

"Jack," I said firmly. "I wish I could help, but my aunt is visiting. She's staying with me for the next two weeks, and I'm completely tied up with family obligations."

"Your aunt? Is she . . . ? What does *she* look like?"

"My aunt?" I repeated crossly. For a moment, I forgot this was a made-up aunt. "I have to go!" Disgusted, I hung up on him. What *is* he thinking? Christ.

THURSDAY, 2/24/00

After stewing over the call from Jack, I decided not to bother discussing it with Allie. But when I saw her today in the cardio room at the gym, I forgot all about my resolve. She was on the recumbent bike, wearing a headset, which she removed when I appeared in front of her.

"Hey!" she said, quite innocently. "I've been calling you for two days! What's going on?"

"What's going on? You'd better straighten your life out," I warned her. "That jerk has been calling me and making strange requests. He says you've been talking to him about doing a three-some with me! And he's bothering Eileen as well."

She looked around to make sure nobody could hear us. Still pedaling, she whispered, "That's ridiculous! I never said that to him. And why is he bothering Eileen?"

"Because he can! You took money from this phone freak and

now he's obsessed. You weren't supposed to see him or talk to him! Much less take money from him!"

Allison stared at the clock behind me and checked her pulse. There wasn't a trace of remorse in her eyes. She was in another world.

"Roxana's meeting me later at Zen Palate," she announced breathlessly. "She's coaching me for the radio show. We're brainstorming. She wants to talk about changing the name of our group. What do you think of Sex Workers Organization of New York? SWOONY. You know, like SUNY? She thinks NYCOT is kind of retro, kind of eighties. Or maybe even seventies. You know, when everybody wanted to sound sexy. But now we're demanding our place on the world stage and we have to be recognized as *workers*, like everybody else."

"I see."

"Want to come? I know she'd love to hear your take on this."

"No, thanks," I said coldly. "I have a regular at three o'clock and a bikini wax at noon. Some of us have *business* to conduct." In other words, *Fuck you*—but I'm too ladylike to put it that way.

LATER

Allie has no idea what kind of trouble she could be courting. She thinks I'm exaggerating the dangers because she doesn't know how unsafe this business can be when you're careless. I've learned, the scary way, not to be cavalier with men's appetites. Aside from that coke addict with the gun, there were a few others. And *all they did was scare me*. But that was enough for me. There was a guy who tied me up—because I let him. Because I was fifteen, curious about bondage, and completely clueless about the dangers. He was my fourth customer ever. But once I was tied up, he gagged me with my pantyhose, despite my objections. Not something I had expected. I was terrified because I thought he was going to kill me. After he came, he apologized for scaring me—and untied me right away. His apology spooks me to this day. I never let anyone do that again. What was I thinking? I was lucky he didn't do any of the things he talked about doing while I was lying there, immobile and frozen with fear. I was lucky, in a way, to meet up with a man who got his kicks from scaring hookers; though I wonder if he graduated to worse stuff.

Allison has always had it easy. Despite all this "sex worker" babble, she hasn't a clue what most hookers have to deal with when they start working. The wild-goose chases and time wasters. The risks you take. The stupid and dangerous mistakes you can make. If she knew what really goes on out there, she would think twice about playing hide-and-seek with Jack. Right now, she's flattered by his air of desperation, by his money, and by his horticultural choices. Okay, so Jack isn't a kinky john she picked up in a bar. He has never displayed the slightest bit of weirdness in bed. But the other day, what was that about hoping to surprise Allison with another girl? Customers are not supposed to plan "surprises."

Straight people wouldn't understand why it's so dangerous for a client to show up at your building without warning. (Unless, of course, he happened to be a sexual freak.) But a customer who disrespects the whole concept of calling first—that guy is already flirting with the dark side of being a john. Especially if the john in question is a middle-aged guy with money. I mean, we're not talking about a construction worker who wanders into a cheap massage parlor. Professionals demand that their clients behave like gentlemen, and while this might seem quaint or silly to the new girls, it's quite a serious matter. It's too easy for customers to get away with mistreating hookers; you can't afford to have guys around who are just barely acceptable. They have to be held to a standard.

How can a girl hook for this many years in a place like New York and still be as naive as Allison? She walked right into being a private call girl, that's how. Without ever working for an escort agency. Without paying her dues. Unlike me, Allison *started out* as one of Liane's new girls.

I met Allie on a call at the Pierre, about eight years ago. I was alone with a client in my panties and heels, waiting for the new girl to arrive and doing my best to keep a very impatient gentleman amused. Roland had a plane to catch, but I didn't want him to come before Allie got there—Liane would be furious, and justifiably so. I tried to distract him by pretending to be impressed with his Central Park view. It worked for about a minute. When Allie showed up, fifteen minutes late, I was immensely relieved. And we actually hit it off. We worked well together, like concert pianists who have practiced their duet many times. We faked it but it was fun, and Roland loved our act. He gave us each a hundred-dollar tip on top of our basic fee. Not bad for a first meeting with a new girl!

As we waited for the elevator to reach the lobby, Allie's cheeks were glowing. She had been working for only a few months, and she was still excited by all the new places and girls, the new situations she was getting herself into. Like being late for a double at the Pierre and trying to find her house keys and her K-Y at the last minute and . . . all those things that can make a new girl so flustered. On the way downstairs, I could tell she was still a bit dazzled by the Pierre Hotel's old-fashioned lushness. There's nothing trendy or Schrageresque going on there; it's a well-oiled, well-preserved Fifth Avenue institution, a very hospitable fortress.

Despite the panic on her way to the call, she had enjoyed performing well and getting paid cash for it. She couldn't wait to spend it. Though she made me feel like some sort of Jurassic tart—I was a veteran by then—I recognized a kindred spirit. Or thought I did. We went to Cipriani's for a snack and a drink, and as we got to know each other, I began to find out how little we really had in common.

4 Origin of My Species

MY FIRST TRICK WAS A BABY-SITTER'S CHILDISH LARK.
I was thirteen and Professor Andrews was a local celebrity,
a neighbor, who caught my eye.

In the quiet Canadian city where I grew up, anyone
who had ever lived abroad or who hung out in Toronto
was considered cosmopolitan. Professor Andrews qualified on both counts. He took *lots* of trips to Toronto,
which struck me then as glamorous. It tickled me to know
that grown women were actually falling in love with this charismatic radical chic author-professor, while I knew the *real* G. Frasier
Andrews. And I knew they'd be horrified if they found out what he had
done with me. I was having a giggle at the expense of all those grown-ups
who said, "You're too young to have sex. You aren't ready for it." I sensed
that there were things *they* would never be ready for.

While my parents knew I was on the Pill, I made sure they didn't
hear about my adventure with our neighbor. My mother created—and
enforced—a ten-thirty P.M. curfew but had no idea what I got away with in
the middle of the day.

It's horrible, really, when you think about it—how cold a pubescent girl
can be in the face of a pedophile's lechery. I wasn't a virgin, but I was
ridiculously innocent. I had never felt full-fledged physical desire. I didn't
know that mature women lusted after men's cocks, didn't know what that
felt like or looked like—which is why I didn't understand the adult
admirers of G. Frasier Andrews.

So when I looked at his cock, I must have appeared more curious
than appreciative. Professor Andrews was part of a summer project I

had assigned myself just before the break: I was determined to start taking the Pill, to start having a Sex Life.

Sex was instinctual for Professor Andrews; I doubt that he'd ever had a Sexual Plan when he was my age. And where I was too clinical to know what passion was, he was unable to control the urges that were most dangerous to his reputation.

Sometimes I think of Professor Andrews as my first adventure in the business. But I was still living at home; I didn't need the money, and it was summertime. I understand that summer has changed, that thirteen-year-olds now spend those months imprisoned in summer school and self-improvement day camps. Not then! I had lots of time on my hands.

The next summer, I ran away—to another country. Later, when I started hooking in earnest, I came to see Professor Andrews as an amateur trick. Having sex for money was, at first, a perverse little game that made me feel cocky and cool—different from my peers. But later, money became a necessity: it was food, freedom, the ability to control my life, to stay afloat and hold my head up without admitting defeat to my parents.

The boyfriend who took me in when I ran away to London was twenty-two, agoraphobic, and given to migraines that could last for days at a time. There were long silences when he would lock himself in the bedroom with a cloth over his eyes. His parents had purchased a garden flat for him in a row of mock-Tudor buildings right next to Hampstead Heath. They believed I was nineteen, an age Ned and I had settled upon as plausible when we set up house together:

"You look as old as twenty," he'd said, rather skeptically, "but you act about seventeen." I'd taken his word for it, though at twenty-two he looked about sixteen and sometimes acted even younger. "Maybe, when they come over to see me, you can just read a book. Look very absorbed. That way you won't have to chat." Neither of us wanted them to catch on that he was harboring a fourteen-year-old runaway.

Had they known that this person who roasted the occasional chicken, watered the hedges, cashed checks for their son, picked up his antidepressants, and ordered supplies from the milkman—*and* had time to explore the hotel bars at night—was actually fourteen, perhaps they wouldn't have been so quick to label his girlfriend "understandably immature." In other words, he couldn't expect to attract a *mature* nineteen-year-old. I accepted the slight as a compliment to my camouflage.

When I told him, over a midnight snack of hot cocoa and oatmeal, that I loved him, he smiled patiently as if his mind were very far away—in another universe. Our lovemaking was one of the best things we had; he was the first guy I ever had time to relax with, now that I had no curfew. So he became the first lover I really *needed* to fuck. I felt new sensations and wavelike emotions when he was inside. And maybe I shouldn't assign all the credit to our circumstances. He was a good lover, and I knew he was very fond of me.

Though he sometimes did strange and terrible things—once, during a twenty-four-hour headache, he tore up a glittery nylon jacket that was my favorite possession—he never locked me out of his home. In fact, he made me feel that this was my home, too, though I now realize that it never really was. He made sure I went to the doctor and the dentist, encouraged me to do all the household shopping (which meant I had a constant stream of cash), and sometimes—very rarely—got into a sufficiently normal mood so that we could go out together. In his own way, he took care of me.

His idea of a really good time was tinkering with the stereo, putting together Revox reel-to-reel tape recorders using spare parts, and then playing Mahler or the Moody Blues—loud. Sometimes I went to a shop on Mornington Crescent with a strange-looking list and picked up the bits and pieces that were required to add the finishing touches to a tape recorder. When I think about Ned, which I still do occasionally, I wonder if he blew out his eardrums listening to *Days of Future Passed* on that big cushiony headset that looked like Darth Vader's helmet. I also wonder if he's alive. I have a feeling he is. Crazy people have this strange ability to hang in there.

Between the help from his parents and the dole money he collected (Mummy and Daddy officially rented the flat to him and then doctored his rent book so he could collect extra money), we had an easy existence. Ned was "on the fiddle"—the middle-class fiddle—and it suited us both.

But his black moods reminded me that I couldn't stay there forever.

The first time Ned locked himself in the bedroom, he locked *me* in there with him, too. When he refused to let me out, I became completely hysterical. At which point he unlocked the door, stormed out, yelling and swearing at me, and locked himself in the music room with a chair up against the door. It was terrifying, but—too young to know any better—I tearfully pursued him, banging on the door, demanding an explanation. Some part of me thought this was romantic. Soon that part of me had been deeply wounded. We didn't speak for days. He called me terrible ugly names that I had never heard before. And when his mood had lifted, he was incredibly sweet again.

"Why did you do that?" I asked him. "Why did you lock me in the room?"

"I don't want to talk about it," he said, sulking. "I'll never do it again."

"But—but—you have to talk about it!"

"I *won't* talk about it," he replied. And on went the headphones.

Only a runaway would tolerate such a housemate, let alone

boyfriend. Only a boyfriend on a steady diet of MAO inhibitors would be so easy to snow. When I started turning tricks, he chose to believe any story I told him. And since he was sleeping off a headachy fit half the time, it was easy to sneak in and out of the flat. Ned had some deep flaws, but he wasn't nosy. He was much too involved with his headaches to be a snoop. And geeks were not yet regarded as hot property. In 1980, very few attractive girls—even runaways—were interested in snagging (or shagging) a geek. And how many geek groupies, even today, would enjoy picking up spare tape recorder parts for a melancholy agoraphobic? We both had a pretty good "deal," if you want to look at it that way; but I never called it that. I really did love him. He gave me a chance to make my way in the world.

When Ned made it clear that he was unable to discuss his craziness with me, I came to a private decision.

What I think of as my first *professional* trick was a guy I picked up at the bar of the Cumberland Hotel in Marble Arch. I was almost fifteen. It never occurred to me that being underage was something I could charge more for, so I told him I was nineteen. Too naive to realize that a pro shouldn't drink, I had my first snowball, a frothy yellow concoction of 7UP and Advocat. A cocktail that could well have been invented by a child prostitute, actually! But it was the bartender's recommendation, and it became my signature drink at that particular hotel bar. While under the influence of my first snowball, I negotiated this date myself—money, condom, sex—and was very soon upstairs.

In bed, I had no idea what a real professional does. I lay back and allowed my new customer, a gentle sweet-faced American salesman, to fondle me. I knew I was supposed to like it, so I made excited sounds. But I didn't know I was supposed to use my mouth for other things as well. I had no intention of including blow jobs in my repertoire; I didn't really like oral sex back then. Fortunately, he was dying to get laid, and very little could have turned him off. He was about thirty—"older" by my childish standards but young in real terms, if you think of him as a john. He slipped the condom on, entered, and came.

Then he started talking about Vietnam. He started crying. I held his hand but was more amazed than moved by his emotions. He had killed a very young woman in Vietnam, a young soldier. He had been treated like a hero when he went home to Houston, Texas, and someone had given him a job, right away. . . .

Then he said something about wanting to marry me.

"I can't marry you!" I told him.

"Why? Have you been promised to someone?"

At first, I didn't understand. Then I realized that the girl he had discovered in a London hotel bar was an exotic Asian flower, a mystery. (I had told him I was Malaysian because I thought it sounded sexy.) My appearance overshadowed my voice, which— to any thoughtful listener—was a North American teenager's bratty twang gone slightly transatlantic. I had never been viewed as an exotic flower before, and I didn't know how to be gracious about it.

For me, of course, *he* wasn't foreign—not in that way. I had grown up in a small Canadian town surrounded by freckled Waspy faces. By faces like his. In fact, I found real Asians quite exotic, just as he did. But we didn't get into that.

"We can't get married," I said, "because we hardly know each other! And I don't believe in marriage."

I didn't, at fourteen.

I sometimes wish I could travel back in time and give this guy the benefit of a grown-up hooker's attention. I'd be nicer. More aware of the subtleties. If I had been aggressive and slutty in bed, would he perhaps have been in a completely different mood? I'm convinced that my amateurish style—i.e., my tendency to lie there—came off as innocence (which, in a way, it was) and evoked his more vulnerable emotions. If I could turn back the clock (an ominous concept for a hooker) and be grown-up, cheerful, professional, my first bar trick would have been lying there with a smile on his face, forgetting his Vietnam stories instead of repeating them to a teenager.

But I wouldn't even be seeing a guy like that because I don't pick up guys in hotel bars. And I wouldn't go near a dive like the Cumberland today. His room was clean but hardly atmospheric, a junior salesman's hotel room. It wasn't so bad, but it was still a dive.

It was very different for Allison. At twenty-two, she turned her first trick in one of Liane's cozy bedrooms, surrounded by Indian-print wallpaper, Jim Thompson cushions from Bangkok, and bookshelves full of travel guides, spanning three decades. Allison—under strict instructions to "be eighteen"—wasn't permitted to imbibe anything fizzier than a Perrier water. Her payment was guaranteed, and there was little for her to negotiate. Her client, a mature businessman in his fifties, had been in and out of Liane's place many times—without ever having to bare his soul. From the very start, Allison was protected by the private girl's private code: When you arrange a date, you guarantee the other girl her share. That's how reputable madams and call girls do things, so Allie always assumed this was how *everyone* did things.

I knew better. When I met Liane, in '84, I had been working for a few years. I kept the details of that first year in London a secret and leveraged my transatlantic aura by casually dropping names—Molton Brown, Harrods, Biba—while avoiding any mention of my other haunts: the Cumberland Hotel bar, the Praed Street clinic (where the bar girls got their free V.D. tests). Liane never heard about the Kontinental—a small downstairs nightclub off Oxford Street, where I worked as a "hostess," hustling bottles of champagne. I allowed her to think I was the kind of girl who gets her V.D. checkups on Harley Street. And I certainly didn't let on that I had started the New York leg of my career working for a tacky outfit like Jeannie's Dream Dates!

I knew, from the girl who'd introduced us, that Liane had "excellent dates," and that she was eager to meet me because she was on the lookout for a pretty Oriental. That's all I knew when I walked in the door of her many-roomed duplex on East Sixty-fifth Street, still—finally—well, *almost* nineteen. I vaguely assumed she was a madam who simply ran a better class of escort agency. The girl who knew her warned me, "Don't tell her how we met. If she asks, you just say a john introduced us. We met in bed. Okay? Let's forget that we ever knew Jeannie."

Jeannie's operation had been abruptly closed down, and I had never been aggressive about giving my number out to Jeannie's clients. So now, without a regular source of new business, without a way to reach the clients I had been seeing, I was scared. Where would I go next? To avoid the police, I had moved out of a new apartment—leaving no forwarding address—into a room at the Allerton Hotel for Women on East Fifty-seventh Street. My brand-new furniture was sitting in a storage unit and sometimes I had disturbing dreams about the other hotel residents—like the formerly chic, asthmatic spinster on my floor who had once been a milliner. On her good days, she was friendly; on other days, she refused to share the elevator and gave me a beady stare.

Most of Jeannie's girls had scattered. Our shared fear—Where was Jeannie? What had caused her to close down and leave town?—spooked us so badly that we could hardly stand the sight of one another. Without Jeannie's couch (where we used to gather on a nightly basis) and Jeannie's ringing phone, our camaraderie was beginning to evaporate. Too late, it occurred to me that this was my reward for not giving out my number, for being a loyal agency girl. I had no clients of my own!

But three of my regulars from Jeannie had given me their business cards. I decided to call.

Wayne lived in Michigan and offered to fly me out to the sub-urbs of Detroit to spend the night with him at an airport hotel. I hedged. The idea of flying to Detroit was daunting. And I wasn't sure about this overnight thing! Would he try to have sex all night? In New York, I could get up and take a cab home if he became too demanding. In Detroit . . . well, god only knows. I made an excuse and he promised—in a rejected-guy voice—to call on his next trip to the city. And never did.

Jeff was a mild-mannered middle manager at Citibank, wore bangs and a beige suit, always smoked a joint beforehand, and liked to go twice. He wasn't a big spender, but he was reliable.

Marvin, in his sixties, lived alone in a high-rise on Whitestone Boulevard and paid extra for the cab. He also gave me a nominal "tip" for letting him take close-up Polaroids of my pussy. I wasn't ashamed of my profession by any means, but when people say that "every woman has fantasized about being a hooker"—well, I knew this wasn't what they meant. A middle manager who goes twice and a retired bachelor in Queens who collects homemade beaver shots.

Desperate to find a reliable escort service, I began combing the ads and discovered that the other agencies were even tackier than Jeannie's.

At one agency, I went on a call with two escorts who invited me to live with them. They both shared a large apartment with some-one whom they described as their "old man." They had two Siamese kittens, a weekend place in the Hamptons, and dressed like fashion-conscious secretaries. Pretty but not hyperchic.

"Thanks," I said, "but I don't think I could live with cats."

Back at the agency, the owner—marveling at my naïveté—spelled out the scenario when I told her about their generosity.

"He's their pimp, Nancy! Get it?"

"Really? I thought . . . I thought that sort of thing only hap-pened in the movies."

The owner was a tired-looking, gray-haired woman in her fifties who did not suffer the naive gladly. "If that's what you girls are looking for in life, be my guest, but don't come crying to me when you want to get out! If you can't stand on your own two feet, you have no business working. *Where* did you say you were from?"

And from that moment on, she seemed to dislike me. In fact, she stopped giving me calls. In her mind, a working girl either lived with a pimp or despised anyone connected to the pimp scene. My neutral puzzlement struck her as snooty, and she didn't like snooty hookers.

I couldn't understand why the two girls who had tried to recruit me seemed so content and normal. It was obvious that they were free to come and go—for good, if they wished. I was intrigued by their general aura of stability, though I couldn't imagine living with them. The owner was one of those people who hates anyone she can't understand. She understood pimps. She understood those two girls. But she didn't understand my curiosity, and this made her hate me. My two-week stint with that agency had yielded very little, and the two girls who'd tried to recruit me—well, I wasn't about to ask them for business now that I knew the score.

So I was feeling rather jaded when I entered Liane's apartment for the first time. And I was worried about the rent. My jaw almost dropped when Liane said, "You mustn't talk to my clients about money—I will pay you if there's ever a problem."

This was not an escort service: Liane was a proper madam with clients she could count on. I had read about such operations in books, a long time ago, as a child. But I had grown accustomed in my teen years to working escort and, for someone who starts out in a bar, working escort is a glamorous self-improvement. Meeting a reputable madam like Liane isn't necessarily in the cards.

In that split second, as Liane prepped me for my first date in her apartment, everything changed. I had never before met a madam or working girl who took so much pride in her clients. None of the nightclub managers or escort-service owners could afford to; they didn't even aspire to. Their prevailing attitude was that johns pay—"they" pay—and "we" collect or get paid. Winners receive, losers give. Liane's ideas about "us" and "them" were different. Johns were not just transient wallets, they were permanent connections—to be treasured. Suddenly, I sensed that Jeannie had been quite barbaric. When I realized how primitive the escort agencies were, I knew how lucky I was to have stumbled into Liane's apartment—and how important it was not to act as surprised as I felt.

I did everything in my power to stay on Liane's good side. Her normal clients were as nice as the best clients I had ever encountered working escort. Her better clients—well, you don't even meet guys like that through an ad. They're much too careful. I didn't kiss the bedsheets in gratitude, but I paid all my cuts on time. When Eddie, that first client of Liane's, asked for my phone number, I pretended I didn't have one—told him I was staying in the home of a prudish relative. This way he wouldn't feel rejected; he could see me again, through Liane. And did.

Liane had one thing in common with Jeannie's escort service: a possessive vigilance regarding girls who give their numbers out. Of course, I'd wanted to give Eddie my number. He was a quick $300, and I was tempted when he said, "I'll be in town next month for two days—at the Waldorf this time. Liane's an old pal, but she doesn't have to know everything, does she? I'll have a nice room."

But if Liane found out, she might stop giving me business, and I could end up working hotel bars and escort services again. And if I did, I was bound to get busted—or something much worse. Seeing Eddie repeatedly, for $180 instead of $300, getting about half as much as some girls were making for the same work, I was deeply tempted. Of course, I wasn't staying with a prudish relative—but I didn't know if I could trust him to stay mum. I played it safe, very safe. I wasn't going to let go of the opportunity Liane had given me: to work at the highest levels with the best clients.

Other girls, well established in their apartments, with private clients of their own, felt confident about taking Liane's clients—especially her hotel dates. When it comes to "stealing" dates, hotel calls fall into the gray zone. You're not in another woman's apartment, where pushing your number on a man is an out-and-out no-no. What the madam doesn't know won't hurt you, and Liane understood that some of the older girls gave their numbers out. But she expected loyalty from new girls. And while other girls could afford to lose her business, I simply couldn't. The reality was that the new girls, the loyal girls, were the ones who got the most business from Liane. She used the other girls only when she had to. (And that's why, today, I hear from Liane only once in a while.)

After my initiation into the rough-and-tumble of clubs, bars, and $200-an-hour coke dates, I was willing to keep seeing Liane's clients on Liane's terms. I was meeting diplomats and famous publishers. Her clients were often mentioned in the *Times,* and their faces sometimes appeared in those engraved portraits on the front page of the *Wall Street Journal.* But most of all, I could relax with a new client; I didn't have to think about whether he was a cop. Or whether he was going to pay. Though I still paid a cut to a madam, I had arrived. My technique was improving. My bedside manner was smoother, more confident. I began to see my previous adventures (and misadventures) through different eyes. I could concentrate on cultivating my clients, not just surviving, and was surprised to discover that I actually liked being good at oral sex. But I wondered if I would get stuck on this lesser track—the unambitious track occupied by girls who don't give their numbers out.

Allison didn't give out her number either. Of course, she had her own reasons—insane reasons. She had this rather dotty idea that giving johns her phone number would make her *more* of a hooker. She did actually have a roommate, a girl from her hometown in Fairfield County who knew her family. So she had to be cautious about hiding her new job. But even after her roommate moved out, Allie continued to work for Liane and to see clients through other call girls, as if direct contact with these men would somehow contaminate her. As if she could hide her job from *herself,* now that she was her own roommate.

"Allison's a natural!" Liane would sigh. "They all want to see her again. If only she had more common sense outside of bed!"

But Allie's guilt was a source of revenue for Liane.

"Working for Liane is easier," Allie once told me in a weak moment. "It's harder to stop when you see guys on your own."

I never could relate to Allie's sex guilt. Hooking always felt like a logical next step for me. Ever since the age of ten, I'd wanted to be a hooker—and before that, a *Playboy* centerfold. Before *that* I wanted to be a librarian. Allison had never had any occupational fantasies as a child. Not a one. I didn't understand those kids when I was a kid—how could they be so unexcited about the future? Allie and I would not have been friends if we had known each other as kids. When she started having sex, she was almost seventeen, and she didn't use anything until she had a pregnancy scare. That's so typically Allison.

But sometimes I think that early financial—not sexual—conduct is the key to what makes a hooker tick. Jasmine, who started hooking in her late twenties, always had her eye on the bottom line. She probably has the first nickel she ever made—"taxing" the lemonade she sold as a child. Jasmine has always had a criminal streak: She took her savings from baby-sitting to buy opera tickets and financed a precocious career as a ticket scalper when she was fourteen. She squirreled away exactly 10 percent of her profit, religiously. Most of the balance was reinvested in tickets.

When she was arrested in front of Madison Square Garden for peddling Rangers tickets, she lied to the cops about her age. She wanted to be tried as an adult. That, in fact, is how she met the notorious Barry Horowitz (who last year became my attorney, too). Back then, Horowitz was an idealistic Legal Aid lawyer paying his social dues. She was incensed when he guessed her real age. He said she could use it to beat the charge. This "went against the grain," she insisted. He told her she had no concept of the future, and he was, she once told me, "so obnoxious that I had to stop talking and listen to him." Horowitz pointed out that many adults in her position would happily pretend to be sixteen if they could: "So, if you wanna be an adult, you'd better start thinking like one. Beat the system."

Horowitz got Jasmine out of jail, helped her finesse the incident with her dad, and made sure that her arrest record was expunged when she turned eighteen. With the money she had stashed under her bed, she started a small franchise as a marijuana dealer, then moved on to bigger and better drugs when she graduated from high school.

At twenty-five, Jasmine was a very discreet Upper East Side drug dealer, living in a nondescript elevator building with no doorman and taking an awfully long time to get her business degree: "Perpetual student's a great cover for a drug dealer. I kept switching my major." But she was getting itchy.

"I wanted to keep expanding my business," she once told me. "I didn't do any of my product, but I was addicted. To growth." Her lawyer (by then he was in private practice) warned her. "He said if I kept selling drugs I would eventually come up against the glassine ceiling: there's no future in being a corpse. If you really want to deal, it's still a man's world. A chick can only go so far.

There's always gonna be some guy with a gun or worse who thinks that because you're a chick, he can hold you up or move in on you. You can't deal drugs as a single woman unless you're content with moderate growth. It's like being on the mommy track!"

So turning to a new criminal enterprise—using her body for the first time—was an admission, as she likes to say, that "anatomy is destiny." And a chance to be good at something where "it's all about being a chick."

One of her pot customers, a good-looking pimp called Rico, started boasting to her about his business. A number of his girls worked for small private houses in Manhattan. The second-tier private madams weren't as stylish as Liane, but they were equally security conscious. Jasmine wanted in, and she wanted to work safely. But Rico dismissed her offer when she suggested that he take her on for six months.

"I could learn that business in *less than* six months," she assured him.

"Well, that's the problem," he said. "You'd make trouble with my other ladies. No, thanks. I don't need it."

Then she offered him $500 to introduce her to a madam, and he accepted.

Jasmine worked in a very private, high-turnover house for about three months—an apprenticeship she insists was worth every cut she paid. She learned how to get some guys in and out the door in less than ten minutes. She managed to make some good connections and, at the first opportunity, bought a book from a girl who was moving to Florida. And that's how we ended up meeting in a luxurious thirty-fifth-floor apartment overlooking the U.N.

We both knew Jean-Paul, a French bachelor who saw girls and entertained his colleagues on a regular basis. So there we were, at a small party with two good-looking Dutch guys (whom every girl avoided because they seemed so young and energetic) and three mysterious diplomats, somewhat more senior, from the Gulf States. The girls had all been hand-picked by the host because Jean-Paul didn't like leaving his party arrangements to a madam. He was one of those self-sufficient bachelors who could decorate his own apartment *and* arrange a successful evening with a few call girls. Probably knew how to cook as well.

The girls kept pairing off in the powder room to compare notes—banknotes. We all wanted to make sure we were getting the same rate. Jasmine was relieved when I assured her that she wasn't undercharging.

But there was instant tension between Jasmine and a pretty redheaded girl, an adventurous Mormon who had escaped from Utah to New York by way of Nevada. When a client asked Jasmine and the redhead to join him, Jasmine balked. I ended up doing the scene and listening to the redhead's giggling assessment as we undressed together: "That girl, Jasmine? She's sooo uptight! I worked with her before, and she thinks every girl she meets is a lesbian!" She was playing with my bra strap, stroking my hair. "It's like, everybody's supposed to be 'after her'! Can you believe it?" I smiled politely. Our client was getting an eyeful *and* an earful. After we were done, the redhead whispered, "I don't usually get into it with girls, but you turned me on. Here's my number." I called her the next day, and we exchanged a few dates. If she hadn't been such a cocaine addict, we would have done more business together. She was pleasant to work with, had soft hands and an interested tongue. I'm happy to fake it with another working girl, but if she insists on the real thing, why not?

Jasmine, on the other hand, is highly paranoid around other working girls. She won't cop to being lesbophobic, but she refuses to see married couples because she won't "do a girl for real." You don't learn how to be smooth and "European" about these things by working in a high-turnover house. Even if it's in a nice building with a doorman, as it had been in Jasmine's case.

You can make good money seeing the cheaper, faster dates, but it's not the kind of work that broadens your mind.

Eventually, I introduced Jasmine to Liane, who decided to work with her occasionally but did not take a deep liking to my ambitious new friend. Jasmine was too well established by then to curry favor with Liane. And it was never in her nature, anyway, to look up to another woman, even if that woman was old enough to be her grandmother.

5 The Folks Who Live on the Hill

Busy e-mail day, even if you discount the junk. Two offers
from the online Viagra pushers, some further come-ons
for an herbal cocktail that will "postpone your [*sic*] ejacu-
lations," followed by the usual "make money without working" ads. Hmmm. Something does not add up.

Then a strange e-mail from Allie—is there any other
kind?—announcing her radio interview. "$exual Empower-
ment at the Turn of the Millennium. Celebrate International
Women's Herstory Month and the Evolving $isterhood of $ex
Workers. Tune in to WBAI-FM 99.5."

WBAI is kind of obscure, but you hear it from time to time if you take
a lot of cabs. Allison will be radiating her message of sexual "empowerment" to hundreds of left-wing cabdrivers. They won't be able to sit still
when they hear that creamy voice of hers. When I pointed this out, she e'd
back: "That means I'll be reaching the escort-agency girls on their way to
hotel calls. And those are my constituents!!" Constituents? Does she think
she's running for office? Most hard-core escorts would regard Allie as a
mere carpetbagger, with her Fairfield County childhood, her monthly
allowance (which didn't stop coming until she'd been hooking for three
years) and her pampered initiation chez Liane. And that cheerleader
thing—oops, she doesn't like to talk about *that*.

An e-mail from Elspeth: "We never get a chance to be alone," she
abruptly began, "and this has gotta change!" Gulp. "I'd like to meet
your other bridesmaids—Jasmine and Allison, right? Maybe we can
all have dinner at Willow. Where do they work?" Oh, boy. "If that's
not convenient, let me know. Miranda is dying to meet Jasmine!"

Miranda? Elspeth was discussing Jasmine and Allison with my cousin? When? At the party? And enlisting her as some sort of . . . what? Assistant in-law? If I don't answer her mail, will Elspeth *know* that I read it? She's writing from AOL, not her work address. But rumors about Carnivore, that spooky new e-snooper, echoed in my head. Surely this is a sisterly overture, quite inno-cent? But if she's supposed to think *I'm* entirely innocent (when I'm not), then what if I think *she's* entirely innocent and . . . god.

Another e-mail from Karen, the real estate broker: "Looking forward to seeing you both Friday. Three lovely 2BRs and a very special 1BR. Have a good feeling about this—especially the 2BR at 93 & Mad. It's that great bldg with the dollhouse shop on the ground floor." Ninety-third and Madison! I fired off a premen-strual e-ply to Karen: "Let's give Carnegie Hill a MISS. It is DEF-INITELY NOT my cup of tea!" (Hey, I'm the customer. I can use ALL CAPS if I want.)

A message from Bloomingdale's, confirming an order for six push-up bras. And from Garnet Hill confirming five pairs of sen-sible Hanro panties along with my new 310-count sheets. Online shopping's supposed to *save* time that would otherwise be spent schlepping between lingerie and housewares. Jasmine claims it's technology's gift to hookers: we never have to leave home, so we can shop while we're on call. But online shopping's a time sink—there's no limit to how much "Windows" shopping a girl can do. In the physical world, at least your feet give out when you over-shop. What kind of wake-up call do you get online? Your finger-nails might chip from too much clicking. And some shopping sites load so slowly, it's just like calling the catalog and being put on hold.

The perils of the Net! I was sitting there, waiting for a snazzy new Bloomingdale's gimmick to load—supposed to give you more accurate colors. But then, seeing the time, I freaked out and abruptly logged off. I think they're right about this Web-addiction thing. I almost forgot to turn a trick—a first, for me.

I threw my Prada heels into a shopping bag, along with some lacy underwear, and raced over to Jasmine's apartment in my jeans. Better to be semiprepared for Harry than late. If you're even five minutes late, you can actually miss him, he's so tightly scheduled. I rang Jasmine's buzzer and looked around anxiously for signs of Harry's Town Car.

While I did a quick change in Jasmine's bathroom, I could hear the intercom. Harry was on his way up when I emerged from the bathroom, clad in my undies and heels, feeling bloated—period due in less than a week—but doing my best to think slim. My panties felt snugger than usual. I pulled my tummy in and stood tall. Heels help.

"Your bra's inside out," Jasmine hissed.

I was fully adjusted, holding a hot washcloth behind my back, when Harry walked in the door, beaming from ear to ear.

"Beware of a middle-aged man in a hurry," he chortled as Jasmine unzipped him. He slipped easily out of his pants and stood before us in paisley socks, black suspenders, and brown wing tips.

I wrapped the hot washcloth around his cock and heard the crinkle of a Ramses wrapper as Jasmine wriggled into a kneeling position.

"Tell me," he said, in an earnest tone. "Have you ever—did you ever catch your brother jerking off?"

"Once, when he was about twelve," I answered breathlessly. I was trying hard to picture someone other than my younger brother at the klutzy age of twelve. Hardly my idea of a sex god. It's easier for Jasmine to chatter away about giving Little Brother a blow job because she hasn't got any brothers. But she was too busy to talk.

"Was he—ah, yes—hmmmm. . . . How big was he? Bigger than you expected?" Harry asked. "Or smaller?"

I tried, instead, to picture a juvenile Harry as the virile sibling. Suddenly, I had a cramp in my calf—couldn't wait to sit down and get out of my fabulous-looking heels.

"His cock was massive!" I recounted. I brought my pussy closer to his thigh, then twisted it away from his wandering hand. Now he was fondling my tender premenstrual breasts. "When I saw it, I couldn't believe how hard he was—I just had to try it— so I put my mouth—" Harry finished my sentence for me, with a long groan of satisfaction.

After he departed, I told Jasmine about the Carnegie Hill 2BR perched high above the repulsive dollhouse shop.

"What's wrong with you?" she said. "Why don't you go see it? I can't believe you're playing it this way. The more apartments you look at, the longer you can draw this thing out. If you narrow it down, you'll just paint yourself into a corner."

"But Carnegie Hill's hateful! Anemic!"

"A Laura Ashley theme park with fake streets," she agreed. "Anemic."

"And fake sidewalks. Is *that* how people see me? Do I look like the kind of woman who wants to live next to hundreds of *doll-houses?*"

"For god's sake. The point is to give yourself room to maneu-ver. Anyone can see that you're in a panic about this."

"Anyone?"

"Well, anyone who really knows you," she said dismissively. "Look, you need to devise a grand master plan. This situation *can* be managed," she insisted. "As for that dollhouse shop—" She made a sound that was a cross between a wheeze and a snicker. "No, seriously. I *like* that—could be a great cover for you."

"Excuse me?"

"Well, how many tricks have you turned in Carnegie Hill?"

"Almost zero."

"Right. You're less likely to get caught by Matt if you guys move to Laura Ashley country. He'll be home watching the ball game—"

"He doesn't watch ball games." I slipped out of my heels and flexed my foot methodically.

"So he'll be home watching Bloomberg in his shorts! And eating raspberry scones or whatever the hell they snack on in Carnegie Hill, and you can say, 'I'm just going out to Sarabeth's Kitchen to pick up some more fucking scones, dear,' then sneak down to the St. Regis for a quickie without running into him. Even if he goes out to buy a newspaper. Use your imagination."

Jasmine's idea of wedded bliss was making me very queasy. Scones. Sarabeth's. Cutting-edge betrayal. Tricks at the St. Regis.

"This is grotesque," I said. "I can't live like that!"

"I don't see you trying to sell your book," Jasmine pointed out. "Or doing anything to make it possible *not* to live like that. You have no intention of quitting, and yet you refuse to face your real feelings."

"Maybe I *will* just quit—turn off my phone. Sell my book. It's worth something."

"Be my guest," she said with a cool shrug. "You could probably sell your book very quickly if you wanted to. And get some real bucks for it. But you're still in your prime. These are important years, the hottest years in a working girl's professional life span. Your skin's firm, the body's good, the guys still think we're twenty-five. Well, maybe twenty-eight. That's why *I* don't fritter my valuable time away on boyfriends," she explained. "I use my leisure time to replenish the capital assets. So while you're wearing out your nerves negotiating personal boundaries with your boyfriend, I'm catching up on my beauty sleep! Getting ready for another day of work. When you're hot, you're hot! Don't just throw it away!"

Looking very pleased with herself, she started emptying a small trash receptacle into a white plastic bag. She scooped up Harry's condom wrapper from the carpet.

"The longer you take to find a place, the more time you have to exploit your thirties," she continued. "Or what's left of them!"

Suddenly, I had an anxious knot in the arch of my foot.

"You need to figure out a strategy." She paused. "When is your period due?"

Is it that obvious?

"Next week," I said. "Maybe sooner." This is a drawback of getting naked on the job. You have no privacy! Your co-workers can actually see the extra pound or so that any normal woman would be able to hide under her business-casual tunic.

"Well, take some dolomite, stay off the salt, and turn that real estate broker into your willing *pawn*," she advised. "And avoid premenstrual temper tantrums—you know that's when you're most likely to say something you'll regret. Sound body, sound mind, sound relationship. Or something like that."

I came home and fired off a friendlier e-mail to Karen: "On second thought, I'd like to see the Carnegie Hill 2BR. We don't want to prolong our search, and in a market like this, it pays to be open-minded. Right?" Then I sent a note to Elspeth: "Still trying to reach Jasmine about our girls' dinner at Willow. Great idea. Thanks for suggesting it!"

SATURDAY, 3/4/00

Yesterday's apartment tour was a small step for the broker—and a giant step for me.

My paranoic fears were on hold: What's happening to my personal space? To my thirties?

For the first time in my adult life, a man will be paying my rent. Can I handle that? Well, I wouldn't live with a guy who *can't* pay the bills. It's against my nature. But it's also against my nature to let someone pay my rent! So where does that get me? Somehow, it gets me to Carnegie Hill. With a view and an extra bathroom. . . . All that hookerish angst sat obediently on the back burner as I got on with my personal life. Or tried to.

There is something about looking at a new apartment, a prospective home that's three times the size of your current one. It absorbs your attention. You cannot enter an empty space like that and fantasize about living there without losing yourself a little.

With a new buzz in the air, Matt and I began to explore living rooms and cupboards and empty bedroom closets. In the spacious 1BR with a breakfast nook at Seventy-eighth and Lex, Matt kissed me in the foyer while the broker's back was turned. In the Ninety-third Street two-bedroom—Carnegie Hill—he pulled my hair to one side and kissed my neck slowly, with a masterful flourish. I couldn't wait to get back to the bachelor pad, where all this premarital stuff really *began*. I gave his fly a mischievous tug.

Then he took my hand and pulled me gently into . . . the master bedroom. Sunlight. Space. New marble bathroom. Just as promised.

"Huge bathroom!" he said approvingly.

I agreed. He looked at the bedroom ceiling for a long time, then looked lovingly back at me.

"Do you know what I think?" he said in a dreamy voice.

Oh, no. Not *that!* I once had this client—a Garment Center playboy with a smoked-glass mirror over his bed. I also knew a girl from Jacksonville, Florida, who thought *her* ceiling mirror was real classy. But the thought of staring at myself in the A.M. before I've cleaned the sleep from my eyes!

There comes a time in every Serious Relationship where a girl must carefully steer her man away from making a totally inappropriate aesthetic decision, so that they can save face as a couple. I was ready for this rite of passage.

"I don't *think* so . . ." I started to say. Where did Matt even *get* such an idea? I looked at him and had a strange thought: Does Matt go to cheap massage parlors in the daytime? No way—I hope. "I think . . . it's *fun* and *kitschy,* but you'd get sick of it." Brilliant. Nothing to link the disapproval with me. He *disapproves of himself.*

"Really? Kitschy?" He looked philosophical. "I never thought of it that way. You have . . . an interesting take on things, honey."

I was feeling very diplomatic and socially nimble when he added, to my astonishment, "But it's so much healthier than air-conditioning. And you're always complaining about what AC does to your skin. But if you don't like the idea. . . . Well, so much for my career as a handyman."

"Oh!" I squeaked before I could stop myself. "A ceiling fan?"

"Right. Uh, what did you *think* I was talking about?" he said, with a perplexed look on his face.

I stood there with my mouth open, at a total loss for words. Not only had I somehow dragged us onto the wrong side of the decorating tracks—I had dissed my future husband's handyman cred! How stupid could I be? I turned beet red.

"I don't know," I mumbled, feeling less like a crossover success and more like a clumsy hooker. Despite my respectable upbringing, I've perhaps been exposed to One Social Element Too Many.

"Getting seduced?" Karen's upbeat broker's echo intruded on my embarrassment. "This place is so darn *huge,* I can't find you!" she called out. "What do you think?"

"Yes!" I exclaimed, with relief. "It's so roomy!" I headed out the bedroom door and announced, "I *have* to see the guest bathroom one more time." And locked myself in there for a couple of minutes, with the water running. With any luck, I figured, Karen will start bending Matt's ear about what a great place this is and he'll forget the entire misunderstanding. *I* know how guys are. Or thought I did.

Today, I told Wendy about the ceiling-fan debacle.

"Why did that bother you so much?" she asked. "Couples miscommunicate. That's what couples do—they try to communicate and they succeed only part of the time." Wendyspeak for *fail sometimes*. "And it's not as if you had a fight."

"I felt like a social outcast!" I explained.

"Come on. Because he was thinking 'ceiling fan' and you were projecting 'mirror'? Do you really think Matt is that prudish? Do you think he'd be so shocked and horrified? Sometimes I think you overestimate his conservative qualities."

"I was projecting some cheesy guy's aesthetic onto my fiancé. Like he was some—some guy with a deep tan and a gold chain." I covered my mouth in horror and stopped talking.

"What's happening? Have you ever wanted Matt to be—more like that? Someone you wouldn't be intimidated by?"

"Intimidated? I'm not intimidated. What are you talking about?"

"Well, you're intimidated by the choices you're making. And you've made it clear to me that you look down on some of your clients."

"I do not look down on my clients! I wouldn't let someone come all over me if I looked *down* on him!" I blurted out. "Do you look down on *your* clients?"

"No."

Wendy wasn't pushing the issue. I, however, was remembering Bob.

"There's this guy, I saw him last month. I hardly ever see him because he lives in Boca. Do you know what Boca's like? Boca Raton?"

"Of course. My parents hang out there." It's obvious *she* doesn't, though. Wendy's more of a Key West type. "It's not my favorite place, but I know it well," she said.

"He's a very sweet man. He's easy, clean, very gentle and considerate. He's a self-made guy, in real estate, and he wears a gold chain! And he bakes his skin to a crisp, and he—he reads thrillers, and he has a Brooklyn accent! He's like a truck driver who made good."

"And?"

"And the last time I saw him, I thought about Matt. I wanted Matt to be different for a moment. I wanted him to be more like this guy!" I confessed. "Because then he would still have money but he wouldn't—he would have different attitudes. I wouldn't worry about telling a guy like Bob that I've had sex for money, even if he were my boyfriend. Maybe I would soft-pedal it and say I've been kept by a few guys. For a man like Bob, that's a polite way of saying you're a hooker. Those guys understand—they don't have this view of the world where every woman's supposed to be a yuppie. Or a Jane Austen fan. They think girls who play for pay are just part of life. And I've known girls in the business who really like these guys because they were brought up differently. Like, there's a girl I know—Eileen. We're not close friends, but we work together. She has no intellectual hang-ups at all! I can see her having a very satisfying relationship—with a guy who wears a gold chain."

"And if Matt were more like that?"

"I wouldn't know how to love him! Eileen would. And I—I would be embarrassed to introduce him to my family! I realized that after Bob left."

"And how did that make you feel?"

I blinked hard and forced myself to say it.

"I felt a little ashamed of myself."

"Shame: Why?"

"Bob. He's hustled all his life, he has a lot of money, and he hasn't got good taste. But he knows that working girls have normal feelings."

I told her how Bob had assured me that *he* thought I was a Nice Girl. I explained about how a pro shouldn't care: "It really doesn't matter what a john thinks of me. But when he told me I was a 'Nice Girl,' I did care. He wanted to say something kind. And he touched . . . some part of me."

"Which part?"

"Well, *some* part," I said stubbornly.

"He touched your heart," Wendy said softly. "It's normal and expectable."

I made a frantic grab for the Kleenex and pulled out a wad of tissue.

"I think we're really getting somewhere," Wendy continued.

"I don't want to talk about this anymore!" I wailed. Brown eye pencil was dripping all over the tissue.

"That's okay, too," she said. "We have to stop soon, but I want to pick up this thread next week. Can you spend some time with your journal and explore this? I think this is core material for you. Failure. Success. How we define these things . . ."

I sniffled my assent, came home, and turned off the business phone. Then changed into a flannel nightshirt and crept under the covers with a small pack of moisturizer-infused tissues. Better not to rip one's nose to shreds. I should suggest this brand to Dr. Wendy if this keeps up.

I was napping when the phone next to my bed—my personal phone—began ringing. I let it go into voice mail, but it started again.

"Nancy? Are you coming?"

Allison, sounding like she was on a roller coaster. Or in a wind tunnel.

"Coming?" I was confused.

"You said you'd come with me to the radio station. I'm in a cab. I'll stop in front of your building—"

"I never said—" I suddenly recalled a half-assed statement I had made at the gym some days ago. "Look, I can't go out now. I'm sorry, but I can't leave the apartment."

"But I need your support!" she exclaimed. "I've got stage fright! And Roxana's out of town! And you said you would come with me!"

"Allie, I just had a *breakthrough* in fucking therapy! Two hours ago! I can't fucking handle it, okay?"

"Oh." Her stage fright was trumped. "A—really? I didn't know you were in therapy again. I think that's—that's so great, Nancy! Why do you sound so upset? Don't you feel *empowered* now that you've had this breakthrough?"

"No!" I shrieked. "I'm lying in bed in my pajamas and I feel like I've been through a Cuisinart! Have you ever been in therapy? I mean real therapy—not those stupid twelve-step groups you used to attend—"

"Well, uh, therapy . . . I once had a very interesting encounter with a Jungian therapist—"

"Well, no fucking wonder you have no idea how I feel! I'm not some Jungian airhead! And neither is my shrink!" I half sobbed, half shouted.

I slammed the phone down and blew my nose. A minute later, the phone rang again.

"I just want you to know," Allison burbled emphatically. "*Two things*. First, I think you should respect my choices. Every woman arrives at self-knowledge in her own way. And secondly, I realize this is not *you* talking—it's your anger and pain talking."

"Thanks," I sniffled. "Thanks, Allie. Now, if you'll just let me—"

"Three things, actually! I think I'm over my stage fright! Focusing on your emotions has cleared my— You don't have to come with me. But I do want you to tape the radio show."

"Oh, please."

"I know you think this movement's a waste of my time, but this is important to me. And I hope you'll respect my feelings and honor our friendship enough to—"

"I'll tape the fucking show!" I yelled.

"I have never heard you say the F word so many times in one conversation!" she exclaimed. And then, with a faint crackle, she was gone.

WEDNESDAY, 3/8/00

"Actually," I told Allie, when I saw her at the gym this morning, "taping the show cheered me up. I was feeling very raw and— You know how people regress when— Well, anyway . . ."

Remembering that Jungian business, I suddenly didn't feel like discussing therapy with Allie in the girls' locker room.

"You see?" she said happily. "You've made a contribution to the NYCOT archives! The process of political involvement empowers us at the most personal level. It made you feel better. NYCOT has added something of value to your life. And you have added something of value to the sex workers' movement."

"By taping your interview?"

"Well, we're creating an archival record for future generations of sex workers. So they can see how stigmatized we were during the dark ages of patriarchal oppression." Her face lit up at the prospect.

"Really?" I said. "Well, Jasmine missed the show because she was working. Can she borrow the tape?"

Allie frowned at the cassette, which was lying on the bench between us.

"I don't want anything to *happen* to it," she hinted.

"Oh, don't worry. Jasmine—"

"I don't trust her! She might erase the whole thing just to spite me! Or part of it. Like Nixon. The most *important* part."

Suddenly Allie was bent over in knock-kneed agony, moaning quietly and rummaging through her gym bag.

"What's wrong?" I said, holding the bag open for her. "What are you looking for? I'll find it."

"Ooh, ooh," she gasped. "I—I have to pee and I can't find my Quito sticks!"

"Quito—? What do they look like?"

Must be some Amazonian rain-forest rite that Allie's into—but isn't Quito in Ecuador? I looked for something sticklike and vaguely Amazonian or Ecuadorian. Maybe a bundle of tiny divining rods?

"Never mind," she bleated, as she dashed off to a stall. I heard her tinkling and sighing. "You can just keep the tape until the next meeting."

6 As Above, So Below

Allison's sudden enthusiasm for things Latin American is
unnerving. Today she proposed lunch at a Brazilian place
called Circus, one block north of the Body Shop. When
she finally showed, toting her cruelty-free unguents in a
green bag, I was quietly nursing a caipirinha and
meditating on a framed drawing showing a jury of twelve
clowns deliberating over the fate of a clown in prison stripes.

Allie slid into the banquette, almost obliterating the clown
court with her hair, then pulled out a container and rubbed some
slimy goo onto the back of my hand. "Try this. It's made with sesame
seeds harvested in Guatemala by an indigent collective."

I paused for a second.

"I think you mean . . . indigenous."

"Oh!" She opened her menu. "Right! And a percentage of the profits
goes into saving the rain forest. Or gets sent back to the collective! I can't
remember which."

Snapping her menu shut, Allie announced: "My Quito sticks are deep
purple. I've made it through the induction phase."

Induction! Has Allie joined another cult? After last year's bout with
Prostitutes Anonymous and her recent conversion to activism, I know to
steer clear of Allie's new enthusiasms. When she was trying to recruit me
for P.A., it was like having a reverse madam on my tail. Not something I
care to repeat. So I was weirdly grateful when she changed the subject—though not for long.

"Jack asked me to think about a possible arrangement," she told me. "I know you don't think I should see him or talk to him, but he's making a very serious offer."

"Oh? Did he make this offer in person? Or on the phone?"

"On the . . ." She looked away. "In person," she finally admitted. "I *had* to talk to him. He was leaving all these notes and flowers with my doorman. I told him it was getting to be too much and he agreed to stop, so we met for coffee at Starbucks. And," she said optimistically, "I think everything's fine, now."

"In what sense is 'everything fine'?" I wondered.

"Well, he stopped bothering my doorman when I agreed to meet with him again. And now we're actually talking. About real things. He can't be vulnerable at home or in his daily life, so he needs a relationship where he can be *heard.* I agreed to listen. We're not having sex, though."

"He should never have bothered your doorpeople in the first place," I snapped. "You had to *bribe* him with your company to get him to stop?"

"Not exactly. But what harm can there be in my listening? I told him we could meet for lunch or coffee but not, you know, in my apartment. When I agreed to be part of this blacklisting thing, nobody said anything about denying Jack his most basic human rights."

"His . . . what?"

"Well, his right to be heard by another," Allison explained in a soft reverent voice. "To have coffee with a friend! Or lunch."

"Nobody thought you would come up with such a ridiculous excuse for talking to him!" I exclaimed.

A plate arrived bearing my lunch: two baked acorn squash stuffed with shrimp. Their tops had been artfully opened, then replaced.

"They look so sweet, almost like little faces!" Allie said. "The stem is just like the top of a beret! And the *body* of the squash—"

Catching my horrified expression, the waiter placed Allie's

salmon dish in front of her. "And this," he said with a wink, "looks just like salmon."

Allie peered at my caipirinha.

"I think I'll try one of those," she said. "What's in it?"

"Rum, lime juice . . . it's good." The waiter smiled engagingly.

"One for me, too. For the vitamin C! Do they drink them in Costa Rica? I'm going in the fall!" she told him.

"To Brazil?"

"No—Costa Rica."

Costa Rica? Oddly enough, she didn't elaborate.

"Well," Allie said, "the Quito sticks *are* reassuring. I'm allowed to have a very small helping of rice and beans. *And* a drink. And maybe some french fries."

With that we tacitly agreed to cease discussing Jack—a circular topic if ever there was one—for the rest of our meal.

MONDAY, 3/13/00

Today I felt a trifle guilty, listening to Allison's taped radio show with Jasmine—who couldn't stop chuckling at "the blondness of it all." Allie was waxing enthusiastic about the Joy of Hooking in that smooth yet breathless voice that has inspired so many other kinds of calls.

"This," Allie was saying, "is an *empowering* career. I see this as goddess work. I don't do it just for the money. Society benefits from the healing sexuality of women like me! We are responsible for relieving countless headaches, for teaching men about safe sex. We are not just sexual healers. We are social healers. And yet we're being persecuted. By the patriarchy!"

"But," Doug Henwood, the host, replied in an earnest tone, "I think we have to acknowledge that many people, not as privileged or attractive as you, are forced into it by circumstance. How healing is it for them?"

"The New York Council of Trollops represents all the sex workers in this city!" she simpered. "And we're collecting used clothing in good condition for the NYCOT Street Project." She spelled out NYCOT's website for Henwood's listeners. "We accept shoes, clothing, accessories. A pair of designer boots can help a sex worker in Hunts Point command a higher price for her services! And a pair of pajamas will keep a homeless sex worker warm when she's *not* working. If you have blankets, coats, mittens—"

"What about the darker side of your industry?" the host asked. "Have you ever had a problem with a customer?"

There was an awkward pause.

"Well, for those of us who freely choose to be sex workers," she finally chirped, "we have learned to define our own boundaries. You see, Doug, this is an integral part of our job. We define the terms!"

My jaw dropped as I pictured Jack importuning Allie's doorman, overloading her voice-mail box, plotting a "surprise" orgy behind her back—all because Allie was foolish enough to take money for services *not* rendered. So much for Allie's terms and definitions.

"I've heard enough," Jasmine cackled. "The boundaried one has spoken."

"Wait, wait, you have to hear the phone calls!"

We listened to a few abbreviated calls from lewd listeners. The host cut them off quickly.

"As I was telling Allison, there are seven words you can't use around here—we'll lose our license," he remarked dryly. "Bye for now."

Then a sweet-sounding elderly widower from Queens bemoaned a recent roundup of street girls in his neighborhood. "It's been a lonely two weeks," he told Allie. "Maybe your organization could send some ladies out to Roosevelt Avenue?"

"Oh, I wish we *could*," Allie burbled, "but that's illegal. We don't want to be charged with promoting prostitution. We're a support group for sex workers at every stage of their sexual and political evolution. Not an outcall service."

"Sexual evolution, eh? Well, you sound like a very interesting young woman. Good night."

Jasmine's response to all this was, at first, predictable. "Allison's throwing away the best years of her life! She wouldn't be wasting her time on this movement if she had any sense." Then she looked pleased. "She's giving that ex-hooker Roxana what's-her-name a run for her money! Has Roxana ever seen *All About Eve*? She'd better watch out! Allison's no brainiac but she's more plausible than the current leadership. For one thing, she's good-looking. *And* she waxes her snatch!" A partisan note was creeping in here. "That's more than we can say for Roxana! I mean, if there has to be a hookers' movement, I'd rather be represented by a chick who waxes. Wouldn't you?"

"I'm not sure Allison's going to be in this movement for much longer," I said skeptically.

"Oh? Roxana's edging her out? Well, that's to be expected—I always knew power sharing wasn't Roxana's bag. She's probably jealous of the way Allison looks!"

"No," I interrupted. "It's something else. Allison joined a new cult. She said something about her *induction* the other day. I'm afraid to ask."

"Really! So that was a short love affair with social justice. More like"—Jasmine looked vaguely disappointed—"a one-night stand! What's this new cult?"

"No idea. She got into a panic when she misplaced her— She's got these ritualistic skewers. Or stalks or something."

"Skewers?" Jasmine was intrigued. "What kind of . . . skewers?"

"I've never seen them. I think she uses them to tell the future. They're like yarrow sticks, I guess, but they're purple. She calls them her Quito sticks. Do you know anything about Ecuadorian folklore? Because I don't. And she's going to Costa Rica for some reason—"

Jasmine let out a sharp yelp.

"What did you say? What kind of sticks?"

"Quito—"

"You fucking idiot, she's on Atkins!"

"Atkins?"

"Here, let me show you."

Jasmine marched off to the bathroom and I followed, fearing the worst. "See?" She was holding a small white cylindrical jar, which she rattled in my face. I looked at the yellow label— "KETOSTIX"—and noticed some pink and purple squares.

"What are they?" I said blankly.

"They turn purple if you're burning fat."

"Excuse me? Have you lost your mind as well?"

"Oh!" Jasmine laughed. "No, I mean, you have to dip them in your pee—*then* they turn purple."

"Why do *you* have them?"

"You're kidding. You really don't *know* about the Atkins diet?"

Could my two best friends be on the Atkins diet without my noticing? Could I be that self-centered?

"Bunless hamburgers? Fried eggs? But Allison was eating salmon this weekend."

"Atkins is misunderstood," she said airily. "It's the best way to burn fat. And you can eat all kinds of stuff—veal, salmon tartare, lobster bisque, pastrami. You can't drink Kir Royales, but you can drink vodka martinis. My kind of diet."

"But you have no fat to burn. You never did."

"I do Atkins just before my period. You should try it. It gets rid of food cravings. And water retention. You have a terrible problem with water retention."

"Thanks."

"Hey! Water retention happens! I used to have it too! *This* is the diet that resembles what our carnivorous ancestors ate. Before they yoked themselves to the plow and got hooked on wheat and potatoes." Jasmine paused and gave my waistline a critical appraisal. "And rice, in the case of your ancestors. But it's likely that our prehistoric grandmothers never suffered premenstrual bloating. Because they didn't eat starch."

I rolled my eyes. "And what *did* they eat? Lobster bisque? I seem to recall a recent excavation of Absolut vodka etchings on a cave wall somewhere . . ."

"Well, mankind has adapted! *Now* we have cream-based soups and hard liquor! Back then, we had the freshly killed meat of some hunted beast. Prehistoric pastrami! So now that we're all becoming hunter-gatherers again—think about it! Of course we're returning to our original high-powered, high-protein, beast-hunting, fat-burning diet."

Of course. But . . . what's for dessert? Or should I say who?

"Hey. That's the most sensible thing Allison's done in years!" Jasmine was saying. "I may actually develop some *respect* for that girl." She hardly noticed how miffed I was at the prospect.

TUESDAY, 3/14/00

Another misunderstanding was revealed today, when I unwrapped a box of six identical push-up bras, ordered recently from Bloomie's online. I was hoping to model one of these new acquisitions for my two o'clock—Ted, the undies voyeur. But the new bra I ordered is all wrong! It's filled with "lifelike" liquid cups that weigh so much I can feel my deltoids working when I try it on. A good work bra has to reflect your actual shape. Your breasts must live up to the promise of the underwire. Plus, you might have to remove it while performing a blow job, and how can you gracefully slip out of a lingerie item that weighs five pounds? What if, god forbid, a john should take it into his head to "help you out of" your bra?

It should also be possible to hide your money in one of the cups, in case you have an outcall. (Those slutty-looking half-bras that daringly expose the nipples are only good for incalls.)

Time to rinse off my cellular renewing pack and pick out an appropriate bra for Ted. And find the Ziploc bag where I stashed all those G-strings and thongs.

FRIDAY, 3/17/00

Saint Patrick's Day has paralyzed the city. Tomorrow, everyone (including me) will forget the entire affair but today, for a window of about eight hours, it's sheer madness. The streets, the trains, even the foot traffic. You have to plan your day very carefully. I thank my lucky stars I don't have to brave real traffic or commuter trains to go to a straight job every day.

Milton just called from JFK, to make an appointment for Monday. "You're my first local call," he said. "Have you been misbehaving in my absence?"

I giggled, ignored the query, and asked, "How was Japan?"

"Japan, Malaysia, Hong Kong . . . exhausting! I'd love to see you *today*," he growled. "But that parade screws everything up. The Irish are conspiring against the sex life of the Jews. I hope I can survive until Monday. How's eleven A.M.?"

"Noon," I countered, remembering my shrink appointment. I've switched to the early morning because, well, I miss out on the best part of the business day when I use the afternoon for therapy. Or so I thought—until Milton requested the morning slot. Best-laid plans!

Yesterday Etienne showed up ten minutes early, looking awfully *sportif* in leather boots and an interesting green neckerchief.

"What's all this?" I asked. "No work today? Are the auction houses closed for Saint Patrick's Day?"

"My brother-in-law has decided we should observe casual Fridays. So I set an example for the entire group," he said with a shrug. "As for this wearing of green, it is an honest coincidence, I assure you."

Etienne and his half-Brit, half-French brother-in-law run the _____ department at _____, which is handy. Etienne walks around the corner to my apartment in the middle of his workday, and he's back at his desk before anyone knows he's gone. I sometimes think our long business relationship owes more to geography than he'll ever admit. Etienne's vanity (as an accomplished flirt) requires that he respect *my* vanity. So he insists that what really brings us together every week or so is my seductive laugh, or my unique skin texture, or the way I look in a simple white G-string. Still, I've grown attached to his visits. And his flattery.

Etienne was sipping on a Pellegrino, updating me on his outfit: "These jodhpurs I obtained at a riding shop downtown, though of course I do not ride. They are the best I've ever owned. Simple, well-made . . . excellent leather . . ."

I admired his shopper's acumen and shifted slightly on the couch. Provoked by my saucy smile, he began to approach my face. His intent was clear. When I pulled away, his kiss landed on my neck.

"That really is not friendly," Etienne said crossly, but I slid away, pretending not to hear his dissatisfaction.

"It's what keeps you coming back," I giggled. I was heading toward the bedroom, conscious of my back view. In high-heeled mules, a long transparent blouse, and little else, I felt confident that he would get over this kissing thing—for at least five minutes.

"Not really," he said. "It most definitely is *not* your most appealing aspect." Then he wandered off to the bathroom to freshen up.

"Aha!" he announced, a few minutes later. I was kneeling on my bed, in a revealing bra and some tiny panties, examining myself in the mirror. "That's a lovely circumstance to be in." The nonsensical bedroom chatter continued, as he caressed my bare neck.

I had not done very much (yet) to provoke his hard-on, but he was semierect—which, for a man over sixty, is not a given. Sometimes it takes Etienne a long time to get hard.

"I suppose I have *some* appealing aspects?" I asked.

"I suppose," he chided me. "But I'm not sure they make up for the disagreeable ones."

I positioned myself horizontally across his long limbs. On my hands and knees, I coquettishly straightened my back, so that my body formed a bridge across his pelvic region. He was content to lie on his back gazing at me, while I pretended that my torso, thighs, and arms had accidentally arranged themselves into this submissive pose.

"You have to examine Claudia's handiwork," I said, giving him a soft nudge with my right knee.

He made room for me to lie down. "Ah, the infamous Claudia," he said, pulling my panties aside. He stroked the soft hairs lying against my pubic mound. Two weeks ago, all my hair was removed, and now there's a short silky growth. "This is more graceful," he said. "More graceful than nature's alternative. You must thank Claudia personally for me."

I giggled agreeably.

Noticing that his fingers were traveling closer in, I twisted my pussy away gently, replacing his hand with my own. "Would you like to watch me?" I murmured.

He purred his assent as I finessed my rejection of his fingers. Now I was pretending to manipulate my clitoris. My finger was rubbing the spot where my outer lips begin to open, causing a more manageable sensation to travel through my smaller lips. With the workday just beginning, I didn't want to overstimulate my nerve endings.

"I've heard that some people prefer the natural look," I mused.

"*Bien sûr.* But I do not care for an impenetrable forest. I like to rest my eyes on what I will be getting."

During my teens, I cherished my pubic hair because it made me feel so womanly. Now I'm more invested in feeling girlish, and I don't like to see a single hair left standing when I go for my bikini waxing. Also I secretly enjoy the attention lavished on my pussy by the meticulous Claudia (who likes to remind me that she was doing this sort of thing "long before all the hype about those J. Sisters").

"Why do some gentlemen prefer an untrimmed bush?" I asked Etienne.

He looked thoughtful.

"Some prefer Nature's bounty, others appreciate your tasteful—and tasty—topiary. That's what makes a market," he replied.

I laughed, slipped out of my panties, and knelt beside his face.

"You and your market theories."

"It would be boring if all participants had exactly the same parameters," he said, as I parted my lower lips. "You scoff at my comments because women do not really favor free markets." He gave my pussy a fond kiss. "The female is a natural monopolist," he continued. "Nine women out of ten do not even object to Bill Gates. The moral argument against monopoly means nothing to a woman."

I felt the tip of his tongue near my clitoris. "Nor to this little lady down here—she is happiest when she has her monopoly."

I couldn't argue with *that*.

Later, while Etienne was primping in the bathroom, I put in a quick call to Allison.

"Are we still on for three-thirty? The parade's today," I reminded her. "People can't get around. He could cancel."

"He just called—we're *on*," she assured me. "And I owe you a date. You *have* to come!"

When I got to Allison's apartment, the session was already in progress. A large flowery sheet was draped over the couch, and her client was half-reclining, half-sitting. Naked, except for his glasses and toupee, he was smoking a joint and watching a porn movie. The sound was turned down, but not off, so the grunts and sighs of the actors were creating a small distraction. A little background sex.

"Meet Stan," Allie said cheerfully.

"Make yourself comfortable!" he chimed in.

I was wearing a sleek black pantsuit and pumps with very high heels. But Allie, in high black boots that reached her thighs, looked about a foot taller than usual. She was wearing masses of lipstick, a red lace teddy, and big teased hair. She giggled professionally.

"Isn't this *fun?*" she said. "I feel like one of those girls on the Howard Stern show! And Stan brought us some poppers!"

"Terrific!" I said gaily. "I'll be right back!"

I disappeared into the bedroom. Poppers give me a headache! But you have to make a guy like Stan feel that his drugs are as welcome as his wallet. The polite fiction is that the drugs are there for *all* of us to enjoy. I've known call girls who like to smoke pot, and quite a few with a weakness for coke. But I've yet to meet the working girl who can abide the smell of poppers.

I changed into my "party outfit," a bustier with matching garters and lace stockings. As I emerged from the bedroom, I wondered if my feminine pumps were vampish enough. Confronted by Allison's towering boots, I felt like an erotic midget. But Stan was quite taken with me. He patted a spot on the couch and offered me a hit of his joint. I held the joint to my lips, looked off to the side, and blew out, anxious to keep my brain unfogged. Allison was prancing around the living room, saying things like: "Isn't Suzy gorgeous? She just loves to watch me giving head. And she has such a delicious pussy!" Stan was nodding amiably. He handed me a bottle of hand lotion and closed his eyes as I began to massage his cock with lubricated fingertips. My hands slid down to caress his balls, and a small pool of hand cream collected on the sheet. Uh-oh—Allison's couch! I scooped up the cream as best I could and rubbed it into his thigh. I heard a cracking sound and averted my nose from the popper aroma that was now filling the room.

And so it went for the next three hours, with Allie and myself taking turns, getting our pussies licked for what seemed an eternity while we dodged the unsavory vapors. The living room now smelled like old gym socks. At one point, to get free from the fetid smog, Allison draped herself over an armchair so that all Stan could see from the couch was her smooth round ass perched above her thigh-high boots.

I knelt behind her and pretended to lick her. After a few minutes, Stan came over and knelt beside me. He was trying to figure out whether this oral display was for real, but he was too tactful to say that. Instead, he presented himself as a member of the orgy, a voyeur without an agenda. Neither of us girls wanted him nosing around, but Allie had prepared for this contingency. On a small rosewood table behind the armchair, a bulbous dildo was standing on its base—dressed for action in a lubricated condom. Allison squirted some extra lube onto the head.

"I want you to watch while Suzy fucks me," she moaned loudly. "It's Suzy's turn to fuck me!"

Stan returned to the couch and slowly began to massage his cock while I made a big point of manipulating the larger-than-life plaything—eyeing it lasciviously, inserting it between Allison's thighs.

Allie was making so much noise that I wondered if I had accidentally shoved it inside of her. (We have a standing agreement: just the tip, and only when absolutely necessary.) She used her hand to guide the oversized dildo to a safe harbor between her folds.

This was hot enough for Stan, and it provoked his competitive spirit. We somehow managed to get ourselves into a daisy chain of activity that would have impressed Busby Berkeley. (But I felt more like one of the upside-down creatures in a Hieronymus Bosch triptych than a 1930s showgirl.)

Stan was pumping me from behind while I played the assertive role with Allie. But soon it was obvious to all concerned that Stan wasn't going to come this way. Actually, it became obvious to me first, then to Stan. Allie, who couldn't see what was happening behind her, figured it out through a combination of past experience and deduction.

We all agreed that Stan should roll another joint—which he did, while we took turns wrapping hot damp washcloths around his relevant body parts. Then, after loading a new porn video, Allie disappeared, to rinse off and apply fresh K-Y. I followed suit, hoping that Stan would be ready—finally—to come.

There's a point where the client begins to sense that his orgasm is becoming an issue. Stan was getting there. And his impending orgasm was causing intergirl tension. Allie sensed that I might be getting pissed off with her client and, by extension, with her. Which made me sort of paranoid about *her* mood. So I did my best to reassure her, and knelt between his legs on the couch, teasing him with my hands and my tongue.

Was he ever going to ejaculate?

When he finally came (thanks to Allie's handiwork) I was astonished. Despite having declined multiple poppers, I had a major headache just from breathing the fumes. At $400 an hour, I couldn't complain. I had exceeded my weekly quota—and I wasn't the one with an entire living room to defume.

As soon as he was gone, Allie rushed around, naked except for her thigh-high boots, opening windows and turning on all the air conditioners. The draft was so intense that our nipples stood up.

"Where did you get those boots?" I said. "They must be about six inches high."

"Oh," she squeaked. "They're not as uncomfortable as they look. And they're great for work. Listen, um . . . I hate to throw you out of here but I—I've got to change real fast and . . ." She looked flustered. "I have to be downtown in half an hour and I'm running late! I don't want to keep Roxana waiting."

As I walked out of Allison's lobby, I couldn't wait to get into the fresh air. On the sidewalk, I heard a familiar voice and turned. In the early-evening darkness, I could see a short man in a winter coat; the back of his head was slightly hidden by his plaid scarf and he was talking on his cell phone.

Jack! Had he spotted me? As he entered Allie's building, I hurried to the other side of the street. I reached for my phone and punched in Allie's number, but her voice mail picked up. "Hey, it's me," I said, after the beep. "You might have to delay your exit. Jack's bothering your doorman again!" The last thing she'd want is another embarrassing scene in front of the building staff.

I moved behind a parked SUV, where I wouldn't be seen but could still view the lobby. The doorman picked up the intercom phone. Jack's hands were jammed into his coat pockets, and he looked nervous. But Jack didn't leave the building. Instead, he walked right past the doorman to the elevator. I slowly realized that—whatever I might prefer to imagine—Allie was definitely expecting him.

No wonder she was so anxious to air out her apartment! And change out of those slutty boots! Jack, as I recall, prefers Allie in sweet pink teddies and white lace. How could I have believed her ridiculous explanations?

7 Johns and Lovers

Allie has been avoiding me, and it's just as well. She has to know, if she got my voice mail, that I saw what was going on Friday night. Her flimsy falsehood—"I hate to throw you out of here but . . ."—had the briefest shelf life.

This morning, while Matt was in the shower, I checked voice mail on my personal and business landlines. Then my cell phone. For one rueful nostalgic moment, I recalled a time when life was harder yet simpler. When I was a new girl—a young overworked call girl—with zero boyfriends, *one phone,* and one simple goal: I had to build my book. I mean, how the hell did I end up with three voice-mail boxes, anyway? Most girls do fine with just two. Once you've got a nice apartment, some decent clients, and enough time for a personal life, things get horribly complicated. To further confuse things, most of the girls have access to my business line only. But Allison has *all* my numbers. And, despite my irritation, I've been hoping for a message from her.

There was a message from Liane (in business voice mail), followed by a call from Milton. A confirmation from my shrink on the personal phone— but still no voice mail from Allison. My fingers were itching to call Jasmine and Eileen. It's reached the point where Allison's "business decisions" have become everyone's business. The other girls have a right, perhaps a need, to know about Allison's betrayal. But Matt's presence—he could have emerged from the shower at any moment—stopped me in mid-dial. As did the nagging realization that I've been covering for her. Would the other girls see me as part of the solution or part of the problem? I'm not sure I really want to find out. Allie has entangled me in some airtight knot of evasions that I cannot afford to untie. Did she do it on purpose? Could she? I prefer to think it was entirely accidental.

Later, at Demarchelier, Matt picked up on my anxious mood. We were waiting for omelettes, and the sound of my brooding silence was driving us both nuts. "Something's bothering you," he said, in a romantic, masculine take-no-prisoners tone. "What's wrong?"

I never mention Allison to Matt anymore. That's been my policy ever since she went off the rails last year. I don't even want him *thinking* about her, because he might put two and two together—which would be a disaster. But I couldn't help responding to his concern. Some part of me was reassured—and turned on—by the effort my boyfriend was making. I felt interesting, attractive and lucky; mine is a guy who *listens.* I should, of course, be careful when he starts listening too closely, but if you keep your *entire* life a secret, what do you talk to your boyfriend about at brunch?

"Well," I said, frowning a bit, "it's about Allison. I'm sort of worried about her." I chewed my lip to buy some time. While contemplating which version of the truth to tell Matt, I was already feeling much closer to him. What girl is not flattered when her guy jumps through an emotional hoop to reach her, to know more about her feelings? Even if she is also hiding something?

Matt was temporarily distracted by the arrival of our food. He popped a french fry into his mouth, then refocused, a tender look of concern in his eyes. Did I really want my fiancé to comfort me? Or do I just like to see him making the effort?

"I saw her the other day," I ad-libbed. "We were looking at china patterns." A bit of a stretch—from dildos to dishes! "She's being such a big, um, help. And we're going to Vera Wang next week to look at dresses." His eyes brightened at this reference to the wedding plans. "So I took her to lunch, and you know what she told me?" Strange pause. There must be a way to get some emotional support without getting my hands dirty. It's the feelings, not the facts, that matter here. "She's been seeing a married guy!" I blurted in exasperation.

"She has? For how long?"

I detected a voyeuristic twinkle, a hint of boyish interest in sleaze. Hoping to jog him back to Better Boyfriend Mode, I explained, with a womanly sigh, "They've been on and off for a long time. I was so relieved when she told me it was over! And now I find out she's still seeing him. It's just awful."

Matt looked thoughtful, more like a Sensitive Boyfriend again. "You know what I've never understood about women?" he said finally.

"Um . . . I give up."

"Why does a woman take it so personally when a friend is doing something to *herself?* You act like—well, like she's cheating on *you,* honey."

"Well, in a way she is." I blushed with anger. "She lied to me! And it's—it's sort of disturbing to think that one of my bridesmaids is seeing a married guy!"

"Don't be so uptight," Matt advised me. "When I first moved to the city, my roommate was seeing a married woman."

"Oh?" I tried to hide my curiosity. "And didn't that bother you?"

"No." Matt looked amused. "Of course not. We had to change our phone number because she was always checking up on him—he said married women were even more possessive than single women. Look, I'm the guy's buddy, I'm not his guardian. Guys are different, honey." He gave me a paternalistic squeeze. "I'm glad you take marriage seriously, but Allison's a different kind of person. Maybe she's not ready to settle down."

He's only met her three times! It spooks me to think that he's given any thought at all to what "kind of person" she is.

"Isn't she a couple of years younger than you?" he added slyly.

"Only three," I said sharply. I didn't like being cast as the interfering fusspot—how frumpy—who moralizes about married men because *her* partying days are over. But I couldn't afford *not* to be frumpy at this moment. "Let's get the check," I said in a frosty voice. "I don't want to miss the preconcert lecture." When Matt started to organize his wallet, I glared at him with a flash of annoyance.

At Lincoln Center, I ducked into the ladies' room to check my messages. Nothing from Allison. And two beseeching messages from Milton trying to move our noon session to the evening. Damn! Didn't Matt say we were having dinner with Elspeth and Jason tomorrow? Can I squeeze Milton in at five-thirty? But when I called Milton's car, I ended up in AT&T limbo. And still felt vaguely frumpy.

MONDAY MORNING, 3/20/00

Last night, while I was bleaching my elbows with a fresh lemon, the phone rang. Thinking it might be Allison, I struggled to disengage from the lemon halves without getting pulp on my bed.

"Guess what!" Jasmine said cheerfully. I put the lemon halves down on the towel and picked some stray pulp off the pillow. "Allison and I are going to Patroon this Thursday. I made a reservation for three, just in case you want to come. They do the greatest creamed spinach!"

What? Allison can't be bothered to return my call from *Friday?* And she's making dinner plans with *Jasmine?* She has quite a nerve. Here I am, protecting *her* professional reputation from Jasmine and the other girls. Does she take my loyalty for granted?

"Why did she call *you?*" I asked.

"Well, she was trying to find that tape from the radio show and then she remembered that I had it. Now she's trying to get me to attend the next 'union meeting,'" Jasmine chuckled indulgently. "So we got to talking about Atkins." Her entire attitude toward Allie is much warmer, ever since she discovered that they're on the same diet. But I could change that pretty quickly by telling Jasmine about Jack's visit! "So? Are you coming with us? You really should."

I'm the one who brings *them* together! What the hell is going on here?

"She asked *you* to attend a meeting?" I said in a shrill voice. "Why?" Suddenly I felt like a pitiful schoolgirl tagging along in the shadow of the in crowd.

"Who knows?" Jasmine replied. "Sexual socialists have strange ideas. Maybe I'll attend her political circus, if I don't have business that night. What's wrong? You don't sound like yourself."

My other line, the business phone, was ringing.

"Nothing," I said more stoically. "I'll try to make it Thursday but I have to take this call."

Milton, sounding distorted but happy. "I've been trying to reach you! Quick. I'm about to enter a tunnel—can we do it at six tomorrow night?"

I resumed bleaching my left elbow. "That's too late for me! How about . . . four-thirty? Then we'll have time to relax." But I knew we would settle on five. Never one to argue about money, Milton is a haggler when it comes to setting a time.

LATER

Today, I had one of those therapy sessions where you spend half an hour nibbling on your appetizer and, finally, when it's almost too late, the main course appears. The appetizer course being my weekend with Matt, the entrée my nagging sense of displacement when I heard about Allison's dinner date with Jasmine.

"It seems," Wendy said, "that you view Jasmine as the more reliable friend. Aren't you closer to Jasmine?"

"No. I'm closer to Allie. Well, you see, I've had dinner with her parents, and that's a sign of trust in this business. Allie and I met each other's *relatives*. I don't even know if 'Jasmine' is Jasmine's real name!"

"So you've never met Jasmine's family." Wendy paused. "And what did you think of Allison's parents?"

"Normal to the point of weird! Mom's a housewife and Dad plays a lot of golf. But they like me. They're glad she has a friend who doesn't look like a character on *Sex and the City*. I looked very Lands' End catalog that day," I said, unable to hide my satisfaction. "No makeup. And thanks to me, they're less afraid of Manhattan. Less nosy."

Snowing the straight world is one of the perverse little perks of this business—but I sometimes wonder: Is it mature to take so much pleasure in getting away with stuff? Shouldn't I be outgrowing this streak of delinquency?

"Who was your closest friend when you were small? Growing up?" Wendy asked.

I sat up sharply and looked at my watch.

"Why? Uh . . . Vanessa. My dad and hers were in grad school together. We were best friends until . . ."

"Until?"

"Until we outgrew each other."

I left Dr. Wendy's office clutching an invisible doggy bag containing my hastily prepared and leftover emotions. In the cab, I sank into bittersweet reverie. I remembered a muggy afternoon, late in the day, when I was about five years old. I was sitting on the swing set in my backyard, conspiring with Vanessa against one of the local baby-sitters.

We told each other dirty stories about Debbie, the tall freckled sixteen-year-old who lived across the street. We had no idea what sixteen-year-olds did with their clothes off, but we did our best to keep a tantalizing narrative going. Debbie was forced to strip by groups of marauding boys who broke into the girls' bathroom. We imagined high school to be an unspeakably wild place where bigger girls lost their intriguing inhibitions. In one of our Debbie Stories, she was locked out of her house, naked, because her entire family had gone to the beach without her. She slept over in the home of a neighbor who took her in but refused to lend her clothes.

The houses where these imaginary atrocities were supposed to take place lined the quiet city block where I lived, a picturesque street with tall trees, small bushes, and modest patches of green grass. Debbie lived across the street with her five younger siblings and her parents, next to a shop with an old sign that read JIMMY'S CONFECTIONERY.

Vanessa lived in the suburbs, thirty minutes away from our Centertown neighborhood. There were vistas instead of shops, wide lawns, no shadows on the bare curved streets. Everything was so new, and there weren't many trees. When I slept over at Vanessa's house, we waited for everyone to fall asleep, then tip-toed around in the basement without our pj's on. We would lie in bed, exchanging lurid Debbie Tales. We also found ourselves exploring each other's bodies—comparing, looking, touching. We both entered puberty early. But Vanessa was a year older, so I felt slightly left out when her breasts began to sprout first. I bemoaned my flat chest.

"Don't worry," she said smugly. "It's going to happen. You're only eight!"

We both read *Anne of Green Gables*. On a cold March day, we stood over a puddle and reenacted a ritual we'd read about, when Anne and Diana solemnly vow to be faithful bosom friends. We discussed the plot twists of *Harriet the Spy, Black Beauty,* and *Little Women.* We overcame some differences: She didn't share my fascination with the boarding school tales of Enid Blyton; I found the Trixie Belden series flat and boring. My parents were from a British colony and hers were not. She couldn't understand why on earth I'd be so caught up in the soap opera of an English institution. I couldn't grasp what it was like to belong so easily to the present, to have parents who used *Webster's* instead of *Oxford,* who regarded most things British as irrelevant and dusty—and vaguely humorous.

But we had many shared rituals, and not just at bedtime. We spent Sunday mornings melting the butter on our toast by popping the buttered toast back into the toaster—much to our mothers' shared dismay. For a brief time, we shared a craze for preserving autumn leaves between waxed paper, using a hot iron without asking for permission. Another eccentricity of ours that brought our mothers together.

As Vanessa had predicted, my breasts began to grow—and sooner than I expected. The tenderness in my chest revealed itself one afternoon, just before spring break, when I was moving my desk to the back of the classroom. I bumped into the desk. Though I had no bruise—the impact had been minimal—I was still feeling sore two days later. But my breasts took forever! When I finally qualified for a training bra, I was nine and a half.

One afternoon, I came home from school and called Vanessa. I told her I had graduated from a puerile AAA to a full-fledged A-cup. She was already a bodacious 30B.

"I think we should cool it," she said abruptly.

"Why?" I asked.

"I just think we should."

She had recently started attending a prestigious girls' school located in a ritzy suburb. A school with no boys—and she had *asked* her parents to send her there. Although I had voiced my surprise, I had accepted this as a difference we could both live with. It never occurred to me that going to this new school would interfere with her feelings for me. And it struck me as odd that the girl who had been so dismissive of my school-story fetish chose to attend a girls' school. I would have been horrified if my parents had removed me from the company of males.

I ran into her, a couple of years later, in the lobby of a movie theater. She was the tallest member of a uniformed gaggle: Five charismatic teenyboppers in pleated green tunics, white blouses, and wedge-heeled shoes with ankle straps were loudly purchasing popcorn and Coke at the concession stand. Vanessa saw me and waved.

"Nancy!" she shouted, rushing over as if we were the most terrific chums. I suddenly felt like a member of another species in my desert boots, frayed jeans, and loose plaid shirt. I had never worn a school uniform and found it remarkable that she had chosen to attend a school where you had to wear one.

I also felt tiny—never having worn heels—though I knew I was now the cooler kid. I traveled to the movies by bus and bicycle. In fact, I traveled everywhere in our small town by myself and even knew how to get two fares out of one bus ticket. These girls, dependent giants bred in the 'burbs, never went anywhere without a ride. They had no idea how uncool it was to be driven places by a parent because, apparently, they had their own code of coolness.

"Come sit with us," Vanessa said.

I had just finished watching the movie, but in any case the thought of sitting with these Stepford Teens repelled me. And I didn't entirely believe her invitation.

"I have to go," I told her. "I'm baby-sitting." If I left now, I would have just enough time to eat supper at home before my baby-sitting gig.

"Veeeeee!" someone screamed. "Vee! Do you want a Fresca?"

Vee? My bookish, dirty-minded childhood friend was now an eighth grader called Vee. I sauntered off to the bus stop, sadder but wiser. I was still hurt by the way she had dropped me two years ago. So efficiently! At eleven, she had grown sick of playing childish sex games with a ten-year-old. Now I was an earnest twelve-year-old with avant-garde aspirations and a small baby-sitting income. And Vanessa was a silly thirteen-year-old who ran with a pack. In their confusing outfits—childish uniforms, heavy lip gloss—her friends were foreign to me. My casual outfit—no makeup, frayed denim, natural hair—was, I felt, consistent. I was sure I had put more thought into my appearance than they had.

On the bus, I opened my paperback copy of *Knots* and got so engrossed in R. D. Laing's stark mind games that I almost missed my stop. And my dinner.

But that was *more than twenty years ago*. And that was Vanessa.

Allie and I are not small-town teenyboppers torn asunder by competing codes of coolness. We're call girls, for god's sake. In our thirties! And I'm the one who is now in a position to devastate *her*—if I spilled the beans. Oh, Christ. What is wrong with me?

***

TUESDAY MORNING, 3/21/00

Milton was mercifully late for his appointment yesterday. I was sitting on the couch repairing some chipped toenail polish when, five minutes before his session, he called from his car. "There's an accident on the FDR," he shouted into his car phone. "Nothing's moving."

"Don't worry," I said sweetly. "I'll keep everything nice and warm for you. There's plenty of time to relax."

(And time for my polish to dry!)

"Boy, do I ever need to see you, kiddo. Did you rewind—" Terrific honking drowned him out for a second.

"I rewound the video, you filthy dog, to your favorite scene."

"That's the spirit! I'll call when I get to Sixty-first Street."

Our long-awaited reunion cheered me right up. Formative betrayals disappeared in the warm glow of Milt's easygoing lechery.

"It's been too long," he said, when I answered the door. "And I've missed those firm . . . fresh . . . *natural* breasts." They were spilling out of my afternoon costume—an uplifting one-piece number that wouldn't look out of place at a midtown lingerie bar. "I'll bet you're going out with your boyfriend tonight."

"As a matter of fact, I am." I rubbed up against Milton's suited self, and we hugged—a brief but noticeable hug that felt as spontaneous to me as it did to him.

"And you'll be wearing something sweet and wholesome, almost preppy, won't you?"

"How'd you know?" I said, loosening his tie for him.

He reached around to fondle my exposed rump.

"Because I know you . . . and you're just a little too excited about wearing that—what do you call this?" He laughed. "Anyway it looks great on you."

We settled onto the couch, where Milt revisited a truly awful porn video—*Back Door Girls*—left behind by another customer. (A "runner" who never returned to reclaim his dirty movie! I forget his name, but his video has served me well. Glossy erotica for couples this definitely is not.)

"Come on," Milt insisted. "Are you telling me that doesn't turn you on just a little?"

"Maybe as a *fantasy,*" I allowed, showing as little enthusiasm as permissible.

Three guys were doing something rather gross with a tall siliconed blonde on a tatty-looking bedspread, and I didn't want to encourage any of this unladylike stuff in *my* bed.

"She's hot looking," I added, though I thought she looked a bit, well, plastic.

"How does she do that? Is she double-jointed?"

I snuggled up to him and unzipped his pants. "*This* is what really turns me on," I hinted. "You're awfully hard, Uncle Milt! How do you do *that?*"

"And you're a thoughtful hostess," he added congenially. "Do you think she's really into it?"

"Oh, no doubt. . . . But why are guys so obsessed with anal sex?" I asked him. "It's not exactly necessary for a woman's pleasure."

Milton never tries to follow through, but he's always up for watching it on video. (A balance I can live with at work—though I think I'd *freak* if my boyfriend even tried to *discuss* anal sex.)

"Because, as we've established many times, we're lowlifes." Milton chuckled.

"And you're one of the lowest," I said affectionately. "Let's get these pants off, Sir Lowlife."

My feelings for Milton don't make sense. His lewd tastes do nothing for me. I've never had an orgasm with him because I'm too conscious of what I'm doing. I can't relax long enough to get turned on; though I can tell, objectively, that he has some oral talent. He's a gentle bedmate, and his graceful caresses are at odds with his trashy taste in videos. But he's also a lot of work. Last night, I felt like one of the figures in that art deco A-to-Z poster—naked women turning themselves into letters of the alphabet. It's not just the constant changing of positions, it's the effort that goes into looking smooth, svelte, and chipper, no matter what part of him I'm sitting on . . . or how long he's taking to come.

And yet Milton is the only client I feel possessive about. A girl can't stop a client from straying—and Milt knows that I know that he knows. But he's sensitive to my feelings. He shows up almost every week (unless he's on the road), and when I arrange a threesome (or a foursome), he's *financially* faithful—never asks for another girl's phone number. This way, I always make some extra cash when we party with a third or fourth. Of course, we never discuss those finer points, Milt and I. When it comes to money—and feelings—he's a polished professional john, a gentleman.

The extra work when we're alone is a labor of . . . not love, exactly, but something like it. I avoid fucking for too long with other clients—even the clients who make me come. But Milton, who *doesn't* turn me on, gets what I won't give others. For one thing, I don't have to be as guarded. When a client turns you on, that's when you have to walk the line. Milton is hard work, but he's easy in other ways.

"Your boyfriend's a lucky guy," Milton said, after he (finally) came. He has no idea how lazy I am when I'm not working! "I hope he appreciates you."

As Milton got dressed, I tried not to look impatient, but I was anxious to bring out the Velcro rollers! My hair was in desperate need of a pick-me-up after our marathon.

Finally alone, I breathed a sigh of relief and wrapped my hair in large purple rollers, then hopped into the shower, where I treated my body to an aromatic reunion with its favorite bath gel. For business, I have a big supply of unscented soap because, well, a hint of perfume can really mess things up for a client. Men rightly fear the olfactory powers of their wives and girlfriends, so perfumes are forbidden at work.

But now, covering my legs with lotion, spraying my neck, I was a smooth, scented "civilian" again. I pictured myself on my back, luxuriating in my laziness. I enjoy being a girlfriend—but would I enjoy it if I didn't get to be something else the rest of the time? If there wasn't something exotic and sneaky about being Respectable?

I zapped the crown of rollers on my head with the blow-dryer, then finished my makeup. Dressed for dinner in a smart houndstooth skirt, girlish sweater, and Gucci loafers, I left the apartment, feeling rather pleased with my day: This afternoon, in my slutty lingerie, I shunned perfume. Tonight, demurely skirted, I feel like one of those perfumed women whom other women might pay homage to—by not wearing perfume . . .

When I got to Chez Es Saada, Elspeth and Matt were already seated. They were conferring over their cocktails, heads bowed together so you could see from their profiled jaws that they were siblings. It's not so obvious from the front.

"You," Elspeth said, "and Jason are the culprits tonight. If it weren't for Matthew we would have lost our table."

Matt kissed my cheek as I slid into my seat, and it felt like a married kiss. Though, never having been married, how would I know?

"You smell so pretty," he said under his breath. Making a cell-phone gesture, he got up from the table. "I'll be back—gotta call the office," he said, kissing me again.

"Mmmmm," Elspeth commented, sipping on her drink. "The honeymoon continues! Matt says you're going to Vera Wang next week with Allison. I have to meet the bridesmaids," she reminded me. "When are we all having dinner?"

How I could possibly have imagined that having a matron of honor was a smart idea? My problem is, I'm too impulsive where respectability's concerned. I should have given the wedding party more thought before assigning Elspeth that role!

"The fabric you picked out for our dresses," Elspeth was saying. "Is your heart really *set* on that? It makes me look sort of washed out. I think it's too dark."

"That's interesting," I said. "Jasmine was telling me just the other day that the color is too light for her."

"Oh, really?" Elspeth laughed in despair. "Maybe it's just right, then! So what does Jasmine *do?* I asked Matt and he couldn't remember."

God, what does Jasmine say when people ask her what she

does? I tried to remember; I had temporarily forgotten because I so rarely have to deal with Jasmine's alibis.

"She's . . . involved with real estate," I said.

"Oh? A broker?"

"No, investments—I really don't understand what she does. It's all mumbo jumbo to me!" I sighed. "I was never very good at math."

"Really? She manages a REIT?"

I felt my skin getting warmer, my bra clinging uncomfortably to my body, and saw, with relief, that Matt was returning.

"I think she manages some buildings." Then, forced to embroider on Jasmine's behalf, I added, "For one of her relatives."

"Oh, a *landlord.* Well, why didn't you say so? In New York?"

"No," I said faintly. "I'm trying to remember—somewhere in New England or maybe . . ." I realized with alarm that Jasmine would never forgive me if I were to discuss her New Hampshire property deals with Matt's sister—an assistant D.A.! "Delaware," I said more decisively. "I'm sure she said something about some apartment buildings in Delaware."

Matt slid into his seat and looked around for a waiter.

"Delaware?" Elspeth persisted. "Where in Delaware? That's a strange place to be investing in real estate." Elspeth cocked her head to one side. "Delaware, hmmm. I can't wait to meet her."

A waiter appeared, and Elspeth loudly announced, "A round of French whores for the table."

I almost dropped my menu. Elspeth flashed a sly smile at her brother. "Oh, come on, Nancy." Elspeth pushed her glass toward me. "Try this—it's called a French whore and it's delicious. Want one?"

"I think I'll, ah, just have my usual," I said, backing away from her glass, wondering privately if the Kir Royale should be renamed. Manhattan call girl? Paranoid prostitute?

Elspeth's cell phone emitted a few bars of electro-Bach, causing a nearby diner to glare at us. She picked up the call and quickly hung up.

"I thought it might be Jason," she sighed.

I was getting edgy, due to the arrival of some communal appetizers—another Elspeth initiative. Like most hookers, I have an acute respect for germs. Sharing food is something I like doing with Matt when we're alone; but sharing food with his *sister* is a bit like having to kiss a client. And while I have the stamina to resist clients, I find it harder to dodge my future sister-in-law. If you don't participate in communal appetizers, you feel like a food prude. If you try a polite nibble of what everyone's having, it's not enough.

"Have some more," Elspeth was saying. I stared at the spoon and wondered if straight people just assume they're above germs.

Fortunately, Jason appeared, saving me from a second helping of shrimp.

"How about Jason?" I insisted. "He must be famished."

"I *am*," Jason agreed, happily accepting whatever Elspeth was offering.

"How'd it go?" Elspeth asked him.

He nodded in reply. This is their version of a kiss hello? But they seemed so relaxed that I almost envied them. For a minute.

"I kept calling your cell phone!" Elspeth announced. "You said you were leaving at six-thirty!"

"Oh. Sorry. I know. *Endless* negotiations. Deal's turning into a casualty zone," Jason half mumbled. "And their lawyers leave town tomorrow morning."

He wasn't so relaxed after all. He looked a little flustered—or annoyed. I couldn't quite tell. Jason had saved me from the communal appetizers, and now they were saving Jason from Elspeth's queries. He chewed as much food as he could for as long as he could, then turned to face me.

"Matt says you've found a place!"

His eyes were darting around, and if I were his wife or girlfriend I'd think something was up—but Elspeth's face was buried in her menu. She had delivered her semiaccusation, ruffled his nerves, and moved on. A marital moment so seamless and surreal that I wondered if I was imagining it. The kind of thing you can't even talk about because it almost didn't happen.

Why *was* he more than an hour late? Does every husband of means disappear into an illicit twilight zone around six P.M.? Until last night, I never thought of Jason as somebody's john—even though I've met plenty of guys just like him on the job. I guess I don't like to think about the obvious: Could I bump into my future brother-in-law while I'm working? Maybe Jason and I were late for . . . roughly the same reason.

WEDNESDAY, 3/22/00

Last night, snuggling on my couch with Matt, I rested my head on his shoulder and found my comfort zone disturbed by further thoughts of Jason, unreachable on his phone the other night—at the "usual hour," like so many husbands. Like so many johns. And why should I care? He's not my husband, I wasn't born yesterday, we're all adults here. But . . . what *about* my future husband? Is that what Matt will end up doing? I doubt he's ever *been* to a hooker. If we settle down—and if he can afford it—shouldn't I just take this in my stride? We won't be thirty-something forever . . . and I wouldn't want him to cheat on me with a civilian!

"What are you thinking about?" Matt asked affectionately. He was now in the process of muting the NY-1 weather and surfing silently toward CNN.

"The other night—" I paused. "Elspeth got me thinking about . . . my dress!" I looked up at him. "Why did you ask me that?"

"Your neck got sort of tense. Stop worrying about your dress," he teased. "You'll look great. You could get married in a beach towel for all I care. Just tell me where to show up. Listen, there's something I want to ask you about."

I stretched out on his lap and looked into his eyes while he played with my hair.

"You know," he said, "that apartment is still empty. It's been empty for almost two months." The Carnegie Hill two-bedroom.

"And?"

"The owners don't really want to rent. They want to sell it. Should I buy it? I want to know what you think."

"If *I* think . . . ?"

"This is the right time to buy," he said. "Prices are climbing, rents are crazy, and it makes more sense to own—but you keep saying you don't want to have the wedding until next year, and I just want to make sure . . ." The look in his eyes made me gulp hard. "I want to make sure you feel okay about this because if I buy it now it's not going to be in your name—until we're married. I discussed it with Karen, and she says the board will never allow us to put it in both names—unless we're married."

"Can't we wait? Until we're married?" I sat up.

"We can't," he said, putting both arms around my waist. "This is a really good deal and this market is—" He paused. "We have to decide this together."

I blinked. He's asking me how I think we should spend his hard-earned money? He's never done that before. This is something my previous boyfriends never thought to do, never had to do. This is—this is what really sets the perfumed wives and fiancées apart from the nonperfumed girls who charge by the hour. Oh my god. I am in over my head.

Suddenly, I wanted to bleat, "But I'm a teenaged runaway—I have hardly any savings and I can't handle money! You can't ask a hooker who spends all her money on handbags and Hermès scarves how you should be investing your money!"

"What's wrong?" Matt asked.

"I—I don't know what to say," I told him. I had the urge to run away. *But I'm not a teenager anymore—and we're in my apartment on my couch, drinking my white wine and watching my TV. Which is to say, I'm where I hoped I would eventually be—the first time I ran away. So where would I run to now?*

Then I remembered how I once faked it with Liane: By pretending to be part of her milieu, instead of the scrappy little bar hooker turned escort, I effectively became a scrappy escort turned private call girl. *I should be able to think of something to say!*

"You're asking me to help you make a huge decision," I finally said in a solemn voice.

"Well, who else would I ask?" He seemed genuinely charmed by my puzzlement. "I don't *want* to make any more huge decisions without you." *It's so much easier for Matt to come right out and talk about* his *big decisions. If he had any idea what decisions I have to make . . . but those decisions a girl has to face on her own.*

"Just think about it," he said. "We'll talk about it in a day or two."

"A day or two?" I was getting a bit high-pitched.

"Yes." He was firm. "We don't have that much time, but we can't make this decision overnight. If you think we should set the wedding date for this year, it's up to you."

"Why . . . this year?"

"I know you want everything just right and you want the day to be perfect—" *Not the real reason I've been insisting on a later date, but let him think it!* "This market has its own momentum, though."

Later, in bed, I began kissing him and couldn't stop. But Matt pulled away from my mouth and held my arms firmly in his hands.

"Do you want me to spell it out?" he said. "Maybe I should."

"Okay," I whispered, having no idea what he was getting at—but I could feel something happening; he was somehow taking charge of things.

"Well, I really want to buy the apartment—I want to put in a bid at the end of the week." His fingers around my upper arms were gently loosening up. "I don't want you to feel like you're just shacking up with me—I want this to be your place, too. *Our* place. But sometimes I'm not sure what you want. If the real estate market wasn't so insane, I would wait until after the wedding, but—"

Seeing the look in my eyes, he reached down and stopped talking. His fingers slid over my skin. It wasn't just the surprise that made my heart beat faster—the surprise of being pushed into such a tight corner. It was a feeling of both victory and fear that I couldn't talk about. I pulled him closer. My secret panic, the excitement, his nearness, his touch; the flood of emotions was overflowing elsewhere. I could feel myself getting damp. More than damp.

This is the most serious deal a girl can make with a guy, and I have no idea what I'm doing. I've charged men by the hour—that was one kind of deal—but this, this makes my business look like some kind of child's game. What if I say the wrong thing? What if I say what ought to be the right thing but it turns out to be the wrong thing for me? *If only I knew what I wanted!*

His questions, his offer, made me feel like a total amateur, flustered and needy, instead of the sneaky professional I like to be. I enjoy playing the amateur with clients and boyfriends—especially with boyfriends. It's my secret indulgence. But this was scary. It wasn't a secret game or a private fantasy; it was real.

I closed my eyes and whispered, "Make love to me, I don't want to talk anymore. Please?"

It was a strange sensation—helpless, deceptive, scared, guilty—

and I didn't want to like it. But it turned me on—or maybe not. Maybe coming was the only way I could escape this feeling. At any rate, it worked well enough to relax me so that, afterward, I fell into a dreamless sleep.

When I woke this morning, it bothered me to think that if I quit the business for him, maybe our sex life. . . . Will it change? Am I hooked on having secrets? On getting away with something? Do I ever, really, give myself to him? Or is he just one of the more emotional rides in a working girl's erotic Disneyland? Should I reconcile myself to . . . giving back the ring?

If I work on the sly, I'll always be lying to him, and I'll never really settle down. If I settle down, quit my past . . . then what? I'll have to invent some future version of myself, and who exactly is that supposed to be?

8 One of the Girls

This morning I was reaching optimum aerobic heart rate when I spotted Allie—heading for the locker room. She was dressed for Pilates class in loose navy sweats, lugging two huge shopping bags, a white Duane Reade and a Big Brown Bloomie's. Her wavy ponytail protruded from the back of a denim cap that was pulled down over her forehead, so I couldn't tell whether she was avoiding me or just blinkered by her choice of sportswear.

After nearly a week of silence I wasn't about to make the first move. But I *had* been pumping away for at least fifteen minutes, so I cut my cardio short, hopped off the Lifecycle, and headed for the shower. Allie was crouching in front of a locker, trying to cram one bag on top of another. A bright red ankle-strap sandal fell out, scratching her forearm with its spiky heel. She gasped in pain, turned to grab it, then saw me enter, glistening with fresh perspiration.

"I've been looking all over the gym for you!" she exclaimed.

"You have not," I said grimly. "You've been avoiding me all week, and we both know it."

"I can explain! Oh, help," she said to nobody in particular, as she fiddled with the bags. "This isn't working." She pulled off her cap, threw it on the carpet, and leaned back against a locker. She was sitting on the floor looking very resigned.

Peeking into the locker, I saw some slutty-looking shoes way past their prime; they had once been pretty expensive, judging by the labels. In better condition were some staid-looking flats and once-trendy Olive Oyl platforms, unused, wrapped in plastic.

"Where'd you get all these *shoes?*"

"Donations! I'm taking them downtown after Pilates. Roxana's meeting me at the women's shelter, and we're going to help Gretchen do a safe-sex workshop for some homeless teens. And I'm learning how to be a peer counselor!" Allison looked as excited as a farm boy attending his first county fair, and I feared for the street waifs who were about to become a way station on her journey to personal fulfillment. Would they be able to withstand all that compassion? From a thirty-something call girl with a weakness for middle-aged stalkers—who thinks of herself as the right-on "peer" of a street urchin?

"I've been picking up old shoes and used clothing all week!" she sighed. "For the homeless street girls."

"Silly me! I just assumed you were sitting in a Starbucks holding Jack's hand for the last six days. I had no idea you were engaged in such worthy activities!" I replied.

"I—" Allison faltered and began to look embarrassed. "I can explain about Jack. You—um—haven't said anything to Jasmine or Eileen, have you? About Jack?"

"No," I replied in a cold voice. "But sometimes I wish I had—a long time ago."

I turned around and marched off to the showers, then realized that I couldn't enter in my sneakers. I pretended to look for a fresh towel and made my way back to the bench, where I began to untie my shoes.

"This is not what you think. Jack and I—" She paused. "We've come to an understanding. But I didn't think you would understand our . . . understanding. And I was right. You don't understand." She pouted. "I was afraid if I told you in the *middle* of our negotiation—well, you were being so negative. Anyway, Jack's helping me now."

"Helping you?" I was now standing in front of her, in my gym bra and nothing else. "I'm afraid to ask what this entails."

Allie's eyes grew filmy with tears, and she looked away. I handed her my towel—too large for the job, but we practical girls know how to make do. She dabbed a tear off her cheek with the corner of the towel, then added, in a solemn voice, "I'm at a crossroads in my life. Believe it or not, Jack has helped me see that. When we met at Starbucks for coffee, he told me one of *his* secret dreams, and I told him one of mine."

"Oh? Well, he didn't meet you at Starbucks last Friday—so I presume his secret dream had something to do with visiting your apartment?" Some secret!

"His secret wish is that, if things were different, we might have a life together. Well, that's what he says. I told him very honestly that this was not something I could see myself doing. *My* secret dream is to get an MSW."

"A social work degree?"

"Yes! And he's committed to helping me do this. And I believe I can also be a healing force in his life. If he's helping me to achieve my goals, I can help Jack to be a better person," she insisted, her voice rising to a breathy plea. "And that is one of his goals, by the way—to be the best person he can be." Now, if I were a guy, I'd be persuaded by Allie's voice alone. But unfortunately, being a girl, *I hear the actual words,* not just the ear candy of her breathless babble. "My openness as a person helps him to see me as a person! To experience my humanity in three dimensions instead of two. He no longer feels the need to stigmatize me."

"He used those words?" I was surprised by Jack's new vocabulary. Last time we spoke, he was talking about, well, much baser things than his personal growth.

"Well, not those words exactly. I sort of helped him see it. I'm—you see, I'm healing Jack's sex-negative phobias."

How much does it cost to heal such a deeply ingrained phobia? I wonder.

One of the trainers entered the room, and Allie continued quietly: "So he's going to help me get my master's degree. He wants to make a positive contribution to my future. We have an arrangement now. And he's being very generous! I got my first installment on Friday—all cash." She was blushing with pride, and who could blame her? It's not every day that a john becomes your sugar daddy. But still . . . Jack? Why Jack?

"People make mistakes, but people can grow from their mistakes. A negative can become a positive! In order to heal Jack's sex negativity," Allie explained, "I have to forgive him. In order to forgive him . . . well, his offer of financial assistance was very positive. Jack and I are both growing as a result of this experience. I am growing *financially*, and he is being challenged emotionally. I feel so blessed!" But Allison suddenly looked very uncomfortable. "I have to pee," she said abruptly. She pulled her container of Ketostix out of the shoe-filled locker and disappeared.

How many times a day do these Atkins freaks have to test their—? I don't think I want to know.

I changed into my antifungal flip-flops and hopped into a shower, hoping she would just leave and get on with her exercise routine. I'd heard enough. But Allie was padding around in *her* shower flip-flops, looking for me.

"Nancy?" she called out. "Are you—? There you are! Ummmm. Nancy?"

I gritted my teeth and made a consenting gurgling noise under the water as she pulled the curtain to one side.

"Close it, would you? I'm getting a chill."

"I just wanted to make sure I was talking to *you*."

"Good idea," I sighed, as the hot water ran down my back.

"Jack finally admitted—he told me about the phone calls," Allison said. "I'm sorry about the way I doubted you. He even tried to blame me for the fact that he was making all those crazy phone calls to Eileen!" There was an edge of down-to-earth annoyance as she marveled over Jack's audacity. "Anyway, I've been telling Jack, we're all responsible for *how* we channel our sexuality. I think he's starting to see that! He's not bothering you anymore, is he?"

For a fleeting instant, I actually felt sorry for Jack. If I understand this correctly, he's paying Allison to lecture him about her New Age beliefs. They're obviously having sex again, but the more he pays her, the more nonsense he has to listen to! I doubt that he's getting extra sex for those thousands. What a fitting punishment! And, though I hate to admit it, Allie might be responsible for the fact that Jack hasn't bothered me lately. There haven't been any hang-ups and Eileen hasn't said anything about Jack for a few weeks. How long *has* this sugar-daddy arrangement been going on? A little longer than Allie cares to admit. I decided not to say anything about that—for now.

"Are you coming to Patroon tomorrow?" she asked. "Jasmine says it wouldn't be the same without you."

"Really. What else does Jasmine say about me?"

"You know what? Jasmine's a nicer person than you give her credit for."

"Excuse me?" Why is *she* defending Jasmine to *me?* Jasmine is *my* friend, not hers, goddammit.

"Jasmine's donating all kinds of things to the NYCOT clothing drive. Like those shoes."

"The moth-eaten disco pumps?"

"No! The *new* shoes, of course. She got one of her, you know"—Allison's voice lowered to a discreet mumble—"regulars, a guy in the shoe business, to donate some discontinued styles. He's sending a bunch more next week. And she has another guy in the Garment Center who says he'll donate some 'missy loungewear.' You see? Jasmine is just a good deed waiting to happen. Like Jack, she just needs the right emotional environment—"

"And who donated the disco pumps?"

"Well, that's a good question. A man called up after I did the radio show. He said his sister had died and left behind all these shoes and he can't think of a more worthwhile cause to donate the shoes to. He was inspired by my dialogue! He left a nice card with the shoes, but there's no name on it. It just says A NYCOT ADMIRER. I've never met him. But he wants to help the street girls."

Inspired by her dialogue? Dead sister? No name? This sounds weird.

"You let this . . . admirer deliver shoes to your building?"

"Of course not!"

"Then how did he get the shoes to you?"

"Well, it was complicated. But I got him to leave them here, with the receptionist."

"Now he knows your name! And where you work out!"

"Just my first name," Allison assured me. "I only used my first name on the show . . . and lots of people work out here. Listen, Pilates starts in five minutes. So I'll see you tomorrow night? You're not mad at me anymore?"

As I dried off, I was vaguely spooked by the shoe story. Something about it gives me the creeps. I keep thinking about—what was his name? That sick guy who chopped off the hands . . . and feet! . . . of his victims to cover his tracks. I remember when he was on trial and all these moms were gathering at the courthouse, telling the reporters that their dead daughters weren't hookers.

"Typical," Jasmine said at the time. "A serial killer chops you up into fifty different pieces and your mom's worrying about your sexual reputation."

The morbid mood stayed with me, as I contemplated that bag of sexy shoes. Then, as I headed home for my appointment with Steven, it passed.

Yes, we finally connected, Mr. Stockings and I! What an easy yet weird date. While telling me an elaborate and nostalgic story about a girl who made him come in his pants at the age of thirteen, he stood next to me, holding his cock against the top of my stockinged thigh. When I felt the head grazing the intersection of sheer stocking and smooth skin, I looked down. And when I started to touch him—he came!

With a quiet smile on his face, he slipped an envelope into my hand and left.

LATER

Eileen is thrilled to hear that I finally got around to seeing her client "Steven Stockings."

"Do you want the cut or a new date?" I asked.

"Well, I'd rather have the date," she said. "But my nephew's tuition payment is overdue. So let's do the cut. My sister is a bloodsucker," she complained. "And that useless husband of hers! Can you imagine what they'd be like if they knew what I do for a living?"

Eileen tells her family she has a rich boyfriend footing a lot of her bills. I can't help wondering: Aren't her parents horrified? I know mine would be. I could never get away with telling relatives I'm being kept by a guy. That's even weirder (to them) than doing nothing at all. But Eileen's family is satisfied, despite the fact that they've never met this phantom boyfriend (which would imply that he's married). And they're happy to have one adult child who makes up for the financial failings of her siblings.

SATURDAY, 3/25/00

Last night, I waited until the last possible minute, then called Jasmine's cell phone from a cab.

"Hey!" she answered. "Are you coming? Allison just got here." I could hear the buzz of a bar crowd in the background.

"I just had a cancellation," I lied, not wanting to seem eager. "Maybe I'll drop by for a drink. After I finish up at Bloomie's." Okay, so I was having a Junior Moment, playing hard to get with my girlfriends; but my decision to hit Bloomingdale's on the way downtown was eminently mature.

"What are you thinking? They won't seat us unless we're all here."

"I have to return some bras—it won't take long. I want the credit to show up on my statement before my payment date."

"Well, you'd better return them fast! If you're not here soon, they'll give our table away and we'll be eating in *Siberia*. Or maybe Buffalo!"

"Oh, nooo!" I moaned.

"Are you still there? What's going on?"

The sky had disappeared. Raindrops were beating against the window of my cab, and I had no umbrella. "It just started pouring. My god."

"You'll never get a cab at Bloomingdale's in the rain. You'd better get over here!"

"Okay," I conceded. "I'll return the bras tomorrow." I now had a perfectly good excuse to meet the girls for a huge steak dinner. (Without any guy-related worries about after-dinner bloating.) The driver was deeply engrossed in his *own* cell phone conversation, which he was reluctant to end. "Excuse me!" I shouted for the third time. "I have to change my destination!"

Grudgingly, he turned around, still wearing his headset.

"Where it is you wish to go, miss?"

As we pulled up, I calculated a dry dash to the restaurant door using my tote bag as a shield for my hair. But the bag was too heavy due to its cargo of liquid underwear, and I had to dry off in the ladies' room.

When I returned to our table, Jasmine was ordering a Grey Goose martini.

"A martini is on Atkins. A Kir is *not*," Jasmine said.

"I'm not *on* Atkins," I protested.

"But we are. And Allison shouldn't be having white wine."

Allison sheepishly consented to Jasmine's choice.

"So! How was the trollops' teach-in?" Jasmine inquired, in a voice that betrayed an earlier martini. Our fault: She had been waiting at the bar for us both.

"Very uplifting!" Allie replied. "But the project manager wouldn't let Gretchen use a dildo for the oral-sex demo. She said it was exploitive and possibly controversial. Or did she say controversial and possibly exploitive..." Allison frowned. "Gretchen says they're afraid of a dildo scandal because they get funding from the Health Department. The project manager made her use a banana!" Allison looked thoughtful. "You know, I've never seen such a large banana."

"Are you sure it was a banana? Maybe it was a vegetable," I suggested. "Or a plantain."

"Plantains are *off* the diet," Jasmine remarked. "How big was it?"

"Huge." Allie tried to estimate the size with her palms. "We used a large Trojan."

I glanced around in the vain hope that nobody was listening, but two young guys in suits were sitting right behind Allison—openly staring.

"Nancy's right," Jasmine said. "A large plantain! That's, like, eighty-two grams of carbohydrate! *Gag* me."

"There was never any danger of *anyone* consuming carbohydrates at the workshop—" Allison began.

"I guess condoms protect you from carbs, huh?" Jasmine snickered softly, then turned to my tote bag and peeked inside. "Let's have a look at those bras."

"Not here," I pleaded, but she was already poking around.

Allison craned her neck to look. "Brand-new bras?" she said

brightly. "We're taking a van over to Tenth Avenue tomorrow night. With two boxes of free condoms. Maybe we could give the bras to the girls who need them most."

In a low voice, I explained, "They're water bras. Not very good for work."

Jasmine held one of the black bras in her lap. "You're right," she concluded. "You can't wear this with a guy. Let's face it. Tits don't weigh this much, and guys aren't stupid!"

Allison giggled inanely, causing the twenty-something boys at the next table to smirk.

"Can you two calm down?" I said sourly. "You're making a spectacle of yourselves. People can hear what you're saying." The Atkins acolytes were staying away from the bread basket but not the cocktails, and I was the only one nibbling on a roll. Hence my relative sobriety. "Have a roll, Allie. Before you get alcohol poisoning."

Allison was about to take me up on this when Jasmine reached over, efficiently snatching the basket out of Allison's reach.

"I had two pieces of focaccia last night and my strips were medium purple!" Allison protested.

"But we want to keep them purple," Jasmine said. "A piece of focaccia here, a roll there, and next thing you know . . . pale pink! Or *beige.* My strips are consistently dark purple."

"Must we discuss all this at the table?" I inquired in a testy voice. "I'd like to be able to enjoy my meal without having to hear about your personal habits."

Allison looked subdued for a while. Later, having demolished her grilled salmon, she began once more to zoom in on the bread basket. The diet of the loaves and fish?

"If you're not careful you'll stop producing ketones, and then you'll be right back where you started," Jasmine warned her. "Have some creamed spinach instead."

"I'm not sure about this diet," Allison sighed. "Even though

I'm producing ketones. I inhaled that salmon and I'm still in the mood for a sourdough roll."

"That's because you have this stupid New Age hang-up about red meat! Woman does not live by brook trout alone. Or boneless chicken breast. You need to start eating more beef, pork, and fatty birds. A nice duck. A juicy lamb chop." Jasmine sliced into her porterhouse steak. "Look at me! I eat this stuff all the time, no problem. And I never crave starch."

Allie gave Jasmine's sleek seated figure a sideways look.

"Aren't you worried about cholesterol?"

"No. My cholesterol count is amaaaazing. And my doctor is, like, 'Whole grains, low fat, you know the drill,' so I just play dumb. He has no idea I'm eating *no* grains and lots of fat. And he's thrilled with my cholesterol results."

"Why," I asked, cutting into my own juicy steak, "are you lying to your doctor about what you eat? That's like lying to your lawyer about what you do for a living! It's crazy."

"Doctors will just lecture you to death. They're in league with the powerful cereal companies. Did you tell yours?" she asked Allie.

"Not yet."

"Being on Atkins is sort of like joining the Resistance," Jasmine explained. "When you go to the doctor you're, like, *underground.* You have to think like a fugitive. The medical establishment's totally against what we're doing. These people are the food police."

Food police? Could Jasmine be projecting just a wee bit?

After ordering dessert—a cheese plate, of course—and making sure Allison didn't get anything sweet, Jasmine stood up. "My phone keeps vibrating! I'll be right back." As she sailed off, phone glued to her ear, the twenty-somethings were checking her out. She did look intriguing, in her hand-tailored black velvet jeans and her steel-tipped cowboy boots. True to form, Jasmine pretended not to notice—though her walk hinted vaguely at a swagger when she passed their table.

Allie turned to me with a worried look on her face. "I saw Jack this morning—he had to come over at six-thirty!" she said quietly.

"In the *morning?*" I gasped. "I hope he's not going to make a habit of that."

"Well, sometimes it's the only time he can fit me in. He comes over before he goes to the office. His wife thinks he's going to the gym."

"Strange. He used to see you in the afternoons, when he was a normal customer! What time do you have to get up?"

"Very early," she said unhappily. "The thing is . . . he said something today that I didn't like. My next installment is due any day now, and he's—he's giving me a hard time about my major. He wants me to change it."

"Hang on. He agreed to what, exactly? To send you back to school?"

"To pay for my MSW. And help with the rent for the next two years."

"And what's the problem?"

"He wants me to withdraw from NYU and go to *interior decorating school.*" She looked deeply hurt. "And I don't want to! I really want to study social work."

"Why?" I asked. In a strange way, I could sort of *see* it—Allison as an interior decorator. But . . .

"I want to give something back," she said earnestly. "And this is the right time in my life to do it. I was so inspired by the safe-sex workshop today! And I'm doing outreach tomorrow night with Gretchen on the van—this is what I love to do! If I get an MSW, I can do what I love and make a living at it!"

Before she started hooking, Allie went to Marymount and graduated with a B.A. in art history. Which led to a nice job at a Madison Avenue boutique selling dresses and suits to party girls and bored housewives. She also amassed a collection of great outfits at a nice discount—which, when she entered her new profession, came in handy. There was a logical trajectory: low-pressure private girls' college, followed by a cushy clothing store job . . . followed by an even cushier stint as a call girl. But this is where the trajectory sort of wobbles a bit.

How does any of this prepare Allison for life as a social worker? "Doing outreach" on a van in the middle of a dangerous neighborhood? When all the drunks and yahoos, the bridge-and-tunnel drivers, are cruising around the streets of New York! Tenth Avenue is not where Allison should be spending her Saturday nights. But I didn't want to take Jack's side. She was visibly upset about the prospect of studying interior decoration.

"Are you sure social work is really right for you? Maybe that van won't be as fulfilling when it's a real job. And you do have an art history degree," I added. "You could use it—"

"That's what *he* says!" she objected. "But I didn't know what else to study when I was eighteen years old! I didn't *like* art history. I just didn't know who I was at that point. I have no interest in decorating rich people's homes. I want to help the people who don't *have* homes. I've found something that gives my life meaning, and I want to make a difference. You'd be amazed at the number of women on the street who are homeless and addicted and persecuted—and the risks they take every day just to survive. If I go back to school, I can help those women full-time, and I'll be taken more seriously."

"Taken seriously. What do you mean? By who?"

"Everyone. Well, people like Gretchen."

"You have to get a social work degree so that some sanctimonious ex-streetwalker will take you seriously? What kind of a movement *is* this? Why do you care what she thinks of you, anyway? She was horrible to you!"

"They have access to *jobs* and U.N. health funding! You can't get paid unless you have all the right credentials! Right now, I'm just a volunteer!" Allison explained. "It's sort of like working for a madam—that's fine, but then you want to branch out on your own, make something of yourself. You know, I'm going to this conference in Costa Rica and Gretchen's airfare is being paid for with UNESCO funds out of Venezuela, but *I* have to pay my own way! The *professional* activists never have to pay!"

Last time I looked, airfares were ridiculously low. Clearly, it's the principle of the thing—being wanted, being paid for—not the price of the ticket.

"I can't just see guys for the rest of my life!" Allison was saying. "Jack said he would get me started on a new career path, he said he would help me realize my dreams, but now he's—I feel like he wants to *destroy* them! It's not fair," she added. "He says he won't give me the money we *agreed* to unless I pick something else."

"Jack is unstable," I pointed out. "You can't allow him to direct the course of your future." I tried to look as sympathetic as possible, but secretly I was rejoicing. Maybe this signals the end of that arrangement, and we can all get on with our lives.

Jasmine sauntered toward us, looking very focused after her phone call. She sat down with a decisive smile on her face and began attacking the cheese plate. "Hey, remember that dot-com investment banker?" she said. "The guy I met at the benefit? We're having lunch tomorrow for the first time. Jesus. What do you wear to the Lotos Club? I've never been."

"Something low-key but expensive," I suggested. "You don't want to stand out. How old is he?"

"About . . . forty-eight? Fifty-something?"

"Go conservative, but not matronly."

"Mmm. Look young enough to feed his ego." She nibbled a forkful of ripe Brie.

"Right. But not *too* young. And wear your Bulgari knockoff, the bracelet. This way he'll know what kind of present to buy you."

"Maybe I'll get some real Bulgari earrings to match the knock-off," Jasmine mused.

I feel quite envious. Of course, I have the freedom to sneak around, but everyone seems to have that freedom. Big deal. Now that I'm engaged to a guy who's an up-and-coming player, I can't exactly run around town cultivating Wall Street sugar daddies, enticing men into buying me love trinkets. In fact, the only men I can play with at this point are straight-ahead johns.

Jasmine was impressed with my vicarious game plan.

"Wear black or brown," I told her. "A great scarf, and how about that V-necked blouse you got at the Bergdorf sale? You can *hint* at cleavage. Maybe . . ." I hesitated. She's not going to sleep with this would-be sugar daddy tomorrow. She's just introducing herself. "Maybe this is where a water bra comes in handy. Can you wear a 34C?"

"You're right! And I can!" she said happily. "Even though I'm really more like a 36B. I guess dating isn't such a waste of time, after all. You seem to have developed good instincts."

I was discreetly tucking a bra into Jasmine's Ferragamo back-pack when I noticed Allison staring at me, looking wounded.

"Maybe I can spare *one* for the street van?" I suggested. "I really do have to return the others, though. And I have some shoes you might be able to use."

"Oh, that would be nice!" Allison agreed. "I know there's someone out there right now, working on one of those avenues, who could use a new bra. If we would just think of ourselves as a community—"

"Get out the violins," Jasmine muttered.

"We could change the world!"

"I just hope that bra doesn't start a civil war in the outreach van," Jasmine said. "The road to hell is paved with the intentions of do-gooders."

Out on Lexington Avenue, Jasmine hailed us a cab. I was relieved when she encouraged me to sit in the middle. I should have known that all those two needed to set them back on the path of discord was an evening in each other's company.

But now I'm two water bras lighter! I really must return the bras *today* before I meet Matt and Karen—before anyone else persuades me to give one away. Karen's taking us to see some more co-ops, and the first one is at— Yikes. Really? That's not possible, is it? I thought 444 was still a rental.

MONDAY, 3/27/00

I used to be the kind of girl who worries about whether to sleep with a "freebie" on the second date or the fourth. Whether I should or shouldn't put the condom on my boyfriend with my mouth; I didn't want Matt to think I was a lot more experienced than he was. I like being seduced, being treated like a Nice Girl, being taken by a guy who does most of the work in bed—when I'm not working, that is. Letting your boyfriend put the condom on is key to passing for a Nice Girl in bed. (Once, I maneuvered a condom onto a boyfriend while he wasn't looking. We had been fucking for a good ten minutes before he noticed what he was wearing. I admit I was feeling mischievous—but I didn't think he would take it *that* way. He gave me a resentful puzzled look, and things went from weird to worse in that relationship. I've never made that mistake with Matt!)

But now—now that I'm wearing a ring—I worry about how to advise my boyfriend on a real estate deal. I'd like to go back to worrying about my sex life. Real estate makes me feel . . .

". . . like an imposter," I told Dr. Wendy this morning. "I'm afraid to make a wrong move with this co-op. So far, he seems to think I'm very serious-minded, looking at all the angles. The truth is, I'm afraid to offer any opinion at all." I paused to brood. "If he buys it before we get married, I don't have to go before the board!" I added.

"And you're afraid of the co-op board?"

"Nooo, not exactly. Well, yes."

"What are you afraid of?"

"Now that he's thinking about buying, we've been looking at lots of different apartments. And this weekend, the broker took us to a building where I used to work!"

"Really!" Wendy looked either amused or curious. I wasn't sure which.

"Yes, I worked in a house for about two weeks in this really great building just off Sutton Place. When I was about twenty-three. And the apartment we looked at this weekend is in the same line! The same layout, three floors down from the place I worked in! The J line—it's a two-bedroom with an extra powder room."

"How did you feel about *that?*"

"Well, I would have preferred two full bathrooms."

"I meant—" Wendy massaged her temple for a second.

"Oh!" I said, giggling nervously. "I was spooked when I realized where we were! But I felt like the cat that ate the canary," I admitted, "because Matt was really impressed. Now it's a very fussy co-op building, but it was just a rental when I worked there. Well, I used to fuck men for money in basically the same apartment, and Matt was slightly *intimidated*. It gave me a sick thrill, I guess."

"When did you reveal this part of your life to Matt?" Wendy asked. She was adjusting her glasses and sitting forward, ready for some major therapeutic action.

"He was intimidated by the *apartment*," I said vehemently. "He doesn't know anything about my past, and this is hardly the time to tell him!"

"Oh." Wendy relaxed in her chair. "Say more—about intimidation."

"You have to put down fifty percent, and we—he—can't at this point. The other building's only ten percent. And the tax-deductible portion—" I stopped chattering and took a deep breath. Jesus. Co-op hunting is making me crazy—almost as crazy as the Atkins diet is making Jasmine. I must stop thinking (and talking) like a real estate ad. "Look, it was just a little too close to home, okay? I realize now that if I have to talk to a co-op board, well, of course, I know how I'll dress for the interview. But what if I run into a client? A lot of my clients are on the boards where they live! Last night I couldn't sleep!"

"Okay," Wendy said, in a calmer voice. "Most people experience self-doubt before an interview with a co-op board."

I wondered if Dr. Wendy was disappointed: Instead of a confessing hooker who just blew the lid off her personal life, she's getting another co-op board story. This can't be her idea of a great day!

"You just said that Matt was intimidated by the requirements of the building where you once worked. So, you see? You're not alone in feeling this kind of fear."

"But he's not afraid of the co-op board at the building where he's really hoping to buy. It's a ten-percent-down building! I'm embarrassed to admit that—" I caught my breath. "Look, it's one thing to be intimidated when a building wants fifty percent down. But I can't admit to Matt that I'm afraid to face the board at a building that only requires ten percent. He won't understand!"

"Okay, but you can talk about it here. So, what's the worst thing that can happen at the interview?"

"What if they ask embarrassing questions? Co-op boards want to see your tax returns, they can ask you where you went to college! What if we get turned down because of *me?* Because I can't account for my past?"

"Many people are turned down by co-op boards. It's more likely, since he's buying, that if you're turned down, *he* will be the cause. As a therapist, I dislike co-op boards. I advise anyone who asks—not that most people think to ask a therapist for real estate advice—that condos are less intrusive and less confrontational. And less stressful for relationships like yours."

"Really. I should tell Matt to look at condos? But what reason would I give him?"

"He's marrying you? As his future partner, you have a say here. Condos are easier to resell, but you may simply prefer to look at all the options. Since he asked you to help him make this decision, why not express a desire to look at some condos?"

"I don't know! I feel so out of my depth! I've never really shared a man's money or his financial decisions. It's one thing when a boyfriend takes you out to dinner or buys you a dress or a piece of jewelry. And, of course, there are money issues with a john. But this is different."

"How?" Wendy asked.

"A john—no matter how much you like him—isn't your partner. He's a customer. You get money from him, you don't help him make decisions about money. Matt's not acting like a john *or* a boyfriend."

"No. He's treating you like his future partner."

"But I don't know what I'm supposed to do!"

"There's no script," Wendy assured me.

"There must be!"

THURSDAY, 3/30/00

This morning, a call from Liane: "I know it's short notice, but Bernie's in town, and he so wants to see you!"

Short notice from Liane probably means that one of her newest girls has stood her up. But she's too diplomatic to admit that. And I guess I'm enough of a sport to play along.

"Bernie?" I said. "Have I ever seen—"

"Dear, he'll be here in an hour. If you get here soon, I'll explain it to you. Dress simply. No lipstick. You saw him last summer. Remember? He thought he was your first client!"

Bernie! Right. The guy from Chicago who thinks I'm a college sophomore. When in fact there are people my age who *teach* college. Bernie thinks every girl he sees is doing it for the first time. Or (if he sees her again) the second time.

I threw some condoms and K-Y into my purse, changed into a pleated skirt and low heels. Were I to look like a real college student, I would have pierced eyebrows and tattooed buttocks or thighs—and Bernie would be horrified. So would Liane, for that matter. Both have a rather sanitized notion of what a "college girl" looks like. And it's just as important to please the madam, a habit that dies hard with me, even though I don't exactly need Liane's business these days. But maintaining a Good Attitude—a better one than you need to have—keeps a working girl young.

Bernie is about sixty, very toned and virile looking with a full head of salt-and-pepper hair. He likes to think he's either ruining a girl or helping her. It was hard to say which, as he talked me through his blow job.

"You're getting better and better at this," he said, pushing gently on my head.

I twisted my mouth away and looked up innocently.

"Do you like the way I suck your cock?" I asked in a breathy voice. "Am I doing it right?"

In fact, I just wanted to get his damn hand off the back of my head—and it worked. His cock stayed hard as I knelt in front of him. I reached into my panties, a look of quiet desperation on my face.

"That's right, make yourself come. You're learning to like this," he said, "I think I'll see you again, Suzy. Keep playing with yourself, baby . . ."

The fact that he was wearing a condom while I sucked him—a

distinctly professional touch—didn't mar the scenario for some reason.

I was sucking harder and faster, like a schoolgirl possessed, and he reached down to pinch one of my nipples. Ouch. This broke my concentration. I held his wrist and guided his hand toward the back of my head. After a few seconds of that, I brought his hand back to my breast. It's okay to take a john away from one body part if he thinks he'll gain access to another. I kept up the bait and switch, moving his hand every time he got too intrusive. Finally, to my great relief, he came. I moaned rather loudly while his cock was in my mouth and—a prerogative of all defiled co-eds—allowed him to dispose of the condom himself. No hot towel aftercare from *this* virgin hooker. But Bernie didn't mind. While he dressed, he advised me to "be careful—don't let Liane talk you into doing anything you're not ready for."

After Bernie's exit, I emerged from the bedroom fully dressed. Liane was sitting in her favorite armchair, knees together, long slim calves almost slanted, looking me up and down.

"You're taking such good care of yourself! Nobody would know how long we've been friends," she said. "I don't know what you did, but he insists he wants to see you next time. Why don't you sit for a moment?" She smiled and gestured to a pot of mint tea on the small tiled table. "And how is it going with your boyfriend?"

I watched Liane pouring tea into two white porcelain cups. She wears two very tasteful rings on her right hand at all times. And her long pale fingers are always perfectly manicured, with the palest pink polish.

"He's pushing for us to get married sooner—"

"Good!"

A beam of approval transformed her face, still pretty and delicate at seventy-something. Liane is long and slender and has stopped coloring her hair, yet looks positively intriguing when she smiles.

"He wants to buy a co-op now before prices get much higher."

"Oh, he's right. And don't let any of your friends in the business get near him or his family before the wedding."

"But I asked Jasmine and Allison to be my bridesmaids. Along with my cousin. And his sister's the matron of honor—she already expects to meet them."

"Don't let that happen," Liane said. "They're your friends and they're nice girls, but you can't afford to risk it. His sister and your cousin will be in constant communication with them. You can't mix these two elements of your life, dear."

In her long pencil skirt and striped blouse, with a ladylike bow at the neck, she looked as relaxed as I would in jeans. I imagine she hasn't bought new clothes in recent years; her suits and silk blouses are so well made, and she settled on a style she likes long ago. I've seen photos of her from the sixties, in Pucci pants and elegant dresses, with full wavy hair, but you never see her in a dress or pants these days. And her hair is a bit "smaller"—cut to the neck, professionally styled four times a week, like clockwork.

"Times have changed!" I protested. "And I can't turn my back on my friends. I don't want to be alone on my wedding day."

"Times never change," Liane said, gently rolling her eyes. "In 1959—or was it '58?—I met a pair of sisters who worked together. Beautiful girls. But Daphne was so jealous of her older sister that she actually *spilled the beans* to Suki's fiancé—and ruined their courtship. Suki would have been *so much better off* alone."

"Her . . . sister? Did they actually do *scenes* together?"

I could almost see it. Elizabeth Taylor in *Butterfield 8* and Audrey Hepburn as Holly Golightly—doing all the things I've done with Allie! Or Jasmine! Sixty-nining, sometimes for real, sometimes not . . . but—*sisters?* Ick. Elizabeth Taylor would have to be the mean destructive one.

"They were a strange pair, from a small town in the Midwest, and I can't remember exactly what they *did* in bed," Liane said.

"But they weren't shy! And they *were* successful. I didn't judge them. Apparently they were once very poor. But the worst thing is that after Suki's fiancé broke off the engagement—he was very upset, called her all sorts of horrible names, all because of Daphne's poisonous tongue. After all that, Suki continued to work with her. Now *that* was hard to believe. Poor demented Suki, heartbroken and sleeping with the enemy! It made me wonder whether this routine of theirs was . . . perhaps a bit unhealthy?"

We both digested this horror story—Liane for the hundredth time, I for the first. Good grief.

"Well, there's nothing like that going on with Allison and Jasmine. We're not, um, related, and we have no reason to envy one another," I said firmly. "And they both have very good reputations with all the girls."

"True," Liane mused. "Though Jasmine can be a bit pushy with her phone number."

"But she won't be giving her number out at my wedding!" I pointed out.

"Of course!" Liane agreed. "That was never a question. But let's say somebody in Matt's Wall Street circle recognizes Jasmine. She's a striking girl; a man wouldn't forget her. You know what a small world Manhattan can be."

"Yes. I do." (Last year, one of my clients had a daughter who was working for Matt's boss as a summer associate! Now, *that* was weird.) "I don't know what to do," I confessed. "About this whole situation. I don't know if I can bring myself to stop working, to stop seeing guys. And I'm having second thoughts about Matt—about settling down!"

"Second thoughts? Everybody has them, dear."

"I can't decide whether a boyfriend is a luxury or a professional liability!"

Liane looked exasperated. She put down her teacup and shook her head.

"Women's lib has completely twisted your way of thinking," she told me.

"Women's . . . lib?"

"Yes. Why can't a girl with your experience understand that a man who cares about you properly is not a liability or a luxury but a necessity?"

"Because it's not! It's easier to be alone. You know that."

"When I was your age, if a working girl found a man who was husband material, she was ready to quit. She might have to work to pay for her wedding dress, but she would tell him the money came from her family, and most of my friends came from so far away that they could hide their families. Many of them had to, really. Or should have . . ." She was dwelling on Suki again. "In those days, when a working girl married, she devoted her energy to keeping the marriage alive. Now all the married girls want to work on the side. They call me up on their free days and they actually sound guilty if they can't sneak away to see a client! Of course, I'm very happy to work with a girl if she's right for the client, but I don't know what today's girls are thinking."

"But if I quit—"

"*When* you quit."

"—I won't be one of the girls anymore. These are my real friends! It's not the same when you retire."

Despite what I've been through with my two best friends, the idea of leaving the fold makes me panic.

"You must outgrow this. You are facing a golden opportunity. Your fellow is how old? Thirty-five? He has a bright future that he hopes to share with you, and you can't walk away from this man just because of some silly nostalgia that every girl feels about the girls she used to work with. Eventually you have to let go of these connections and form new ones. And you can do it," Liane assured me. "You're lovely, intelligent, and you've had a decent upbringing. Nobody has to know where you've been or what you've done, and you'll be a wonderful example to girls like Allison who haven't got as much sense as you. You'll be a better example if you forget them, really."

"But, Liane, you haven't done any of this. You still run your business and *you* know these girls and you're telling me to forget them!"

"Well," Liane said, "life hasn't been as kind to me as it may be to you if you play your cards right."

I gazed at the paintings. Okay, they're not multimillion-dollar old masters, but she's got some valuable stuff. At the Brunschwig & Fils wallpaper and her beautifully upholstered, yet perfectly mismatched chairs. The chandelier on her ceiling. What is Liane saying? She bought this duplex in the '60s during a downturn— it must be worth almost two million dollars! If she hasn't sold it by now, why not? Because she doesn't have to and because it's her trophy. She bought it with her bedroom manners and the money she earned. And she looks healthy—delicate but not frail. Despite her weirder ideas, her mind is sharp. She goes to all the concerts and plays and gets the best seats. She traveled all over the world— and did it in style.

How can she say life has been unkind? Does she have any idea how other women her age live? How they look? My grandmother, for example. Her life was all about sacrifice and childbearing and she's helpless now, completely dependent on her six adult daughters and her oldest son.

"But you own this place," I said. "You make it sound as though. . . . How can you talk this way? How can you sit here and tell me that settling down with a man is a necessity? It wasn't true for *you*."

"I've earned the right to sit where I sit and to say what I think." She sipped some tea. "Sometimes people have to go without necessities."

There was a look of brave suffering before she got down to

business. Liane often makes poignant allusions to a past tragedy, but she's never gotten specific. I can't figure out whether she had a hysterectomy at thirty-five or a boyfriend who died in combat or a married lover who promised her the moon and stars and delivered only the stars—or all three!

She pulled some folded hundreds out of her skirt pocket and handed me exactly half. When you see a guy on her premises, she takes half; when it's an outcall, you get exactly 60 percent. It's pretty much the same deal when I work with Jasmine or Eileen or Allison—except that we always do a 60-40 split. The 50 percent cut is a madam thing.

"Promise me one thing," she insisted with a vehemence that surprised me. "Whatever mood you might be in, whatever doubts you're having, don't ever tell him you see men for money. It's one thing for people to *think* you do this, it's another thing for them to know. People may occasionally guess. Let them wonder, but you never have to admit to it. And after you're married, you can introduce Allison or Jasmine to your new circle and his friends won't be able to hurt you."

LATER

Liane doesn't see it, but I'd be attracting more attention to my situation by dropping my best friends! Matt would find it bizarre. Jasmine and Allie are part of my emotional background noise. He doesn't see them much, but he's met them briefly, and he takes their existence for granted.

They're my alibis when I have to sneak off to work!

If they *don't* get involved in my wedding party, he'll think something is wrong—like I've lost both of my best friends! And what guy in his right mind wouldn't find that suspicious, even scary? A girl with no close friends looks distinctly unpleasant. Or he'll wonder why I suddenly have to hide or avoid them. If he doesn't ask questions, his sister will.

Not a good idea, even if I had the ability to pull it off. Avoiding my friends for, what, a year? Two years? And then somehow rekindling ties with girls you've abandoned? I don't think so.

Maybe in Liane's day this somehow worked. Maybe in the fifties you could get away with being that ruthless; maybe Liane's girlfriends accepted it. Liane doesn't see that "normal," today, means being respectable *and* open-minded. You can't just drop people! Extreme prudes don't blend in; their behavior, no matter how subtle, is noticed.

Jasmine and Allie would view me as an uptight snob, not a crossover success, if I treated them like that. Allison would be hurt. Jasmine, well, she'd be disgusted. Not so much with the hypocrisy, but with my cowardice. Jasmine figures she can finesse just about any situation if she has enough nerve; and she expects no less of me.

9 A Hooker's Home Is Her Castle

I should have "called in sick" last night and stayed out of Matt's way. He would have understood if I had stayed home with a headache. But instead, we got together. At his place.

I wanted to reassure myself. After that ghastly tête-à-tête with Liane, I wanted to believe that things with Matt were essentially modern—and normal. And they were—until midnight, when we were lying in bed, sipping brandy, reading our respective magazines and listening to Diana Krall on his new speakers: "Someday," went the song, "we'll build a home on a hilltop high, you and I, shiny and new. . . . A cottage that two can fill . . ."

"Talk of the Town" wasn't holding my attention. Respectability, looming large on my landscape, now seemed tempting yet remote.

"Someday we may be adding . . . a wing or two . . . a thing or two . . . we will make changes as any family will. . . . But we will always be called 'the folks who live on the hill.'"

As the words drifted through my head, I tried to banish Liane's dark warnings about back-stabbing call girls. Those twisted sisters and their tragic perversity. Liane makes marriage—love between a man and a woman—sound so lonely. And she's in favor of it! Yet there's a certain wisdom to her advice. Working girls today want to do it all, and you really can't.

I felt a terrible, confused longing, and I desperately wanted my boyfriend to hold me.

"What's wrong? You look like"—he kissed my shoulder—"a sad kitten."

This tender reference just made me sadder.

"It's what this song is all about."

"What it's about?"

And what *is* it about? Two people who want to be prosperous, married, with kids and architectural plans. A love song for *social climbers*. But it's tender and sweet and full of longing, and somehow you think these two ambitious wannabes have every right to want to be. To wish they had always been called . . .

"'The Folks Who Live on the Hill,'" he mused. "Who wrote this?" He turned to me with a concerned frown. "Why are you crying?" he said, putting his arms around me—finally, letting his copy of *FYI* slide to the floor.

"Because I think that's what I want. The extra wing and the kids and the house on the hill. Except maybe—not on a *hilltop*. I think I'd rather be in the city."

And not so shiny and new. What I really yearn for is a prewar apartment with some character . . . and infinite bathrooms. Or the impression of infinite bathrooms. And I wish those apartments weren't all co-ops. It's the condos that are shiny and new.

"But I know that's what I want—with you. So what's wrong?" he asked.

"You don't really want it with *me*," I blubbered.

"But I do!"

"You don't," I insisted.

"Honey, you're wearing a ring, and everyone knows we're engaged, so there's no reason for you to be insecure about me," he said.

"That's what *you* think."

"Hang on." He reached for the clock. "I have a seven o'clock breakfast—" Staccato beeps interrupted his comments as he set the alarm. "And I have to look at Gary's spreadsheets . . ."

Curling up into a ball, I sniffled against a pillow.

"Honey," he said, with an edge of worry, "what is this all about?"

"I can't tell you," I wailed.

"What do you mean? Why not?"

"Because it's—I don't know how to tell you!"

"Look, you have to tell me what's bothering you. What have I done? Why do you say that? You don't believe I want to spend the rest of my life with you?"

"You don't." Fresh tears poured out of my eyes, and now he was sitting up, trying to find a tissue. You can never find the tissues in *his* bedroom. "You don't really want to spend it with— with someone like me," I sobbed.

"Someone like you? What have I done to make you think that way?"

"Nothing."

"Then why are you saying that—or even thinking this way? Is this about the apartment? Just tell me if you don't like it, and we'll find something you like. I can withdraw the offer."

There was a long silence as I sobbed into the pillow. My tears felt like proxies for words or explanations never offered. My body was aching for the enormous relief that might come if I suddenly told him everything. But, of course, I wasn't ready to tell him *anything*.

Finally he said, "If you want to wait until we're married to buy something, we'll do that. But you have to set a date—this market is just going to keep climbing. We should buy soon. I can understand that you'd feel more secure if the apartment was in your name too, from the start—"

"That's so typical of you!" I cried, in frustration. "You think everything is about money!"

He pulled away. "Look," he said angrily. "I can't do this anymore. I have to get up in five hours and I'm—you can't do this to me when I have a fucking meeting at seven in the morning! I'm giving you everything I can possibly give you at this point in my life and you refuse to set a date, and now you tell me you don't trust me or something—I don't know what you want! If it's not about the apartment, then what *is* it? I have to get up at five-thirty and you're carrying on like a child! If you don't stop this self-indulgent bullshit, I'm sleeping on the fucking couch! My biggest mistake was getting engaged to a goddamn attention junkie!"

Suddenly, I felt like a woman who's been lingering all afternoon at the makeup counter while her husband is hard at work, trying to construct a gigantic pyramid from scratch.

Then I got up and pulled open the top drawer of his dresser. I covered my nakedness with one of his freshly laundered shirts, spitefully hoping it would inconvenience him to be short one clean dress shirt. Exiting into the living room, I ignored Matt's objections.

"For god's sake," he said plaintively. "Don't turn this into— I have to get some sleep, Nancy. Don't do this."

I rested on the couch, still burning from his accusation. Attention junkie! Am I? Well, he really *doesn't* want to build his life with me, with an attention junkie, with. . . . I cried for a while, wiping my cheeks off with one of his floppy French cuffs. Then I drifted off, exhausted and horrified by my own behavior. At some point, I felt a layer of warmth enveloping my naked legs, and Matt was tucking a sheet around my torso.

I opened my eyes and started to reach out for him, but my arm was caught in the sheet.

LATER

After last night's tear-strewn disaster, getting back into work mode wasn't easy. It took me three hours to prepare for a half-hour date. I switched all my phones off while I transformed myself from paranoid wreck into frolicsome sex kitten. In between facial masks—a yeast mask for my pores followed by a renewing pack for that tingly confident feeling—I reread Matt's note, the note he left behind when he tiptoed out of his apartment to make the breakfast meeting. "Sleep tight. I love you very much," he had written in small letters on a Post-it note. I found it on his bathroom mirror. I slipped the note into my souvenir box, then lay on my couch with cucumber slices on my puffy eyelids.

My personal phone started ringing, followed by my cell phone. I wanted to pick up but had to lie still for the sake of my swollen eyes. A professional must never look unhappy on the job. And misshapen eyelids are a sure sign of mishap. When I got up, there was voice mail on my home phone: "Sweetheart, I'm sorry. I lost my temper last night. I didn't mean to hurt you. We'll find the right place, don't worry."

He really believes this anxiety can all be pinned on the co-op crisis. The sound of his message made me teary again, but I forced myself to stop. Twenty minutes before Etienne arrives!

I applied more eye makeup than usual—even mascara, which I hardly ever wear—then slipped into a new pair of Bottega Veneta heels and smoothed out my silk robe. I loosened the top—the better to flash my lacy cleavage when I open the door—and studied myself in the mirror. I checked my Ramses supply. Only three condoms left! By the time I rushed to the intercom, to buzz Etienne into my lobby, I was feeling—and looking—like myself again.

MONDAY, 4/3/00

Today, a call from Howard, urging me to set up a three-way with Allison. We're still his favorite show. But when I got through to Allie, she was evasive.

"I don't know if I can. I may have to see Jack that day."

"Oh, come on. Can't you move Jack around? You know Howard likes to see us together and I hate to disappoint him. Anyway, I need to set this up—and I need to know."

"Well, the thing is . . ." There was an awkward silence. "I promised Jack I wouldn't, you know, *see other guys.*"

I was taken aback. "After all that *nonsense* about not wanting to pay for your tuition—? What are you thinking?"

"Oh! *That!* I agreed to stop seeing other clients—if he would stop talking about interior decorating school. And now everything's okay! I'm going ahead with my MSW."

"You're kidding." Just when I've been thinking that Jack would be on his way *out* of the picture, he seems to have replanted himself like an evil seed in Allie's life. "So you're just supposed to be seeing Jack?"

"That's our agreement. And he's been holding to *his* end of the deal. He brings cash every week. *Lots* of it."

There was no point arguing, but I let her know that Howard was definitely eager. "I can get him to see me with someone else, but I could probably *raise* him if I saw him with *you,*" I hinted. This promise of extra money did not move her. Jack must be delivering the financial goods!

"I haven't even got the time!" she protested. "I'm so busy dealing with school now! And with NYCOT and the outreach van, I really can't, Nancy."

But if Jack is such a great provider why does she sound so . . . cornered? Shouldn't she be proud of her good fortune?

"What exactly did you agree to? Are you supposed to forsake *all* other guys for this—this—arrangement with Jack?"

"He says he doesn't want to share me, and I don't want to rock the boat right now. I know he's more in love than I could ever be with him," she said in a quiet voice. "But I've always known that. And," she added, "this is the choice I've made."

I didn't like her tone, that cornered quality. How long can this continue before Jack tries to extract some new concession? I called Eileen—she's always happy to see Howard—and then made my way over to Dr. Wendy's office.

Toward the end of our session, Wendy asked, "Hasn't there ever been a boyfriend who knew about your work?"

I shook my head and changed the subject. "Listen, I have to ask. Have you ever lost money on a real estate deal?"

"No," said Dr. Wendy. "Because I rent. It's so much easier to rent."

I had no trouble looking her in the eye as I left, but it's such a waste of money to lie to your shrink!

I wonder if she can tell. Shrinks like to call everything "material," whether it's true or false, perhaps to excuse their own bullshit detectors for occasionally failing. Like hookers, they have to know that some "client lies" are harmless, part of the ongoing relationship. And even smart people get fooled.

One of my clients had me fooled for an entire year. He called himself Dr. Albert and claimed he was . . . a shrink, actually. One day I said something to Jasmine about Al and she almost fell on the floor laughing: "Al's not a shrink! He runs a toy business!" I guess he thought a shrink has more appeal than a guy who wholesales Betsy Wetsys? And he did persuade Eileen to chatter about her family problems—until she found out he was in toy sales. So he wasn't all wrong.

I also knew a client who told me he had been in the Foreign Legion. Turns out that he's a CEO at a major insurance company. Why do some guys do this? If you're just trying to protect your real ID, you don't make up soldier of fortune stories. And of course the most common lie is from the married client who pretends to be single. As if it mattered to me! But it may be his fantasy that he's a footloose single guy and I'm a willing single girl.

Compared to these fantastic fibbers, I think I'm pretty normal. At least I'm not lying to my shrink about what I do for a living! Still. A girl who plays along with a john's lifestyle fantasy is giving him his money's worth, while a girl who lies to her shrink is just wasting her own hard-earned money.

But maybe I wasn't lying. Didn't she ask me if there's ever been a boyfriend who knew about my *work*? Well, I didn't really call it "work"—because my idea of work, at thirteen, was baby-sitting.

TUESDAY, 4/4/00

This morning, an appointment chez Jasmine.

The ultimate quickie: Harry waits for no girl, and you have to be on time—or risk losing him to someone who's punctual. When I saw a black Town Car parked in front of Jasmine's building, I thought: Yikes! Harry's *early.*

But when I got upstairs, he was nowhere to be seen.

"There's a Town Car downstairs," I told her. "I thought it was Harry!"

"Oh, that," she huffed. "Do not get me started. *Don't* even go there!" She reached down to adjust her stockings.

"Huh?"

"Somebody—I don't know who—is up to something," she said in a sinister tone. "I have to brush my teeth. Help yourself. Evian? Club soda? Whatever. Go for it."

She stalked out of the kitchen and I opened the fridge. A riot of white plastic containers assaulted the eye. In the good old days, Jasmine's spotless fridge contained nothing more than white wine, vodka, and club soda, the occasional yogurt, and the ubiquitous box of baking soda. Now the baking soda was obscured by mascarpone cheese, blue-cheese dip, and Alfredo sauce from Agata & Valentina. Three plastic tubs of D'Artagnan truffle butter. And a large container of . . . rendered goose fat from Schaller & Weber. There were two boxes of omega-3 eggs and two cartons of whipping cream. An Atkins cornucopia.

I poured myself some filtered water and shook my head. But when she reappeared in thigh-high stockings and lacy underwear, I had to admit, her waistline *does* look more defined. To think that I've forsaken butter and cream for virgin olive oil, while she's eating all this sinful gloop and getting away with it.

"There's something going on, and I don't like it," she was saying. "Town Cars parked outside my building all fucking day and into the evening! Well, not all day—but enough to draw attention."

"You're kidding! How often?"

"Three, yesterday! And you say there's one out there right now? It's not even fucking noon and they're already open for business!"

"Who? What?" I glanced up at the clock. Almost eleven-thirty, and our client was due any minute.

"Some . . . somebody is seeing guys in this building, and I don't appreciate it."

"But you're seeing guys—"

"That has nothing to do with it. I don't have *volume*. This is the kind of volume that gives a building a reputation!"

Jasmine's building is a co-op—not a serious co-op, just a six-story elevator building that converted when the converting was good. But still. There's a board. They might notice these things.

"Whoever is doing this has some fucking nerve," Jasmine grumbled. "Wait till I find out who it is. Eviction's too good for them!"

The buzzer restored her to a more social mood and I peeped out the window. Two identical Town Cars parked in front! I had to agree: It looks strange, and "our" car—Harry's—is the one that belongs out there. Except that I couldn't tell which was his; they look alike.

Harry was in too much of a hurry to notice (or comment on) the other car. He whistled as he undressed, and Jasmine wandered away to run water and heat up his washcloth.

Standing in his socks, suspenders, and wing tips, he grinned. "Ready for some hanky-panky, ladies?"

Jasmine wrapped the towel around his cock and I began to play with her panties.

"She's got a hot tongue today," Jasmine murmured. "Do you want to watch?"

After he left, Jasmine resumed her tirade. "In a small building like this, you can't be too careful! What if people start thinking those are *my* customers? You know, *I* am a fucking *lady,* I do not have this kind of volume! I charge enough so I don't have to see twenty guys a day in my own apartment! What kind of operation produces all this goddamn traffic?"

The kind of operation Jasmine started in—when she "turned herself out," as she likes to put it. But that place was in a huge anonymous building where you could pay off a doorman. This is different.

"Are you saying there's a *house* operating? Somewhere in this building?" I asked.

"Who knows. Could be that two-bedroom on the top floor. I saw a girl coming in the other day—I've never seen her before. She was going to six."

"You don't think they're advertising! Have you seen *guys* in the lobby?"

"They're probably on the Web! Or Channel 35! People have no goddamn sense. . . . No, I haven't seen guys in the lobby, but I'm sure everyone else has. *This* is the kind of thing that hookers' union should try to eliminate! But no, they're trying to make it *easier* for people to do this. I can't stand it!"

As I dressed, she continued.

"They have no right to behave this way in a co-op. And if the board gets curious, well, I have—" She paused. "Never mind. It's not going to happen." She was mumbling to herself.

"Stay calm," I counseled. "You can't control what other people do. Anger won't solve this."

"Oh, great. Now you sound like Allison."

"I do not! That's unworthy of you!"

"Fine, fine, unworthy, whatever," she grumbled, "but I have something to lose!"

"I know, but maybe the traffic these other people cause—"

That set her off.

"Guys don't like to think they're going to a building where there's a hooker on every floor! At least our guys don't. Obviously, these idiots parked outside have no qualms. It looks absolutely terrible."

"I know. But Harry was in too much of a hurry to notice! Maybe the other tenant will get blamed for your traffic, too. It doesn't have to work against you."

"Yeah, well. The other tenant won't get blamed for what I—" She hesitated, then went on. "I have never attracted a scintilla of suspicion, and that's why they've never been able to—" She stopped again.

"I know all this. Get a grip."

"No, you *don't* know! It's not what you think, dammit." Marching over to the walk-in closet, she beckoned to me. "I want to show you something."

A new fur coat? A cage for locking up kinky clients?

"Promise not to tell anyone," she said.

"Of course."

"Not even Allison. Or your boyfriend."

"Not even!" The boyfriend part was a joke. She knows I don't share secrets with Matt.

She flung open the door and I saw a good-sized walk-in closet transformed—into something that now looked rather small. There was a gleaming white hand basin with a small cupboard below. An oval mirror with a burled wood frame. Four neatly folded green towels hanging from a rod, beneath a small makeup shelf. Oh, and a small but elegant toilet.

"I have an illegal bathroom," she said in a hushed voice. She was standing in the doorway, arms crossed, a look of prideful paranoia on her face. This room is like her secret child! "If they find out, I'll be sunk! I could get reported to the city! And I'll have to pay a fine!"

"But—but—how long have you had this here?" Last time I opened this door, it was her coat closet!

"Two years."

"But I've never seen it!"

"Of course not. I'm the only one who uses it. Usually when the other one's occupied."

"When did you have this installed? How come I never knew! You had this done without a permit?"

"You were on vacation in France. Everyone was in the Hamptons and this guy I know from ... before"—meaning her cocaine-dealing days—"Vince. He's a contractor now. He did it on the sly for cash. If those busybodies on the board find out, they'll be pissed. I have to keep a low profile! That's why those scumbags with their constant traffic are such bad news. I can't afford the attention!"

She closed the door quietly. Illegal luxury on a small scale but still—very illegal.

"I see what you mean," I agreed.

FRIDAY, 4/7/00

Today, a piece in the *Times* about a Washington archaeologist who recently uncovered a brothel in D.C. While searching for something entirely different, her team discovered buried garbage going back to the 1800s. It was the strange mixture of trash that gave the building's former game away. Hundreds of champagne-bottle wrappers, mingling with humble dishes that weren't good enough to rub shoulders with the champagne paraphernalia. Digging deeper, they found two kinds of china: fancy stuff for the business and sturdy everyday stuff used by the girls when they weren't working. (Sort of like the apartment at 444, where Bianca, the madam, kept two sets of towels! In one closet, the "elegant towels" for clients. We girls got our own from a separate closet filled with clean but faded washcloths that had seen more elegant days.)

Back at the D.C. dig: Almost a century later, after the business had been literally buried, this building could not escape its past. Because two kinds of trash—high-class and middle-class—were revealed in the dig. Whereas the other buildings in the vicinity produced only one kind: common, or garden-variety, working-men's trash. So something funny had to be going on.

There's a moral here. If archaeologists, a hundred years later, can figure out what you were up to, well, think of the present! You can't be too careful about separating your trash.

Ever since recycling hit, I've been religious about separating the respectable trash and the bedroom trash. Never mix the sex trash with old bills or junk mail! Don't even let *female* trash—tell-tale signs of makeup removal, tampon wrappers, and the like—enter the same bag as the condoms. (This way, if anyone should find three discarded Trojan boxes and ten little K-Y tubes, they might assume a popular gay guy instead of an industrious call girl.)

Your landlord might be snooping around the incinerator room. Like the D.C. archaeologist, he's looking for something else. An illegal subletter. A recycling transgression. But he stumbles across a suspicious cache of *sex trash* on the floor where you live. Thanks to an old Con Ed bill, he starts wondering . . . night-mare on East Seventy-ninth Street!

Pleased with my foresight—I've been two steps ahead of all

this for at least five years—I clipped the *Times* article for Jasmine. I bundled my used coffee filter into a partly filled D'Ag bag. Then I trotted down the hall to the disposal area, a four-day "growth" of *New York Times* Metro sections tucked under my arm. After popping the bag down the chute, I gazed at the neat spotless floor. The tall blue bag was empty, and the porter had left behind his signature aroma—pine-scented Lysol, which inspired a wave of regret. It seems a shame to desecrate a tidy recycling area with more of the same old same old!

A minute or two later I was back in my apartment, standing in the kitchen and rinsing out an empty Astroglide bottle, trying to decide whether to recycle it here or toss it into a garbage can on York Avenue when nobody's looking.

At which point, the phone rang. I picked it up with my free hand and scrunched my neck over to talk.

"Suzy! At last!"

A male voice from the past, calling me by my work name . . . Who—? Then my internal voice-ID "software" kicked in.

"Wally! I thought you were—" I gulped hard. "Just one second, okay? My hands are full."

I stuffed the Astroglide bottle into my gym bag and dried my hands on my jeans.

"How are you?" I asked. "It's been ages! Is everything okay?"

"It's been exactly a year and nine months," he said. "I've been counting the days. And I'm very pleased to have my health back."

Actually, I'd thought Wally was never going to call. After twelve months of silence, I had gotten concerned. I'd figured he had gone off me or started seeing someone new. After a year and a half, I'd believed he was dead. Client attrition is something you start seeing more of when a high percentage of your clientele is over sixty.

"You should have called," I told him. "I was worried about you!" But I did my best to sound light and chatty.

What does it mean when you think someone has died—and he resurfaces? Could it be that I'm too vain to believe a regular client would *choose* not to see me? After I hung up with Wally, I stared into the mirror. Vanity, thy name is . . . well, for today at least, it's "Suzy."

10 Only Collect

Wally is a soothing probate lawyer whose passions have been
gently organized into well-tended collections—nineteenth-
century micromosaics, twentieth-century paintings, and
books. Despite the fact that his books are eighteenth-
century editions, he's democratic enough to appreciate my
embryonic collection of significant editions.

Most of these were gifts from the parents after I demon-
strated that a runaway does not automorph into a child of Satan.
When it became obvious that I wasn't going the way of all the other
middle-class runaways—pregnant with an STD, living in a squat, calling
collect from jail or rehab, asking for money to buy drugs, showing up on
the doorstep with self-inflicted wounds—when it became clear that I wasn't
doing any of this juvenile stuff, that I intended to live quite comfortably and
knew how to, Mother started normalizing our relationship. By sending me
things that needed taking care of. A small necklace with my name on it, too
delicate for a child, that my father's mother had given me at birth. Some
Doulton china with a pattern of falling leaves. A silver bracelet that once
belonged to my mother's Chinese grandmother. Last year, I received a
framed picture of my father's half-Indian mother, taken in a Port of Spain
photo studio when she was a sultry flapper. (Any sexy genes in my lineage
must come from Dad's non-Chinese side. So it's kind of funny to me that
clients don't notice my darker bloodlines.)

I'm not sure my parents would have entrusted me with these personal treasures had they known I was turning tricks. They would fear
for my safety, for the security of my possessions and my body. They
think a hooker is someone whose household can be turned upside

down at any moment. It's completely outside their placid middle-class lifestyle to envision a girl like me. If I tried to tell them how it really works, that I can afford to turn down risky business, that I see only private referrals—and if I mentioned the kind of money I make—they would suspect wretched drug-induced denial.

Not that they'd ever believe I'm a hooker anyway, even if I were momentarily nuts enough to tell them. Despite the fact that I've been on my own since the age of fourteen. Parents believe what they have to believe, overlooking major details to determine other stuff: Are you alive? (Basic.) Scarred or unscarred? (In any obvious sense of the word.) Do your eyes gleam with ambition or are they glassy with punk ennui? Do you iron your clothes, look better or worse than they expected?

When I first went back to visit, after a long period of skittish paranoia punctuated by the occasional Christmas card, I was almost twenty. To their eyes, I seemed to be doing well, and I was successful at making the ruse of my "copyediting job" sound tedious, so they didn't pry.

They weren't sure what to expect when they came to meet me at the airport—the only time they've driven anywhere together since their divorce. But I looked a little better than *they* did—more professionally coiffed than my granolafied mom (who never does a thing with her hair) and a lot less rumpled than my dad. (He's Old School Geek, a programmer who refused to work for IBM in the sixties because you had to wear a tie.) Even when I toned my look down for visits to my hometown (no jewelry, no fur), Dad said I looked like a "Reaganite." He pretended to be horrified—Dad always hated Ronald Reagan—but he was obviously relieved. I took more vitamins than my parents, exercised a lot, and sent them art postcards whenever I went to a lecture at the Frick. With details of the lecture in my note.

All this evidence of Right Living was reassuring. They could live with my Reaganite wardrobe. They knew how bad it could get, even if your kids *didn't* run away. My younger brother was dressing like Boy George—and boasting that his "seed" was being nurtured by a lesbian collective in Toronto. My childhood friend Vanessa (whose father had attended grad school with mine) now had an eating disorder. And these were the mild cases.

The only person who suspected anything was my father's second wife, who had a tendency to glare at me across the dinner table whenever Dad wasn't looking. Occasionally, she would ask bitchy questions—about my luggage, for example. (Well, I couldn't resist investing in some Louis Vuitton travel gear, and it *was* the eighties.)

"Who bought that for you?" my stepmother asked when I arrived at Dad's house for a visit. "That suitcase looks very expensive."

"Oh, I got it on sale," I assured her.

"The child descends from a long line of thrifty shoppers," my father explained. "She has her mother's genes—the Laytons have always known how to hunt down a bargain."

Louis Vuitton *never* goes on sale—but this is what I mean about my parents. Neither one has a clue about the most basic facts of life!

On my twenty-first birthday, I received a good edition of the collected works of Robert W. Service—their way of saying that the rupture I caused at fourteen wasn't permanent; these books were older than all that. On my last birthday, Mother hunted down a 1926 edition of Fowler's *Modern English Usage.*

Today, when I showed Wally the Fowler's, he complimented my mother's excellent eye. Wally likes to chat, not so much about the contents of books as their care, their history. The lore of editions.

"Never clean books with a cloth," he counseled me today. "Do you know how they clean the books at the Morgan?" I shook my head and allowed my skirt to ride up as I crossed my legs. "Very gently, with a Dustbuster. I was hoping to read you some poetry, but we got sidetracked. By dust." He checked his watch and smiled.

"Next time?" I suggested, getting up from the couch.

Today I was more relaxed than usual. Wally's hand lingered between my legs and I didn't feel like moving away. His fingers proceeded downward. I never encourage clients to use their hands on me. The average tongue is easier to take than the average man's undisciplined fingers. But Wally's so gentle that I didn't bother to pull away this time. I used to be more disciplined about letting Wally touch me but he *did* "come back from the dead." That puts a different spin on things!

What's more, I was getting rather wet, and he was curious to see how good he really was. His finger slipped, quickly and softly, between my smaller lips and almost entered—probably *did* enter for a second—then slid away. Maybe he was just checking for lubrication. Or maybe he's smart enough to know that you can do these things with a working girl on special occasions—just don't push your luck. He was gentlemanly enough to pull his hand away just as I was about to turn businesslike. Smart man.

A session with Wally is like getting paid to watch Channel 13 when they're not doing a membership drive. "In-cu-na-bu-la," Wally was saying, as he adjusted his bow tie with one hand. He measured out the syllables as he felt around with the other for his wallet. "*In the cradle.* One of the most breathtaking collections of fifteenth-century books is in Philadelphia. Well, all the money was here, you see, and we just went around buying everything up after the Spanish-American War . . ."

One day, just before Wally disappeared, he presented me with a first edition of *High Windows*. He sat on my sofa, reading Philip Larkin in a voice so mellow and accurate that I couldn't help wondering: Who is this man?

"When I see a couple of kids / And guess he's fucking her and she's / Taking pills or wearing a diaphragm, / I know this is paradise . . ."

"Apparently Larkin didn't think poetry should be read aloud," I told Wally, "but he was wrong about that."

It was the right thing to say, but I meant it. A small part of me fell in love—perhaps not with him exactly, but certainly with his voice, with his open yet mannerly mind.

When I didn't hear from Wally again, I wondered, as I sometimes do with older clients, whether he had died. He was having mysterious health problems and what was I to think? When a client is absent for too long, I don't *want* to know. I stopped myself from calling Wally's office to see if he was still alive and kicking. I had my reasons.

There's a scenario that everyone talks about: the well-regarded pillar of society (married, of course) dying in a call girl's bed.

"What would *you* do?" girls ask each other. "Shove him in the elevator? Call 911? Search his address book? Call his office?"

"Remove the cash from his wallet," Jasmine once conjectured. "It's okay if he's dead—and you know that's exactly what the emergency team would do. But only if he's dead," she added primly.

Her notions of proper conduct aren't everyone else's, but she sticks by them religiously.

If Wally or Etienne or Milt were to die in my bed, it would be a disaster! Unlike some clients, they're prominent enough to make the news. It's the classic fear. But if everybody abstained from activities that (in the event of sudden death) could lead to all-around embarrassment, nobody would do much of anything.

Fortunately, this has been entirely theoretical for me. I've never had a client who died in flagrante with *me*. But two of my customers, Bill and Chip, died in '96, and that was a strange year for me.

In Bill's case, I found out when I called his office. I had not heard from him for three months, and he'd had a habit of seeing me every four weeks. A receptionist told me Bill had died of a sudden heart attack, while playing tennis. I was astonished, and she agreed that it made no sense because he was so health conscious. She was a competent and good-natured angel of death who handled the conversation well; it went on for just as long as it had to, and she didn't ask how I knew him.

And, I thought, hanging up, *it could have happened in my bed.*

That night, I dreamed about Bill. I was kneeling over his chest (as had been my habit with him) and he told me I would always be beautiful, that my pubic hair was really part of an epic poem that he was writing. Bill wasn't literary in real life, so I woke up confused, half thinking that he was cultivating new hobbies in the afterlife, sort of like a retiree.

Four months later, Chip, who was being treated for cancer, gave me ample warning. In a whimsical voice, he insisted, "I'm going in with a positive attitude. I have every intention of making it, and I'll see you in a few weeks. With bells on." Three months later, I got someone to confirm his death for me. Chip's son, actually, who is also a client.

I called Chip the Younger and casually said, "How are you?" He has no idea that I also knew his father. (I knew his father better than I knew him.)

"Not too bad. Well, not so great," he added with a resigned sigh. He didn't elaborate—and was politely cheerful—but I could tell.

Chip the Younger doesn't know that most of the girls who see him also knew his dad. He didn't even know I was aware of his father's illness. My detective work yielded a bonus: a paying visit.

When the surviving Chip appeared in my doorway, I noticed his father's quizzical expression more clearly reflected in his face. Had the son *always* looked like this? I had seen him a few times during the last five years and his face had been fuller, the expression more self-absorbed, more remote, the look of an arrogant Wasp Adonis. His face had thinned out, revealing a sensitive shadow effect, and he looked less like the virile smart aleck, more like, well, his thoughtful, sweet-natured dad. Less like *himself*. Perhaps he would now be more of a gentleman on the sheets?

No such luck. Chip the Younger is nothing like Chip Senior in bed, and mourning didn't temper his bedroom style. He was (and always has been) a sexual bounder, cajoling me about the condom, trying to trade on his good looks and his ample cock in the hopes that I might let down my guard and treat him like a boyfriend. He never stops trying. I once saw his face staring out at me from a *New York* magazine cover story on Manhattan's most eligible bachelors. He's young enough and important enough to get free sex from nonprofessionals—and cute enough to inspire nonprofessional enthusiasm in some hookers. But good-natured enough if you don't fall for it.

I see Chip Junior once every six months; I don't want him as a regular. He's too much work, and it would make me miss his father's visits more acutely. The elder Chip never had any problem staying hard with a condom—wouldn't dream of going without one. Chip Senior used condoms long before AIDS paranoia hit the scene. In his day, men wore condoms with hookers, no ifs, ands, or buts. His were the pre-Pill days, a deeply sensible time when everything was terribly clear, and he had never bothered to leave that era.

After the demise of Bill, then of Chip the Elder, I stopped wanting to know.

Because death isn't fair. The customers who die are *never* the ones you merely tolerate to make up your weekly quota. If a customer dies unexpectedly, it'll be someone like Bill—whom I was really looking forward to seeing again. Or a respectful clean freak (like Chip) who always washed his hands before touching me. A guy who pops the instant he's inside (that would be Bill *and* Chip with just about any attractive female). The worshipful client who makes you feel like a minigoddess when you undress for him (Bill more than Chip).

Pushy clients *never* die. They keep trying to kiss you (or worse!) long after more sensitive johns have been cremated and committed to urns. I bet Chip Junior lives to a grand old age.

TUESDAY, 4/11/00

Other people's shrinks disappear in August; mine likes to buck the trend and take off just before income-tax time. She hangs around the city during the summer, then disappears around Christmas. The two most god-awful stress points in the annual cycle—and she's gone, poof. This time, on a tour of the Greek islands with a bunch of her ecotourist friends.

Today she offered me the number of her colleague, June Pepper, in case I felt an Emergency Need. "She's actually much closer to your part of town," Wendy said. "Dr. Pepper is practically a neighbor! She's on Fifth and Seventy-ninth."

"Dr. Pepper?" I echoed. "I don't think so. And Fifth Avenue is practically the West Side," I pointed out. "I'm wayyyy east. Anyway, I've been doing business with *you* all these years. And I'm not likely to have a suicidal breakdown while you're on vacation."

"That's quite true," she agreed. "I see your issues as a very slow-cooking stew . . ." I could sort of picture it. A great cauldron of adult men, adolescent memories, and childhood dreams, simmering gently on a kitchen stove. But which kitchen stove? Well, certainly not my own—I've never cooked anything more elaborate than an omelette in this apartment.

"And I don't think it's likely to boil over and scald you," she was saying.

Maybe the kitchen on Waverly Street, in the house where my parents got divorced. For completely irrational reasons, I think of that as the last permanent household we lived in, when in fact it was the least.

"I'm sorry," I said. "My mind sort of wandered. You said I wasn't going to boil over . . ."

"Don't be sorry. Where did it wander to?"

"The kitchen where I watched my grandmother making steamed pork. I haven't thought about that in years. My father's mother. She lived with us for a while." Many decades after abandoning her flapper look. She was round-bodied and sharp-tempered when I knew her, no longer a handsome girl with smoldering eyes. "My mouth still waters when I think about her cooking."

Wendy smiled. I can tell that she understands pleasure—food, sex, beauty—and that's why I feel okay telling her that I hook. She has the frumpy hair of a West Side liberal, the trim, toned body of an Upper East Side housewife, and a smile that radiates love of pleasure. If it weren't for those last two qualities, I would mistrust her on the basis of the first.

"I have an idea," she said. "How do you feel about homework? Therapy homework. I could give you an assignment to complete while I'm away. But of course you won't get graded," she added with a sly smile.

"Well," I said, crossing my arms. "Maybe this is just to reassure *you*. So you don't have separation anxiety while you're on vacation."

We both laughed, and I took Dr. Pepper's phone number before I left. But I screwed the little piece of paper up into a ball and left it on the seat of the taxicab. Somehow, I would feel unfaithful going to another shrink. It would be like cheating on my hairdresser! And who knows what I might find: A therapist with better hair and a prudish smile? A not-so-great-looking female shrink with a hearty but unsatisfied sexual appetite? The last thing I need now is to start negotiating *that* minefield. And I'd like to keep the number of shrinks who know my business nar-rowed down to *one*.

This afternoon, Jasmine and I shared a cab to Seventh Avenue and stashed our furs for the summer.

"It's so liberating to have that extra foot of closet space! Don't you feel about twenty pounds lighter?" I said.

Jasmine agreed. "Ever since you-know-what I've been so hard up for storage space." Ever since Jasmine turned her coat closet into an illegal bathroom! "But you won't have space problems when you move in with Matt," she added. "You guys are getting a nice big apartment!"

"Oh. Not those kind of space problems."

"Right, well. The other kind. You *signed on* for those! The emotional piper must be paid. Relationships are *supposed* to be a hassle! Why do you think people choose not to have 'em? So," she said cheerfully. "How's the apartment hunt going?" We were on the sidewalk now, squinting into the sunlight. Jasmine pulled out her sunglasses, then her phone. She frowned at the display and began dialing.

"I think we're about to close," I said in a resigned voice. "It's fine. I've joined a bridal e-mail list, and I went to Scully and Scully to look at china, and I called Vera Wang this morning. Sometimes I'd rather be looking at handbags."

"No pain, no gain. You can't look at handbags your entire life. For a girl like you . . . there comes a point when it's time to start looking at china. He's a stable guy. Go for it. Besides, you have enough handbags—for now."

"A girl like me?"

"Well, you never did save any money—I can't believe you've been doing this for longer than I have and you don't own any property! But you do own this guy! So make the most of it!" She was listening to her voice mail. "I have to be at the St. Regis in twenty minutes. Let's share a cab."

When I got home, there was a message from Etienne, one from Milton, a confirmation from Howard, the usual lineup of obligations and opportunities. As I picked up the phone to call Milton, my cell started buzzing. I fished it out of my handbag. Allie, calling from *her* cell.

"I'm at Starbucks," she said in an excited voice. "Why don't you come and join us? It's that guy who donated the shoes. He'll be here any minute. I want you to meet him and tell me what you think."

"I'd love to," I lied, "but I've got a client coming over."

"Oh, too bad. I mean, that you can't come, not that you have a client." She giggled nervously. "I'm just kind of—this is the second time we've had coffee together. He's bringing me a copy of his novel. He says I have a unique perspective and he wants my feedback."

"He published a novel?"

"He's *writing* a novel—about Mary Magdalene, a modern reincarnation of Mary Magdalene living in the meatpacking district before gentrification. Or was that after gentrification? Well, I'm about to find out."

"Why not *during* gentrification?" I pondered aloud, but she ignored the hint of sarcasm.

"I don't know! I'll have to ask him that. He's bringing the manuscript. I'm the only person he's ever—he hasn't shown it to anyone yet. What do you think that means?" she asked in a giddy voice.

"What what means? I have no idea what *you* mean."

"What does it mean if I'm the only person he's ever shown it to? If that's really true, do you think he, well, maybe *likes* me?"

"Who is this guy? What's his name?" I asked her. "Do you know anything about him?"

"I have to go," she said in a stage whisper. "He's coming in the door. I didn't realize this before but—he's really cute!"

Uh-oh. I don't think I've heard that feverish gasp in quite some time. Like any other working girl, Allie enjoys being desired, and she has a tendency to reciprocate a john's admiration with a glowy love of being loved. But this other kind of attraction—the kind that might even cause a girl to lose weight without trying—this is different. And where Allie can resist an extra trick on Jack's behalf, I have a funny feeling about this new admirer. That musical hint of a giggle. It was missing from her voice when she told me about the deal she had made with Jack: fidelity for cash . . .

But the music has returned.

MONDAY, 4/17/00

Etienne was late for his appointment today, and when he did show up, he looked unusually gloomy.

"Tough day at the auction house?" I said in a light voice.

He smiled—a tense, sour smile—and said, "Sometimes I despair for the entire race."

"The Gallic race? The human?"

"Well, the humans in the art business, at any rate. My brother-in-law is a fool," he muttered, referring to the man who is also his boss. "Perhaps—just this one time, I will consent to a small glass of something. Armagnac? No, no, just a thimbleful."

He sat brooding over his thimbleful of brandy while I attempted to cheer him up. He often complains about his business, and it doesn't usually take long to get him over it.

In bed, he was not his usual self at all. I took off the condom and began massaging his cock with oily fingers. Then I removed all the Astroglide with a hot towel and tried to stimulate his naked cock with my mouth. I don't usually remove the condom for a blow job, but Etienne looked so miserable—and I was determined to make him come.

"I must apologize," he said, after I had exhausted my lips. He patted me affectionately and got up. "It's the medication I've been taking for my knee," he added. "If you do not hear from me," he said in a heavy voice, "know that I will be thinking of you during my surgery. I may be out of commission for a few weeks, *cocotte.*"

I nodded sympathetically. This is the first I've heard of his knee. I wonder if he was making it up. But when a guy makes an excuse for his nonperformance, you really don't want to question that. And I was glad that he—not I—suggested the orgasmic rain check.

***

LATER

Etienne's anticlimactic visit is still nagging at me. It's not like him to make up a surgery story. He's proud of his good health. His brother-in-law has always been a capricious boss and Etienne likes to complain about him, but it never affected his performance before. Still, he offered me a piece of advice that makes me question that knee operation. "Don't ever work for relatives," he advised me. And he didn't try to kiss me! That's not like Etienne *at all.* Is he about to get fired? Divorced, perhaps? That might explain his disenchantment with his in-laws. God, I hope not. Nobody wants a client who's going through a divorce.

11 Hetero Doxy

Last night I logged on for the first time in days and found a pile-up of e-mail, mostly from relatives. It's hard to keep up with Mother's family but equally hard to get free of the Layton legacy. For the first ten years of my life, I did not know how my mother's Chinese family got to be called Layton. My Chinese grandmother once told me it was my grandfather's anglicized Chinese name, and I believed her. Later, my uncle Gregory explained that Grandmummy likes to say this because she gave up a Chinese name for an English name. The first Chinese Layton was an indentured servant who adopted his employer's name when he left Canton province to settle in Trinidad. Due to my grandfather's hard work—his small shipping company dealt in soft drinks, condensed milk, and life insurance—Layton is now a name to be reckoned with throughout Trinidad. Layton Marketing Ltd. expanded rapidly while he was alive, then reached a kind of benign plateau under Uncle Gregory's stewardship.

Many Laytons are so proud of being Laytons that you have to look carefully at your e-mail to figure out which Layton is addressing you: gplayton is my cousin Gregory Jr., pglayton is another cousin, Paul; and glayton is Paul's daughter. No other family (including the Chans) has ever really absorbed a Layton. Nominally a Chan, I'm really a Layton. I scrolled through four e-mails entitled "Layton anniversaries, birthdays, and christenings" and found that my birthday was included but my surname omitted because few Laytons can remember it. A birth announcement from my cousin in Calgary who just had twin boys. A recipe for hot-milk sponge cake. And another birth announcement from a

Trinidad cousin: "Olivia Marie Layton, 6 pounds 2 oz. b. ten days ago!"

Sandwiched between Olivia Marie's birth and my great-aunt's sponge cake recipe was a jarring subject header: LOOK FOR THE UNION LABIA! "Featured Guest Speaker from the Bay Area, Cozy Von Booty," read Allie's e-mail. "Cozy led the exotic dancers' union drive at the Lusty Lady peep show in San Francisco last year. T&A—oops—Q&A to follow." Signed with Allison's unique emoticon :)-$->==.

A later e-mail pleaded with me to attend the meeting:

> *I'm facilitating, you know. Gee, it would be reassuring to have you there. Nervous! xxxxx Bring Jasmine if you feel like it! In sex-worker solidarity, Allison. Power to the $isters—but please don't mention to the other sexworking members that I'm now a Kept Woman. They might get the wrong idea and try to prevent me from chairing.*

The wrong idea? I guess Allie needs all the street cred she can possibly project with this crowd. What would they do if they found out how totally unbusinesslike Allison can be? Expel her? Demote her to envelope stuffing?

TUESDAY, 4/25/00

Just got a surprising call from Jasmine. "So, are you coming to this crazy meeting? Allison's playing chairhooker tonight!"

"Well, I *might* pop in for a short while. If I'm not working. Why are *you* going?" I asked.

"She wants to see a familiar face. She's nervous about whether she can handle her new role. I told her: Calm down, it's just like being a madam—but that made her *more* nervous. Ha!"

Hard to imagine Allison as a madam! Jasmine would also make a terrible madam if she actually had to make her living that way, because she barely gets along with other women—and a madam *has* to. But Jasmine lacks Allison's humility. She really imagines that she *should* be one.

WEDNESDAY, 4/26/00

Last night's meeting was larger than the last one—about twenty people crammed into Roxana's living room, inhaling the heady aroma of burning sage. Apparently, Cozy Von Booty is quite a draw on the East Coast. And she makes Gretchen's nose rings and spiky hair look almost *preppy*.

Cozy's red rubber outfit was composed of one-inch strips fashioned into a dress, so you could see her numerous tattoos—front and sides—peeping through the rubber "slats." Like pictures behind a venetian blind. Her Louise Brooks bob was dyed lime green, the same color as her fetish pumps. She was selling buttons that promised (rather, threatened): NO JUSTICE, NO PIECE. When she stretched her arm out to make change for one of her disciples, you could see that she had allowed her underarm hair to grow— it was dyed to match the green bob. And the shoes.

"Are you thinking what I'm thinking?" Jasmine asked in a low voice.

"Well, the *New York Times* says matching accessories are coming back this fall."

"Maybe her pubic hair matches her shoes. It must take three hours to get into that outfit! The exhibitionists are definitely in a majority here," she groused.

A girl dressed in a conservative version of Cozy's outfit— leather instead of rubber—walked in, and Roxana, who was wearing a SAFE SEX SLUT T-shirt, greeted her with a politically righteous hug. A number of members wore buttons that read LIP-

STICK LESBIANS AGAINST GLOBALIZATION. Jasmine and I, in our simpler garb, felt a bit conspicuous. As, I think, did Allie.

"Why do lipstick lesbians always have such bad taste in lipstick?" Jasmine muttered under her breath.

Before Cozy got started, Allison announced, "I would like each person in this room to share something positive about her experience as a sex worker. But please keep your comments under a minute, so that Cozy will have time to speak."

Roxana interrupted, unable to completely give up her customary role as chair. "Or we could share a positive action we've taken to improve the lives of all sex workers."

"And *future* generations of sex workers," Belinda, the gray-haired dominatrix, added.

"Why not previous generations, too, while we're at it?" Jasmine asked me. "Some of these chicks are waaaay past their prime."

Allison caught some of this and looked nervously in our direction.

"Try to be nice," I muttered to Jasmine. "This is her first time chairing. And she's feeling kind of outnumbered by all this . . . leather." And rubber!

Cozy Von Booty was the highlight of the evening. She sat on a high wooden stool, legs strategically crossed, arching her back just enough to show off her hourglass shape.

"Lisa and I have started a new e-mail project," Cozy announced. A few people, including me, looked puzzled. "For those of you who aren't familiar with the sex-positive actions of the adult industry's role model, Lisa Marquis . . ."

The Lisa Marquis? Of X-rated fame? Cozy, proud of her intimate connection to a well-known porn star, made a point of referring to "Lisa's upcoming tour" and "Lisa's commitment to whores' rights."

"Lisa and I are reclaiming the concept of the 'media whore.'

As whores, we need to monitor the way we're depicted in dominant discourses—in the news, in Hollywood movies, on TV . . ."

Allison glowed earnestly at Cozy, causing Jasmine to narrow her eyes strangely and causing me to fidget. Every time Cozy rhapsodized about "being a whore," I cringed. The antiglobalization lipstick lesbians seemed to love it, though.

"So we created an e-mail list of whores who will be alerted whenever there's a negative depiction of a whore in the media, and we'll be able to respond as a unified movement of whores. We need to attack—in a sex-positive way—patriarchal movies like *Eyes Wide Shut* that exploit the theme of the dead whore—"

Without bothering to introduce herself, Jasmine exploded.

"*Lisa* says? Since when is some airhead porn actress an expert on what happens to hookers in real life or in the movies? Are you telling me a *porn star's* going to decide whether a Hollywood movie's acceptable or unacceptable to *me?* That's unacceptable right there."

Caught off guard, Cozy blinked and sputtered.

"Hello?!" Jasmine railed. "Porn stars perform anal sex on-screen for a couple of thousand bucks! Lisa's mom and dad can walk into Champagne video and rent a video of their little girl sticking beads up her ass for money! It's, like, since when do porn actors have any idea what should be portrayed on-screen—when they're doing stuff in front of a camera that no self-respecting hooker does in *private?* Lisa Marquis is not exactly equipped, mentally speaking, to evaluate a Stanley Kubrick movie. Maybe she thinks she can make a better one?"

"You don't even *know* Lisa!" Cozy interrupted. I was beginning to sense that the feminist porn star and the peep-show activist were girlfriend-and-girlfriend. Jasmine should really shut up!

"That's right!" someone else agreed. "Who do you think you are?"

"One at a time—please!" Allison bleated. Her plaintive tone cut right through the hubbub. Everyone, including Jasmine, fell silent.

"There are divisions between sex workers," Allie intoned. "We are here to *overcome* these differences."

"I'm not," Jasmine said firmly. "I'm just here to see what lunacy is being cooked up in the name of hookers' rights. By porn stars, no less!"

Do I really want Jasmine to be a bridesmaid at my wedding?

"I don't think Jasmine introduced herself," Roxana interrupted. "Jasmine, why don't you tell the room how you arrived at this point of view? I think we need to have a dialogue here—*articulate* our differences if we're going to, uh, work through them."

"Well, first of all," Jasmine began, "I've *paid my dues* as a working girl. I have my own business and I have nothing in common with some half-wit who can't keep her clothes on. Why is Lisa Marquis claiming to represent people like me! I don't claim to represent *her*. Porn is ruining a good thing. The guys see all this disgusting stuff on video, and it gives them ideas."

"This is our common struggle," Allison began to explain. "We're all stigmatized by our work—"

"*Porn stars* might be," Jasmine said. "But that's because they haven't got the discipline to make it as call girls. Look, there's no way— Some chick who thinks it's okay to get fucked in the ass is going to defend my rights? She's gonna decide whether *I'm* being degraded? By a movie that I'm not even *in*? I don't *think* so!"

"Anal sex is part of the erotic mosaic—" Roxana began.

"It's a personal choice!" Cozy proclaimed.

"It's disgusting!" Jasmine retorted. "And it's even *more* disgusting to do it for money!"

I was gesturing to Allie with frantic eye movements—could someone please get Jasmine to stop dialoguing?

"Why can't we all agree to disagree on this topic?" Allie asked. "I really don't like this! It's making me . . ." Her voice trailed off and she looked as uncomfortable as I was feeling. In fact I was getting a headache.

"Well, *we* didn't bring it up," Belinda said. "Your elitist friend started it. And now we have to change the subject because *you* can't handle it?"

"We have to listen to this insulting, divisive tirade from one call girl and then we have to *kill* the *topic* because of *another* call girl," someone complained. "What I see happening is an attempt by the call girls to exercise control of the discourse! Anal sex is just a red herring. You're both pursuing the same agenda! Because you have more of a stake in your own shared status as call girls than you have in this movement!"

"That's just not fair!" Allison cried. "If you want a peep-show dancer to chair this meeting, I'll step down. Go right ahead!" She was on the verge of tears. "I didn't ask to chair this meeting!"

Roxana brought the meeting to order. "Allison's right. Let's agree to disagree. Some women find anal sex degrading and some find it empowering," she mooed. "Every sex worker must have the Right to Choose."

"Please," Jasmine grumbled. "Anyone who chooses to is deranged."

"Have *you* ever done a porn shoot?" Cozy asked.

There was silence as Jasmine met her gaze.

"No," Jasmine finally said. "Why?"

"Until you've walked a mile in another girl's G-string, I suggest you withhold your judgments. By the way, Lisa has produced a very woman-friendly video for couples on how to enjoy anal sex—it's very egalitarian. I don't think you *understand* anal sex, and when it comes to human sexuality, people are afraid of what they don't understand."

"You don't know who you're talking to. Listen, I know how to *fake* anal sex, and I happen to be one of the best! I'll bet there's nothing in her video about *that*."

Suddenly the meeting, which had been turning against Jasmine, began to change course.

"You do?" Gretchen piped up. "That's an important skill! Maybe you could teach a workshop at the harm reduction conference in Seattle. I'm facilitating the safe-sex workshop. I promised them three authentic sex workers, and so far I haven't been able to find more than one—me." Gretchen confessed, "I'm starting to forget some of the tricks I learned on the street. Sometimes I have to fake the workshop!"

Jasmine, unprepared for the sudden shift in temperature, looked flinty and suspicious. "Seattle? You want me to fly to Seattle and do what, exactly? Who, may I ask, is paying for this? And who's going to be in the audience? Do you think I'm crazy?"

"There's grant money from the Soros Foundation," Roxana explained. "Outreach workers and peer counselors will benefit from your knowledge and share it with working prostitutes. Think of all the disenfranchised prostitutes who need your advice!"

"Must I?"

As the meeting came to a close, Cozy was giving Jasmine icicle eyes. She wasn't happy about sharing the spotlight, but what can you expect from a nude dancer?

A small coterie encircled Jasmine, and I could hear snatches of her invective: "This business of being dictated to by San Francisco—I don't think you should stand for that!" The Cozy Von Booty wannabes, wearing leather dresses and U-shaped nose rings, clustered together at the other end of Roxana's living room.

I was standing against a bookshelf, recovering from the sheer embarrassment of it all, when a slim freckled girl with delicate features and strawberry blond hair rushed past me. She had slipped into the meeting while Jasmine was bickering with Cozy Von Booty about anal sex. Dressed in jeans and a hooded sweatshirt, she looked about seventeen. But could have been twenty-five. It was hard to tell.

She confronted Allie, a wild worried look on her small face. "I'm Charmaine," the girl said in a half whisper. "I sent you that e-mail about, you know . . . after I heard you on the radio." She looked around warily. "I can't talk about this here! You told me this was a small confidential gathering!"

"You're among friends!" Allie assured her. "We had more people than we expected. But you don't have to be afraid anymore. This is a safe space! We support you in your—"

"Listen, these people scare me—especially that loudmouthed brunette. Who *is* she?"

"Isolation will disempower us!" Allie told her in an urgent voice. "We're here to help you!"

"I need a lawyer! I don't need to share my problems with all these people." The girl looked miserable. "Here." She handed Allison a small piece of paper. "You can call me on this number. It's my cell. I have to meet him at Carl Schurz Park tomorrow at four, it's—" Her voice broke. "Humiliating. . . . I don't know what to do. . . . I'm scared . . . but I told you because I trust you."

Charmaine's quivering words were drowned out by Jasmine, who suddenly appeared at my side.

"Those zealots are babbling about globalization and red-light zones—can we please get out of here?" Jasmine begged. "I need a drink!"

At the sight—and sound—of Jasmine, Charmaine gave Allison a frightened look, then turned and walked out of the apartment, almost as if she were being chased.

When I finally got home, I was emotionally exhausted. At three A.M., I woke, disoriented. I had fallen asleep on the couch, and I was haunted by the face of that girl. What was the word she'd used? Humiliated? I've heard about girls who get caught up in dark S&M games that get out of hand. . . . Or is a sadistic cop taking advantage of her? I've also heard some gruesome stories about *that*.

TUESDAY, 5/2/00

Today Milt called from his car and proposed a late-morning quickie.

"I don't have much time," he warned me. "But we'll manage! I need to see you. The last week has been hell!"

I pulled out a fresh sheet for Milton and opened my secret dildo drawer. Tasteful Lucite? Or garish "flesh-toned" rubber? I picked up a smaller sleeker black number, then put it away. Who am I kidding? The more outlandish and sleazy, the better. Milt gets plenty of tasteful sex at home; his wife is no slouch—I've seen the family photos—and I doubt that she's a prude. It's just that, with kids in the house, you can't exactly come home, turn on a porn video, and get down to business in the middle of the day! People think it's the repressed types who go for kink. Actually, the happier and healthier a client's marriage is, the harder you have to work at keeping things sleazy.

I dusted off a monstrous-looking dildo and propped it against a pillow. I opened a tiny tube of K-Y, wrapped it loosely in a tissue, and slid that beneath the pillow for easy access. Then I rewound the video.

I was still brushing my teeth when the buzzer rang.

To speed things along, I encouraged Milt to watch while I fucked myself slowly with the head of the dildo. I don't do this often for Milt—only when he's in a hurry, when he hasn't got time for more affectionate sex games. First of all, I don't want to overdo it. I worry about the *size* of that thing (and always do a few extra Kegels afterward). Secondly, it's important to do something different every time you see a regular. Make sure you don't get into a rut.

After Milt had showered and paid, I got ready to see Bernie—at Liane's. I really don't need the extra money that I get from seeing Liane's people; it's less than I make seeing my own. But each appointment you keep gets you closer to meeting your weekly quota—and Bernie's so easy.

In Liane's spare room, where clients are entertained, I treated Bernie to some playful theatrics—looking into his eyes while I slowly unbuttoned my blouse, then lifting my skirt to remove my panties.

"Leave that on," he suggested.

"My skirt?" I acted surprised, as if this was the kinkiest thing anyone had ever said to me.

"Just for a few moments." Then he came over and slid his hand under the silk knit fabric. Fortunately, it was a rather slim skirt, and I was able to wriggle away from his finger. A professional could just ask him to go and wash his hands, but as a supposed amateur, I didn't want to come off too clinical.

"I—um—really have to tinkle!" I finally said, pulling away and disappearing into the bathroom.

I washed up, hung my skirt on a hanger, and returned, naked but for my heels.

"Leave *those* on," he insisted. "You look great like that!"

"Really? Should I wear them to bed?"

"Absolutely. . . . And I want to spend some time pleasing you today."

I slid onto the cool white sheet and into character, as the slightly promiscuous "coed" who's never been with an experienced old rake before.

Bernie gave my hairless pussy a gentle kiss, then began to blow on it softly. Because I'd waxed so recently, every inch of my skin was tingling. Sometimes, though your head is thinking that the man you're in bed with is a bit of a fool, your pussy seems to smile back at him with a mind and will of its own.

While Bernie licked me, I lifted my torso slightly—ostensibly to watch him. Actually, I was toning my abs and counting slowly as I raised and lowered myself, in a seemingly spontaneous series of movements. This morning's dildo flitted through my mind, and I did ten more Kegels while he licked me. Then I "came."

"Oh, my god," I said in a wondrous tone. "You're—you're just amazing."

After he left, I joined Liane in her sunlit living room, where she sat on the sofa, wearing a brown silk blouse with a pleated front and a straight brown skirt. Her Chanel slingbacks were brown and white.

She put down her *New York Times* and smiled.

"Bernie is enchanted!" she said, patting the sofa. "Have some peppermint tea. According to the *Times* . . ." She poured my tea. "Ladylike is coming back into fashion this fall! I'm rather excited!"

"Oh? In what sense?" I wondered. One nose ring instead of three?

" 'Covered buttons,' " she read out loud. "I hope that includes belly buttons!" she added. "The other day I had lunch at La Goulue with my friend and the hostess was wearing a pantsuit that showed off her belly button! Or should I say navel? Pantsuits are one thing, belly buttons are another."

Liane still remembers when call girls didn't wear pantsuits to hotels and restaurants because ladies just didn't.

I glanced at the paper. " 'Three Generations of Ladylike . . . Can one be ladylike in a tube top?' " Absolutely, said one young blonde who looked like a sixteen-year-old version of Allison. Nan Kempner was quoted, holding forth on the great pantsuit rebellion of '65.

I'm surprised to read about a teenager who Enjoys Being a Lady. I didn't care about being a lady until I started working. My desire to turn tricks was actually a tomboy's notion; I thought I could just get out there and start collecting scalps, like a guy. But I soon discovered that I had to learn how to behave like a lady.

A lady may let a client perform around the world but she doesn't reciprocate; it's ladylike, after all, to let guys worship you. (Jasmine, who knows how to fake *that* as well, thinks you can pretend to do it and still remain a lady. I'm not so sure! Ladies care about sexual appearances.)

Another thing that distinguishes a ladylike working girl is her groomed and tidy muff. Clients know you make money *with* your pussy, but a freshly waxed, beautifully maintained pussy sends a message: You spend money *on* your pussy. The word *pussy* is ladylike; *cunt* is not. *Muff* is somewhere in between. It's okay to tell clients you have a steady boyfriend, but it's not ladylike to give them sexual details! It's unladylike to count money in front of a john, but ladylike to count the money openly (as Liane does) when two girls are dividing it. As for drugs, cocaine is more ladylike than heroin; snorting coke is more ladylike than smoking crack. Ladies only do small amounts, anyway. And it's unladylike to admit to a client that you went without sleep last night but staggered out of bed in order to see him (which has been known to happen). A lady is more decadent in the daytime than she is at night.

"Last month, I had a new girl up here to see one of the fellows, and I discovered that she was covered in tattoos!" Liane was saying. "She had a nipple ring—it was shocking! I think we're all looking forward to a ladylike autumn." Liane would have fainted if she had seen the motley crowd at the last NYCOT meeting. "I should have asked her to undress when I met her. But I stopped doing that years ago, when things slowed down around here."

Some madams insist on seeing what their customers will be getting. Bianca, who ran that house around the corner from Sutton Place, always examined a new girl to make sure there were no surgical scars or signs of drug use. Jeannie, who ran the Dream

Date service, made new girls undress—to see if we were wired. Now, it seems, madams also have to be on the lookout for tattoos and labia piercings.

"When my business was very active," Liane was saying, "I needed lots of different girls. I had to branch out so, naturally, I *met* more girls. Which meant I had to be more careful about who worked here. I was a lot more demanding." She sighed. "That was before the airlines ruined my business! A man had to spend the night in New York if he wanted to get to Chicago," she reminded me. "Everyone"—meaning the guys—"came through New York! So everyone"—meaning the girls—"had to undress first."

By the time I started working for Liane, her business was beginning to slow down. Her busiest decade was the seventies—the era of the Happy Hooker, whose "public carrying-on" Liane still recalls with horror and disapproval.

"These days I meet so few girls," Liane said. "I don't think I've asked a new girl to undress in twenty years, dear! Did I ask *you* to undress? I can't remember."

Neither could I.

12 Origins Again: The Sex of Money

BEFORE SHE LEFT FOR HER VACATION, DR. WENDY SAID,
"Think about the nature, not the content, of your secrets.
Including your earliest secrets."

Before I was a hooker, I was a baby-sitter—which is (or
was) more like being a call girl than people realize. And,
for me, filled with secrecy.

I had my regulars: Mr. and Mrs. Hersch with their baby
boy; Emily's mom, a thirty-three-year-old divorcée who lived
with her two kids and dated a guy ten years her junior. (She was
big on informalities; I called her Liz.) One evening, Liz came home
to find her kitchen covered in cookie batter—her four-year-old daughter and six-year-old son had conned me into believing they could bake.
Since I was on the precocious side myself, I had been easily persuaded by
their ruse. Emily's mom hit the roof when she saw the mess her kids had
created on my watch—but she forgave the mistake and allowed me to learn
from it.

These were my bread-and-butter gigs. But I was always on the lookout
for new business. I scoured the want ads—nothing there, but why not give
it a shot? I never passed a bulletin board at a grocery store without reading
every single notice—and I got some extra business that way. If somebody
was seeking a baby-sitter, I was generally the first passerby to tear off any
phone number on a strip and make the call.

I loved making my own money. My mother had been trying to teach
me basic budgeting skills. She gave me a monthly allowance for sanitary
pads, bus tickets, acne soap, school supplies, and shampoo. A regular
amount of $1.40 was allocated for Frivolities, and I remember being
overwhelmed by how small this was compared to the total monthly

sum. The temptation to spend the whole thing on Frivolities was unavoidable. At the end of each month, my accounts reflected unrealistic quantities of Kotex and Clearasil. Where did all that money go?

But I had a reputation in the neighborhood—for being level-headed and mature. I was allowed to start baby-sitting at eleven, and the local parents thought I was wonderful! My baby-sitting gigs were all within walking or biking distance. I took my respon-sibilities seriously and enjoyed having them. But money was another matter. I frittered away my baby-sitting money on boarding-school stories and ice-cream cones, on Richie Rich and Millie the Model comics, then—as my tastes evolved—on maga-zines, French pastries, little tubs of flaky halvah from the Lebanese bakery, handmade Turkish delight, and the occasional schoolyard mandrax. No matter how much I spent on these deli-cacies, there was always another baby-sitting gig. I searched for out-of-print boarding-school stories in secondhand bookstores and bought foreign fashion magazines.

There were lots of books at home but not enough magazines. I liked sinking into the sophisticated ephemeral universe of a monthly fashion magazine; it was nothing like the permanence of a book, and it gave me access to a world that was so much bigger and more complex than the one we lived in. Since we didn't have a TV, this was my independent and private bond with pop culture that nobody could interfere with. There were frequent attempts to undermine this bond—magazines were frowned upon because there were so many ads—but I found that I could tolerate my par-ents' hang-ups now that I had my own money. Sweets were another forbidden pleasure in my mother's household, but now I bought them whenever I felt like it.

If my monthly allowance ran out, I got an extra baby-sitting job to avoid having to ask my mother for bus fare. When I discovered that I could circumvent her scoldings—simply by working—it must have been one of the happiest days of my life. I discussed this with nobody; it was a quiet kind of satisfaction, and I didn't want to draw attention to my spending problem. My job was no secret: a baby-sitter has to publicize her work if she wants to stay in business. But the reasons for my working—those were secret. I didn't even mention these money problems to Liz. She was my adult "friend" who liked to be on a first-name basis, but she, like Mom, was still an adult. I sensed that I should not discuss my money matters with adults, period. Money was quite personal. And since adults did not discuss their money openly, I knew that keeping my money problems and issues private would give me some adult freedoms.

By the time I started baby-sitting, I was also planning to be a hooker. Ever since I had heard the word *prostitute* and looked it up in a dictionary, I had fixed upon this as my ambition. But if you had asked me why, I couldn't have told you—nor did I feel any need to explain or defend it. I told a classmate what I was planning to do "when I grew up" and she was horrified.

"You don't know what you're talking about!" she yelped.

"Neither do you," I said.

When I decided, at ten, that I wanted to be a prostitute, I had never even heard of an orgasm. I knew that I wanted sex to be my career, the source of my independence, what I spent my days doing—when I grew up. It was a decision I made before I had even begun to contemplate having sex, and I assumed I would not become a hooker until I could also vote. Ten-year-olds may dream big dreams, but their perspective tends to be somewhat narrow; I didn't know about underage prostitution.

At eleven, I discovered a porno paperback called *Little Girls for Sale* in the back of a poster shop that also sold used books. On the cover was an illustration of a doll-faced child with big round eyes wearing a babyish dress. She looked about eight. But the girls in the story were twelve and fourteen—not little girls at all, I remember thinking. The imaginary and rather infantile cover child was a hoax. Nobody over the age of nine dressed like that! As one who was no longer a "little" girl, I had a stake in these issues. But the title itself gave me hope.

The not-so-little girls were temptresses, instigators. They had secret sexual encounters in public places. A man in a supermarket was lured by a twelve-year-old girl who made her small breasts available to him by leaning over the frozen food section. He touched her tentatively, while nobody was looking. But before all this happened, she had bewitched him in the soap aisle. He had followed her all over the store.

As I flipped through the book, my body surprised and embarrassed me. I was standing in the back of the poster shop, quietly aroused, but it was totally unexpected. I swelled up, my whole body seemed to be more alive, my face felt flushed, and my heart was beating faster. Warily, I looked around. As the feeling subsided, I realized that I was getting away with something. Nobody was paying any attention to me, thank god. I read further. If the little girls were really for sale, where were the passages describing all the things they bought with their forbidden loot? There was no mention of money changing hands, and I grew impatient. I resigned myself to the thought that there were no real opportunities out there for a girl my age, and life went on.

The opportunity to break in at the part-time level came sooner than I expected—when I was thirteen.

My first trick, at thirteen, was the easiest trick I ever turned. Professor Andrews wasn't my first professional trick—that happened later at the Cumberland Hotel. I think of this as my first emotional trick, the first time I experienced what it felt like to have sex for money. If things had gone wrong, if I had been mistreated or injured, I think I would have been scared off. If it had been hard to do in any way, I might never have done it again.

I was the kind of thirteen-year-old who stubbornly refused to do anything that wasn't easy. In the ninth grade, I had the option, finally, to trade gym for another academic subject. Running, jumping, and climbing were boring, stupid, and hard. (Riding a bike was something else—it got you somewhere on your own, without an adult.) It was easy to fill in the form and add another academic subject, but that didn't mean I cared about getting good marks.

"You think you don't have to be good at science because you're a girl!" my mother said to me one day in frustration. Actually, I thought I had as much right to be bad at science and math as any boy had. I only cared about being good at the subjects I liked. Though I was the youngest in my class, having skipped a year, I had this notion that I was too smart to care about school. I was developing a quiet stubborn will. Their hours? Their days? Their rules? I was just going to do what I pleased. So I didn't show up for a week. I hung out at libraries and bookstores. I was surprised when they didn't notice or report me to my mother. I didn't show up for another week. Eventually the computer noted my huge block of absences and recorded it on a report card. It was a point of pride with me that I had gotten away with this for the good part of a school term. While I was viewed as a nerd by my friends—awkward, insufficiently glib, a tame drug user—I was admired for my will. Maybe they thought I was doing something ingenious, but I wasn't. I was just doing what I wanted. And it was not hard; I would have gone to school on those days if skipping school had been harder to do.

As for sex, it wasn't lust but curiosity, a desire for worldly experience, that made me impatient. I was not a passionate teenager. There was never a boy who got me too turned on to turn back, who persuaded me to prove that I loved him. I was never a candidate for pregnancy. I planned my defloration down to the last detail, read up on every method of birth control for an entire year before deciding to have sex. I read about the different phases of the female orgasm and wondered when I would actually have one.

That incident in the bookstore, my experiments with a pillow between my thighs—what bothered me about all this was that I couldn't just make it happen more naturally. I read about masturbation in books and tried to figure out how to use my own fingers.

When other women reminisce about fucking because they got carried away with adolescent desire, I feel more than a hint of envy. Passion, swelling, throbbing, coming—with a guy! At eleven, twelve, thirteen. All this is mind-boggling to me.

My one romantic experiment with a high school boy was Derek. I had a huge crush on him—and every crush I had made me feel like a victim of fate. He was constantly occupying my thoughts; I felt nerdlike, insignificant, and powerless to attract him. A continuing battle with blackheads, pimples, and oily skin had taken a huge toll on my ego.

Then I read an article in *Sixteen* that proved to be quite useful: "How to Make Him Like You Too."

I still remember it! Practice the Mona Lisa Smile—smile with your mouth but not with your eyes. I tried this in the mirror. When you normally smile, your eyes will smile with you, but the Mona Lisa Smile is a Serious Smile. (I recently checked—in my mirror—and found the Mona Lisa Smile supercilious, so it must be one of those things that looks good only on an adolescent.) Having mastered the Mona Lisa Smile, hang out wherever he hangs out. Be around. Do not make a point of talking to him, just *be there*. When you see him, look straight into his eyes and . . . deliver the Mona Lisa Smile. But don't try to talk to him! This combination projects an air of mystery. He will start smiling back at you. Keep this up for two weeks and he will start to like you too.

And he did. His return smiles became sweeter, more personal, and more liquid-eyed. He was tall and soulful, with dark hair to his neck, and he was mine. For about a week.

Derek came over to the Hersch household, where I was baby-sitting their toddler, and we rolled around on a bedspread in a darkened bedroom. When he asked if he could "stick it in," I realized he had never read a sex manual.

What? I'd read a hundred times that the man was supposed to make sure the woman was lubricated! I didn't understand how this worked in real life. I expected him to ask me point-blank, "Are you lubricated?" And since he didn't do that—and I wasn't even aroused—I felt inadequately handled. I had also read about pills, condoms, and pregnancies. He hadn't asked me about that either.

So I just said no.

"We probably shouldn't," he agreed.

"I don't have any birth control," I pointed out.

The next time we got together, at another baby-sitting location, he gently nudged my head toward his cock—and I cautiously kissed it. But I didn't put it in my mouth. (I didn't understand until years later that this was a social overture—his way of asking for oral sex.) I still remember wrapping my hand around his cock and feeling rather thrilled about finally touching my first hard penis; but it was a sense of accomplishment, not a feeling of arousal, that I remember.

Put another way, I didn't know that he wanted me to suck his cock, and he didn't know that I wanted him to get me wet. It was a simple case of mechanical failure, perhaps. I had this huge crush on Derek, but I never felt anything close to the arousal I'd felt when I'd read that dirty novel at the age of eleven.

I wanted to win him and have him and I loved looking at him, but my body didn't need him.

We were sitting in the living room, listening to Neil Young, when he broke up with me.

"I don't think you really like *me*. I think you just like having a guy, knowing that you're going out with a guy."

"No, no, I like *you*—I've liked you for a long time!"

I started crying. Neil Young started singing a breakup dirge, in that god-awful nasal voice that I found so romantic at the time. I wept more intensely, thinking this would change things between us.

"The song always seems to fit the situation," Derek said.

I cried some more, he was gentle and kind, and then he got the hell out of there. In a way he was right. I was finding that the wanting and waiting and scheming to get him had been more exciting. The time we spent together was weird, quiet; we weren't really connecting, and we hardly ever talked. And I couldn't bring myself to admit it. My first loosely defined junior high courtship—and I was ready to behave like some sort of established partner who is just going through the motions! When I think about it, my attitude seems almost like a caricature of middle age. Scary.

But I guess I didn't know quite what to *do* with him. Why didn't I just chatter, the way I could with an older man? I noticed constantly that guys in their twenties and thirties—guys who were no longer in high school—were so easy to talk to.

In May, Professor Andrews offered to initiate me sexually. I liked the attention I was getting from him because he was a local celebrity, but I was not, like the women in his orbit, a fan. Because I was still a girl, I was immune to his romantic appeal.

I told him, "No—I'm not attracted to you" I didn't want this portly old geezer to be my first lover. I knew it was preposterous; he was somebody's dad, for god's sake. Impossibly old!

Professor Andrews asked me what I wanted to be when I grew up. "I'm going to be a hooker," I told him.

"You can start now, you know. I'd pay you" was his reply.

"I'm going to wait until I've gone to university," I said.

"Call me if you change your mind," he said—but I was skeptical.

A month later, there was no special guy to please or be seduced by when I decided to start having sex. But, oddly enough, a special guy appeared on the horizon as soon as I had made up my mind to start fucking. Peter was a nineteen-year-old history major who had taken a few of Professor Andrews's courses. (In our small town, that was not surprising. Many people had.) I was thirteen and a half, and the decision to lose my virginity was made on the day after I took my last exam for the school year, in June.

A week or so later, I met Peter while I was cruising the aisles of a trendy bookstore, trying to decide whether to spend some of my baby-sitting bonus on a copy of *The Bell Jar*. He was carrying around a stack of books, *Survival,* by Margaret Atwood, being the most prominent.

As a small child, I had never been a tomboy; I'd preferred dolls and books to sports, English to science, even enjoyed home ec. I'd never really liked competing with boys when I was small. But when I started having sex, my tomboy streak emerged. I began to see my sex partners as notches on a belt, scalps hanging from my waist—conquests. Though I was extremely charmed by Peter, that didn't stop me from thinking about who I could sleep with next. And not for reasons of passion; I had a Sexual Plan. I didn't know yet that there could be more pleasure in *being* the conquest, letting a man plan your seduction.

Once I had begun having sex, I felt emboldened. I called Professor Andrews and reminded him of his offer. No oral sex (an act I still regarded with suspicion) and no kissing, I told him. "And we have to use a condom."

He had no quarrel with my terms. "But there's something else we should discuss. What are you going to wear?"

"Wear?" I said blankly. I didn't know that people sometimes wore clothes for the purpose of making sex more interesting. Peter and I had an affectionate, ordinary sex life—nothing kinky.

"Well, you're always dressed in these long baggy things and loose shirts. Don't you have a short skirt? Or a pair of high-heeled boots?"

"Boots?" I gasped. "It's August!"

"Do you have a garter belt?"

"People my age don't wear garter belts!" I scoffed. "Are you crazy?"

This irked him. "That is such an arrogant crock of shit! It's one thing for you to express a preference! But don't try to present yourself as a spokesperson for your generation!" he railed.

I knew he was nuts. Nobody I went to school with owned a garter belt. I showed up for my first trick wearing Dr. Scholl's sandals and a denim skirt hemmed with the wrong color thread, carrying a wicker basket.

"I suppose you want your money first," he said. I tucked it into the small lozenge tin that I kept in my wicker basket and used as a wallet.

As he put the condom on, it came naturally to me to say "I like watching you do that."

"Why?" he asked.

"It's the anticipation."

But I was more interested in getting my first trick over with, collecting what I knew to be an amusing scalp. I knew about erotic anticipation from books. I had never lusted for a man's cock. Today, I might get into bed with a client and make him hard with a hungry look; but I didn't know, at thirteen, how to mimic that kind of desire. I had no standard of excellence to maintain or achieve—the way I do today—and I made zero effort to please him, turn him on, or entertain him.

And yet he came as soon as he was inside me—a fact I just took for granted because, after all, adolescence is wasted on the young.

I didn't appreciate how ridiculously easy Professor Andrews was until a decade later, when I was hooking for real and starting to make myself "younger." Most of my clients aren't as quick as Professor Andrews—or as easy—but I suppose most *would* be if they were fucking their thirteen-year-old neighbor. I'm sure my clients today—Milt, Etienne, guys like that—are turned on by pubescent girls. But these guys are big-city players, not small-town pedophiles, and they're less likely to act on those fantasies. They have too much to lose.

I had no idea what an enormous turn-on my age had been for Professor Andrews until I entered my twenties. There was much I didn't know, but I understood that Professor Andrews was being foolish—taking a giant risk to satisfy a curiosity he couldn't control. I should have felt a little bit sorry for the man, and I do today. But when I knew him I thought about him only in very self-ish terms.

He was different from my boyfriend, whose attention and admiration lit me up from inside. Despite my deliberate approach to sex, I had fallen in love with my first sex partner. I couldn't wait to tell Peter about this adventure; he had more sexual experience than I did, but I was catching up with him. Maybe I could even surpass him. Peter was my sexual confidant—the only person I talked to about the realities and discoveries of sex—so I boasted to him about what I had done. Despite my physical maturity (I had the body, the face, and some of the mannerisms of a seventeen-year-old), this was a child's boast. Bragging to my lover about another sexual conquest—I was like one of those people with new money who can't help flashing their winnings around!

Peter wasn't angry; he didn't insult me or judge me in any way. He looked bemused and thoughtful, and he continued to be quite affectionate—but an older girl closer to his age or a young woman in her twenties would have kept this escapade to herself. And when the summer ended, when the school year began again, our age difference began to matter more.

Ignorance is bliss—sort of. I didn't know a tenth of what I know today, but I had some basic instincts down that puzzle me to this day. How is it that some people are born knowing how to feel about a trick while others (at any age—thirteen or thirty-three) can't figure this out? A misfit hooker feels put upon and put down, or she falls for a john and wants his approval. But I felt that fucking Professor Andrews for money made me his equal. I wasn't some student seeking a good mark, or a lonely lover wishing he would leave his wife. Or an adoring groupie flattered by his conversation. And while he seemed hopelessly old-fashioned—garter belts!—and just plain old, he didn't strike me as much of an authority figure. Fucking a local celebrity was a feather in my cap because of other people's infatuations—and I liked knowing that I had seen the mental underbelly of a town icon. I didn't know how to say this at the time, but that's what I felt.

If I could say I regretted fucking him for money, it would have made—would make—a lot of things simpler. I do regret, or wonder about, some other things, though. Three days after turning my first trick, at thirteen, I'd spent the entire sum. Later, when I was fifteen passing for twenty, and picking up clients at the London Hilton on Park Lane, I knew I was making per trick what some real adults earned in a week. But I ignored the older girls who advised me to save money, and I blew it on restaurants and clothes, indulging my whims. They seemed . . . so dour, like my mother. I much preferred the company of frothy types—also older—who enjoyed talking about their boyfriend problems, who bonded with me over food rather than advice, who enjoyed hanging out for hours in cafés and bistros. And I wasn't getting a very good grounding in reality; Ned, the boyfriend I lived with at that point, provided me with a home, and there were no household bills to pay.

New York was different. Where London was glamorous yet somehow familiar (especially to someone from a small Canadian town), New York felt foreign, untidy and incomplete. I was startled to discover that I now had to pay for my V.D. tests; there was nothing remotely like the Praed Street clinic in New York. The greatest city in the world didn't have casinos or free V.D. clinics! Well, not the kind of clinic where you felt comfortable. There was a public clinic in the West Twenties that looked like an abandoned public school—before you even got inside. So I found a private gynecologist who specialized in working girls and their needs—and got used to paying cash for my medical care.

But the American way was also seductive. When I joined the ranks of Jeannie's Dream Dates (a midtown escort service with ads in the Yellow Pages), I was faced with a surplus of johns. I had never been so busy in London—not even at the Kontinental nightclub. Hustling champagne all evening—"punters" had to buy two bottles of Taittinger in order to sit with a girl—I would usually pick up one client and invest a lot of my evening in him. Things moved at a slower pace, and if it didn't pan out, it was a waste of time—too bad.

New York was different not just because you had to pay for everything but also because I suddenly felt that I was in the aisle of a giant sexual supermarket. Why was I so busy? At first I thought it was my exotic loveliness and my good breeding. "You're so well-spoken!" Jeannie would croon at me. Actually, I was too naive to give out my number and skirt the 50 percent cut that went to Jeannie.

I felt an allegiance to the agency for keeping me so busy—but not to the clients for liking me. I still thought of clients as a breed apart from other guys (like Professor Andrews), and I didn't respect them. In my sixteen-year-old's half-invented inner universe, the agency and I were as one, united in the fleecing of the johns.

But all that changed one night when the agency sent me to see Arnie, a Garment Center hippie and the son of a buttons-and-trimmings magnate, with a triplex in Gramercy Park. For the first time ever, I had multiple orgasms. Due to Arnie's abundant cocaine and my extreme youth, I became somewhat paranoid after my fourth climax. Was he trying to get out of paying for the final hour? But no, it was business as usual, and Arnie asked for my number as I was leaving, a request I warily brushed off. When I woke the next afternoon, I literally pinched myself. Why hadn't I given Arnie my number? I realized I liked him in a way that I had never liked a john before.

Arnie made me look at men differently. Before, clients were mere tools, a breed apart from boyfriends, and I didn't care if I saw them again. But now I discovered that you could care about seeing a john again—because you simply hit it off or he did something to your body that nobody else did. For the same reasons that you might want to see your *boyfriend*.

Basically, I'd snubbed the first repeat customer I'd ever *wanted*. When other girls at the agency went to see him, I was secretly jealous. And I wondered about those multiple orgasms. Did the other girls have them, too? Or was it our special chemistry? Why did I assume this was just a job until now, a crude exchange involving a man's pleasure and his money?

Before Arnie, I resented any client who had the ability to make my body feel things. I had strange ideas. I believed, for example, that a client who lost his erection was prolonging the session to make me work harder. Though I never saw Arnie again, my attitude began to change.

I started finding out what my body liked, what it could or couldn't accomplish for itself while making love for money. I finally began to outgrow Professor Andrews. I was still a pro, still working, and as concerned about money as ever. But I wasn't a sexual tomboy anymore. A customer had surprised me—he had changed me. I wanted to see him again. But I never did.

13 The Bad Seed

Two dates this morning, back-to-back. First, Milt, by appointment. Then, Steven, impromptu: "I'm ten minutes away. Can I come over?" I knew he would be the easiest $350 I'd made in weeks. These sudden opportunities— which you must be prepared for (but can't plan for) if you're serious about being a call girl—really get the adrenaline going. The true test of a girl's sexiness and couth is her ability to turn it on when pressed for time. Anyone can be sexy if she has a whole day to prepare! But I still—after how many years in this business?—get flustered, feel the pressure to perform at the last minute. And I thrive on it.

The pressure to *find those special stockings* that he likes. Where did I put them??

I washed up in record time, changed the sheets, put on my garter belt— and was still adjusting my sheer stockings when Steven buzzed. I stood behind the apartment door, listening; I could hear a neighbor and her Yorkie. The woman who lives three doors down from me. With my ankle straps still unbuckled, I stayed out of sight so Steven could slip into the foyer without letting the dog owner catch sight of me—nearly naked in my heels!

While Steven was undressing, I was still dressing, discreetly buckling my shoes and fastening my garters. He came while I was perched on the edge of my bed, rubbing the head of his cock against the lacy edge of my bra. After he left, I washed the residual Astroglide off my chest, soaked my bra in Palmolive and Shout—it was covered with his come—and decided to spring-clean the closets.

The sun is suspiciously powerful these days: time to excavate the hall closet and find my good French sunblock, my protective summer hats. Yesterday, I picked up a fresh tube of Self Tanning Milk (for my legs only—I never tan elsewhere) and booked an appointment with Claudia for my presummer power peel. Soon it will be mosquito season—time to make the switch from Allure to Off! But I'm not just molting for the summer. It's a bit more serious than that. I guess this is the spring-cleaning of my *life*.

Last night, I gathered my winter sweaters into a pile and started folding them. Every summer, I fold and cram as many sweaters as I can into a box and store them in my closet, under the blankets and boots. I felt a twinge of nostalgia for my solitary rites of spring, as I realized that next spring I'll be sorting my sweaters in a shiny and new two-bedroom. Shouldn't I be thrilled? The hall closet here has never been large enough for my needs, or those of my sweaters. I'm losing my sexual freedom but gaining a *ton* of closet space. Isn't that the very definition of maturity?

LATE EVENING

This afternoon, I ran into Allison at the gym. I was on my way in and she was on her way out. Well, actually, she was standing in the locker room, half naked, in front of a mirror, holding a pair of tweezers over her right brow when I entered. She was taking her time, and it was obvious that she was preparing for some sort of well-manicured exit. A small towel was wrapped around her waist, leaving her breasts completely exposed, and her soft pink nipples added to the girlish effect. When I sat on a bench near the mirror, she almost jumped.

"I didn't see you!" she gasped.

"What's going on?" I asked, looking her up and down. She had done her eye makeup—not her usual style for leaving the gym. "Appointment with Jack?"

"No," she said quietly. "Today, I'm a NYCOT observer."

"What is a NYCOT observer?"

Allie pulled out a cylinder of dark pink lip gloss.

"Sometimes we go to the strolls and we watch the vice squad from our van. Today is unusual, though. I'm going to meet Charmaine in Carl Schurz Park. Remember Charmaine? From the meeting?"

Charmaine! *Didn't I overhear her that night? Saying something about "meeting him"—whoever that is—"at Carl Schurz Park"? What is Allie getting mixed up with? And why does she look so pleased if she's about to meet the dread "him"?*

"Why are you going to the park?" I asked as she applied a coat of pink to her mouth.

Lip gloss to go to the *park?* Subtle eye colors are one thing, but lip gloss? Nobody on the Upper East Side gets tarted up to go to Carl Schurz Park. Or any park, now that I think of it. Then, watching Allie press her lips together, I added, "Does this have anything to do with the novelist who donated those shoes?"

"How did you know?" She smiled with undisguised pleasure. "He's meeting us, too!"

"Just a girlfriend's intuition." And a darker shade of pink than is absolutely necessary for hanging out in a park at midday. "Allie, are you— What are you observing?"

"I can't tell you that," she said quickly. "I agreed to protect Charmaine's confidentiality."

The weird things I overheard that night at the meeting were echoing in my head: *It's humiliating! But I trust you!*

"What is this man's relationship to Charmaine? Is that how you met her?"

This was sounding sicker by the second.

"Oh!" Allie looked surprised. "They've never met. He's coming because I asked him to." Aha. She calls and he comes. Maybe it's not so sick after all. "Look, I shouldn't really be telling you this," she said.

"You told this stranger? This weirdo with the shoes? Something that you can't tell me?"

"He's a NYCOT volunteer! He is not a 'weirdo,' okay? And Charmaine felt—well, she felt sort of safer having a guy around. In case things get . . ." She paused. Then she looked overwhelmed. "I don't know if I should tell you. She asked me not to tell the other members. She's very intimidated by NYCOT. She doesn't trust other working girls. She's been mistreated and betrayed so many times!"

"Well, I'm not a NYCOT member," I reminded her. "I'm a bit of an 'observer' myself," I added slyly. "And I'm in sympathy with her because NYCOT sometimes intimidates *me!*"

Allie looked around cautiously to make sure we were alone. "Charmaine's—she's emotionally paralyzed. She e-mailed NYCOT from a Hotmail account after hearing me on the radio, and she asked for our help. I should really be grateful, I know." Allie gave me a worried look. "After all, I went on the show because I wanted to reach the most isolated and alienated sex workers!"

"Be careful what you wish for?"

"Yes," she sighed. "I've never heard of anything *like* this! First she says she wants a lawyer, then she changes her mind. I keep telling her: she's just making it worse! She says her life isn't her own anymore."

"What's going on? Is she paying off the cops? Where does she work?"

Allie threw her towel into the communal hamper. Sprinkling powder on her curves and crevices, she went on: "You're not going to like this. She was working for one of those escort agencies—they advertise in *Screw* and they have an ad on Channel 35."

Those tawdry nymphomercials! With the bridge-and-tunnel

girls posing in their eighties evening wear! And the pseudorefined names they come up with for these operations! Je Reviens. Chanson de Nuit.

"Oh, Jesus. Poor Charmaine. But," I warned Allie, "be careful about getting too close to her."

"I knew you'd say that," Allie sighed. "But I'm her friend—not her co-worker."

"If a girl isn't in your league as a co-worker, you can't afford to have her as a friend. Look, it's one thing for you to make friends with someone like Gretchen. She's had a hard life on the street and you're doing something valuable together, helping the street girls. Gretchen has made something of herself, okay?" Allie was frowning at me unhappily. I pressed on. "But you can't afford to get involved with a cable-TV escort. It's too dangerous. Too close to home. She'll resent you at some point." Even as I said it, I hated being the bearer of this information.

"Charmaine's boss brought in a new partner who wanted to *sleep with her,*" Allie explained.

"A woman or a man?"

"The boyfriend of the owner. And when she complained to the owner, it was a disaster because, you know, the owner is a little older than Charmaine—actually, a lot older. And she's not so attractive anymore. She didn't want to believe Charmaine, she accused Charmaine of coming on to the guy and banned her from the agency." Allison looked distraught. "So Charmaine had to quit, and she went out on her own. She was afraid to advertise in *New York* magazine, because the owner goes through the ads every week. Her boyfriend calls around, and they try to get all the new escorts and agencies in trouble with the cops. They keep tabs on everyone. So Charmaine went to the bar of the W Hotel. She had a scary experience with a guy who tried to tie her up." Allie looked a bit exhausted, and I felt guilty about getting her to recount the story of Charmaine's unhappy career. "Anyway, she designed her own little website and she started picking up clients online. She thought that would be safer."

"Uh-oh. And the agency goons—?"

"No. Something worse."

"A cop?"

Allison leaned forward to fasten her bra, and her long hair brushed against my face.

"Much worse," she said in a tense voice. "Somebody got into a long e-mail thing with her, back and forth, and he saved the evidence and figured out where she lives! And he called her at her home—even though she has an unlisted number. And he mailed her a printout of the e-mail to show that she had really solicited him!"

A creeping sensation enveloped my whole body as she told me this.

"He figured all this out? How?" I wondered.

"I guess it's not that hard to do." The excitement I had seen earlier was fading from Allison's eyes. "If you really know computers, I guess, you can *find out anything about anyone!* Just like the spam says! It's awful!"

"Now look, I know you've been hanging around with those girls at the NYCOT meetings and you want to be their spokesperson, but this is exactly the kind of thing I've been trying to warn you about! This is why you have to work privately. I hope this has cured you of any fantasies you might have about—"

"I know," she said quietly. "Believe me. I don't want to be *out there* like that. Ever! And I know how lucky we are now!"

"So this is the guy she meets in Carl Schurz Park? This creepy blackmailer?"

"Yes, but you won't believe— The worst thing is—" Allie pulled on a pair of hip-hugging Capris, then sat down next to me, in her pants and bra. "You see, the thing is, Charmaine did something she should never have done!"

"Well, that's obvious. Is she having . . ." The idea was making me kind of nauseous. "Is she having unprotected sex with this sadistic creep?"

"No. There's no sex. That isn't the problem."

"How do you know?"

"He just wants money. At first she thought she could handle it by paying him off and then he would go away, a onetime thing. Now she worries about making enough to pay him, and she's afraid this will start eating into her savings! She has a CD that's coming due—and she took some money out of the bank last week!"

"Jesus. This is scary." Scary to think that a girl could be smart enough to have savings, yet foolish enough to pay off a black-mailer!

"Well, it's *really* scary because there's—he's—what she didn't know when she solicited him—" Allie made a helpless gesture with her hands. "And I think she agreed to do a bunch of really explicit, dirty things to him in her e-mail because he asked her to— Oh, Nancy. I don't know if I should tell you this part. She's afraid of people finding out."

"Tell me what? Could it get any worse? And how do you know he's not a cop?"

"Well, I've seen him."

"And? How can you be so sure?"

"Because he's—"

Allie paused.

"What? In a wheelchair or something? That can be faked!"

"He's *ten years old!*"

I was dumbfounded.

"Hang on a sec. Are you—are you serious? How can a ten-year-old boy—how could that happen?"

"Well, think about it! He goes online, he—" Allie made some more helpless hand motions. "And he's ten!"

I thought about it.

"What does he look like?"

"He looks like any other ten-year-old boy. I think he goes to Rudolf Steiner. And he doesn't look as nerdy as you'd expect. You'd never know from looking at him that he's a—" She groped for the words to describe this monster.

"Juvenile extortionist," I suggested.

"Last week, I went to the park to make sure things didn't get out of control. I wanted to see if there was anyone with him, that kind of thing. He didn't see me, but I saw him. And I was—I was a little bit afraid that she might do something foolish if she was alone with him. She's at her wit's end," Allie explained, "and sometimes she—"

"Don't say it." God, what a nightmare. I'd be tempted to strangle him! "That park's awfully close to the river," I observed.

"Well, she won't do anything if she knows I'm there," Allie assured me. "She's afraid her parents will read about it in the paper. Did you see that story in the *Times* the other day about the high school teacher? She was charged with raping a fourteen-year-old boy! It's his word against hers! Charmaine read that and got hysterical. And this—this ten-year-old. He's very smart. He could say *anything*."

I pondered this for a while.

"How long has this girl been working? Where's she from?"

"About three years. She just turned twenty-one in December. Her parents live in Pittsburgh."

"It's time for her to quit," I said bluntly. "She's in over her head! And this is the craziest thing I've ever heard, Allie! You can't afford to get involved with this! And you can't go alone to the park—"

"Well, fortunately, I'm not going to be alone," she reminded me.

The glow was returning to her eyes.

"Does Jack have any idea you're seeing so much of this guy?"

"I've met him a few times for coffee, and we've had some meetings with Roxana. It's not as if I'm— Nancy! He's just a friend! A political supporter." She blushed and then admitted, "Well, I saw no reason to tell Jack about a political contact. It's not as if I'm sleeping with him. Or even thinking about it!" She gasped. "I'd better get going—I don't want to be late!"

She grabbed a gym bag and fled upstairs. I reached down to find my weight-lifting gloves and realized she had the wrong bag—she had taken my cell phone, my house keys, everything I couldn't possibly function without. I ran after her, praying she had not left for the park. When I spotted her on the sidewalk, my black gym bag was hanging over her shoulder and she was looking around anxiously . . . for the guy she's not even *thinking* about sleeping with.

"Hey." I nudged her. "You're so uninterested in that guy you grabbed my bag by mistake!"

She made a light squealing sound and turned. "Oh, my god, yes, I did. Look, here he comes. He *is* kind of cute, isn't he? Butwe'rejustfriends."

"Who?" I peered down the street. "That *delivery boy* in the baggy pants?"

"No, silly. Over here," she whispered, tossing her head in the direction of the crosswalk. "In the blazer."

Walking toward us—well, toward Allison—with eyes *only* for Allison was . . . my future sister-in-law's *husband* wearing a business-casual blazer and khaki pants. He was so delighted to see Allie that I, standing in the doorway, did not even register until—

"Hiiii!" Allie waved at him like a professional activist courting votes. "Thanks so much for meeting me here! I'm really glad you could make it!" she said in her creamiest, most sincere voice.

Jason and I were staring at each other, open-mouthed and rigid with confusion. Allie was oblivious.

"This is Jason! The novelist I was telling you about."

Jason blinked frantically and gave me a helpless look of pure anguish. Whatever Allison might not be planning to do with him, he had guilt written all over his face. *Jason* goes around telling girls that he's writing a novel about Mary Magdalene? *Jason's* going to escort Allie to the park to meet with a ten-year-old black-mailer? And *Jason's* the guy who donated his dead sister's shoes to the homeless streetwalkers? Oh, my god. Those must have been *Elspeth's* shoes.

"Hello," he managed to say in a shaky voice. "I—uh—"

"I bumped into Nancy in the locker room and we switched bags by accident!" Allison was burbling away.

What was she going to say about me? What *has* she said about me? I thought frantically.

"But you left your bag downstairs!" I exclaimed. "Don't you want to come down and get it?" I grabbed Allison's hand. "Was your wallet in your gym bag? We'd better go get it."

If I were Jason, I'd be thinking about making a quick escape at this point, but Allie—unaware of the problem—invited him inside. Bewildered, he agreed to wait for her.

In the locker room, I grabbed Allie by the arm and pleaded with her: "Listen to me. Have you ever told Jason anything—any-thing at all about me? You have to tell me!"

"I can't remember! I don't think so. Why? What's going on?"

"You have to promise me something. You have to pretend that *I don't know anything about you*—tell him I think you're a stu-dent or something. I don't know you're in NYCOT and I don't know you've ever worked in the business. Do you understand?"

"How can I do that? You're my friend, and he knows me from the radio show! He heard me on the radio, and he got in touch—"

"You have to let Jason think that he knows something I don't know."

"I do?"

"Yes. Otherwise, god knows what he'll think about me—or say."

"But you don't have to fear him! He's such a nice person! He's donating his time to sex workers' rights, and he's a NYCOT volunteer. In fact, he's going to be an observer with me—"

"I have everything to fear! He's married to my fiancé's sister!"

"He's what?" Allie's eyes flew open. She shook her head. "Are you sure?"

"What do you mean, am I sure? I *know* him—didn't you notice how he reacted when we met?"

"No." Allie looked crestfallen. "But he never told me he was married."

"Did he tell you he was single?"

"Well, no. He just . . ."

"Let you think it?"

Allie looked puzzled. "But why would he hide that? He's been so open with me, so giving of his time, and he genuinely . . . and he's never even touched me or tried to ask me out on a date. He's not trying to sleep with me! I thought maybe he was *gay.*"

"He's crazy about you! Don't be so naive! Did he tell you he's a lawyer, too?"

"He said something about taking a break from Legal Aid work in the Bronx to write his novel. And he's been meeting with our steering committee. Roxana wants NYCOT to be a 501C charity. He said he would do the paperwork for us. Is he—is he qualified to do it?" Allie looked worried now.

"Qualified? He's an M&A lawyer! I'm sure he knows how to file some corporation papers—but he's obviously mixed up. I mean, if you knew this guy the way I do—" But then I realized that

I don't really *know* Jason, after all. "Please just trust me on this. If he's still there when you go back upstairs, tell him we're gym buddies: I'm a copy editor and I think you're a student and I don't know anything about your other life. You have to play it this way."

Allie looked reluctant. "I'd rather not have to . . ."

"How would you feel if I had opened my big mouth when we had dinner with your parents?" I reminded her.

Apparently, he was still waiting for her when she went upstairs. She didn't come back or call my cell phone. And when I tried to call hers, she was unreachable. I had expected him to run away while we were in the locker room—hadn't I given him a chance to extricate himself? His strange brand of loyalty—or is it just obsession?—surprised me. Who knew that Jason, my future sister-in-law's corporate lawyer husband, could be such a trendy yet romantic dreamer? A novel about Mary Magdalene? A do-gooder lawyer chasing an activist hooker? Wow.

When I got home, I called Matt and left a voice mail, claiming a very bad stomach bug. "I just need to stay in and rest," I pleaded in my best sick voice. "I'll see you tomorrow, okay?" The thought of dealing with my "real" life just now was overwhelming. Then I realized: Tomorrow, we're having dinner with Elspeth and Jason! My god.

TUESDAY MORNING, 5/9/00

A call from Allie, very late last night. I was sitting in bed trying to read myself to sleep.

"I hope it's not too late," she began. "But you left *ten messages* on my voice mail, so I felt like maybe I'd better call you back—"

"Well? What happened?" I sat up, waiting for the worst.

"We went to the park, but Charmaine wasn't there. There were all these kids on scooters, but I didn't recognize any of them. And then we had a bite at Arturo's, and while Jason was telling me about his marriage and his novel, he got a call on his beeper so he had to leave. And he kissed me good-bye—on the cheek."

"That's it? What *else* happened? Did he say anything about me?"

"He made me promise not to tell *you* anything about *him!*" Allie said.

"Yes, but did you remember to tell him not to say anything to *me* about *you?*"

"Yes! And he promised right away. He said he would never do anything to hurt me. But this is all so silly," she insisted. "Here are the two of you—two people I admire and like and trust—"

"It's not silly at all," I told her. "Jason has a lot at stake. So do I. And how did you feel," I pointed out, "when he said he would never do anything to harm you? Did *that* seem silly?"

"No," she admitted. "It made me feel . . . special. But I think he meant it as a friend," she added quickly. "This is so confusing. *I'm* not supposed to tell you and *he's* not supposed to tell you but—you already know!"

"It makes perfect sense!"

"Well, I'm sure it does to *you*. But I don't like lying."

"What are you talking about?" I said. "You lied to me for *weeks* about Jack!"

"That," she protested, "was not my fault! You were giving me such a hard time! And besides, I didn't feel *good* about it. If you must know, I felt terrible."

"Great. You'll lie to *me* when it suits you, but you think you're *better* than me because you feel *bad* about it. Thanks a *lot*." I immediately felt like a harridan—and a very unwise harridan at that. I shouldn't be alienating Allie at a time when I need her cooperation!

"I never said I was better than you," Allie replied in an injured tone. "I have never judged you! How can you say that? I—I have to get off the phone. It's been a long day and I'm exhausted. Charmaine hasn't answered any of my calls. And her e-mail keeps bouncing. I hope she's all right."

"I'm sorry," I told her. "I'm just overwrought. I'm tired too. Let me know if you hear from Charmaine."

Reconciled, we both hung up.

Maybe Charmaine packed up her belongings, quit the business, and went back to Pittsburgh. To a simpler, safer—and saner—life. It's too late for me, but maybe that's the answer, I thought, as I drifted off to sleep. Or maybe it *was* the answer, long before I invested my teens, twenties, and a chunk of my thirties, in this sexual rat race.

14 In-Laws and Outlaws

Just when I need her *most,* my shrink is still on vacation,
touring the Greek islands. A shrink's like a hairdresser for
the soul, an indispensable part of gracious living. When
your hairdresser goes on holiday, you can schedule a
precautionary trim, some prophylactic highlights. But
what do you do about your *shrink?* It's hard to plan for
an emotional crisis. Wendy's "assignment" before she left
was "Think about the nature of your secrets." I'm sure she
never imagined I'd be confronted with something as weird as this!

With Wendy out of town, I contemplated my options. Jasmine is
really the only other person I can talk to about this. In the meantime, I'm
steeling myself for the social showdown tonight—dinner with Elspeth,
Matt, and Jason at San Domenico. If I'm too passive, Jason might start
thinking that *I'm* the one with a secret. How long could it take a man of his
intelligence—and imagination—to put it together? Especially given that his
secret happens to be this thing he's got for hookers. Not even a normal
thing—a strange weakness, judging by his Mary Magdalene fixation.

LATER STILL

"Come early," I told Jasmine before our date with Howard. I felt
somewhat guilty about booking her—she's not really his favorite—but
I really wanted to talk to her. And I owed her a date. "There's
something we have to discuss!"

Instead, she managed to show up at the same time as Howard,
because a previous client had messed up her schedule by arriving

late. My performance adrenaline was higher than usual. Nervous energy made my body more enterprising, and Howard attributed this generous mood to Jasmine's presence.

"She really turns you on!" he said. "Let's have her over more often."

But Jasmine knew better. After Howard was gone, she said, "What's up? You're buzzing around this bedroom like a bee on crank."

While she dressed, I told her about Jason and Allie.

"This is the craziest thing I've ever heard!" she exclaimed. "People should not be allowed to go on the radio."

"What are you talking about?"

"WBAI should be *removed* from the airwaves! It is the *only* station that would give that New Age floozy a full half hour. Do you realize that if Allison had not done that radio show she would never have met your future brother-in-law? We have *nonprofit broadcasting* to thank for this social and psychosexual train wreck. If Allison's babble had been drowned out by back-to-back commercials and weather reports, just think! Jason's life would never have been disrupted by Allison's sexual socialism. Who says ideas don't have consequences?" Jasmine demanded.

"I, uh, guess you have a point. But Jason is so devoted to her cause. Who knows? Maybe they would have met *anyway*. With or without the invention of radio. I'm beginning to think they were just destined to find each other." I told Jasmine about the novel he's been writing and the shoes he donated. "And," I added, "it sort of creeps me out that he said they belonged to a *dead sister*. Those were his wife's shoes!"

"Well," Jasmine said, "maybe their marriage is sexually dead and he feels like she's his sister. It's been known to happen." She shrugged. "I wouldn't assume he's *unhappy* in the marriage. Just happier when he has, you know, a little diversion."

"Some diversion! Why can't he be a normal husband who *pays* hookers? Why does he have to be a hooker *groupie?* This might be a diversion for *him,* but it's a disaster for me. And they're not even having sex!"

Jasmine looked as annoyed as I felt.

"Trust Allison to get into some complicated *triangle* that totally endangers you—and the silly bitch isn't even having *sex* with him. *Or* getting money."

If Jason were Allison's client, everybody would know the rules. If only Jason were a client, as I had recently begun to suspect, capable of splitting his life up into appointments. Instead, he's much stranger than that, capable of splitting his life up into *lives.* Capable? Or compelled?

"He's been leading this double life for I don't know *how* long! Maybe years," I said.

"Well, he just met Allison a few months ago. It's not that long."

"But Allie says he's been writing about Mary Magdalene's reincarnation—and doing the research—for ages. He told her he got the idea listening to *Jesus Christ Superstar* when he was a teenager. And," I added, "Allie thought he was a Legal Aid lawyer—in the Bronx. She believed he was completely penniless!"

"He probably thinks Allison *is* Mary Magdalene. I'm surprised he didn't tell her he was a carpenter! She'd probably believe that, too," Jasmine said. "You're right. People like that will *find each other*—even if it is completely inappropriate."

WEDNESDAY, 5/10/00

Last night Matt and I were in a cab, on our way to San Domenico, when his phone started buzzing. "You're kidding," I heard him say. "Okay, man, feel better. Yeah, sure, I'll tell her. Nancy had something like that too, but she's fine now." He hung up. "Jason's got some kind of bug. And he's going home, but he can't find Elspeth." Jason and Elspeth work at opposite ends of town, and they rarely show up together on a work night.

"What's wrong?" Matt said. "You've been kind of jumpy ever since I picked you up."

"Oh, I just . . . didn't get enough sleep," I said, looking out at Central Park. I had been anticipating a chance to make eye contact with Jason, take him aside, spin our encounter in a way that would calm his fears, reducing the likelihood of an escalation. Is Jason having a nervous breakdown? Or just avoiding me? Shouldn't I be glad if he's a little bit afraid of me? But I wasn't thrilled when Matt told him about my own paranoiac "vapors"— now Jason will wonder if I have something to hide from Matt!

When Elspeth finally arrived at the restaurant, she was talking a mile a minute. "Sorrysorrysorry, kids! My day has turned into madness, and it looks like I'll be insane for the next four weeks. Depends how long this takes, of course. How quickly we can *win* this." She was clearly excited about putting someone in jail, making no secret of it, but observing all the necessary discretion. "Anyway, where's Jason? Late as usual?"

"He tried to call you, but he couldn't get through. He had to go home—some kind of bug," Matt told her.

"Oh?" Elspeth looked surprised. "My cell phone's working *fine*. In fact I've been sitting at my desk all afternoon waiting for calls. What is he talking about?" She frowned, then pulled out her phone. Casting a guilty look at us both, she added, "Just a quickie—to my ailing husband. I promise I'll be quiet." But Jason seemed to be avoiding her call. "Honey?" she told his voice mail. "Call me when you get home. I have the ringer off, so you might have to keep calling. Let me know if you need to know where anything is." She put the phone on the table and eyed it conscientiously. "He seemed a little off last night. He came home around nine-thirty, looking kind of sad and exhausted. Then he went straight to sleep! No matter how many times I go through the drill, he can never find anything in the medicine cabinet, poor baby."

I felt a twinge of sympathy for Elspeth. She seemed to regard his physical discomfort as her own—up to a point.

"Must be something that's going around," Matt mused. "A twenty-four-hour virus. Nancy went to sleep early last night, and now she's just fine."

"So," Elspeth said eagerly. "What progress on your wedding date? Did you make a decision yet?"

"Well, I . . . went to the Leopard, and I'm going to look at La Grenouille. I have to pick a place first. Then I'll decide."

"Really? You'd rather have it in a restaurant? Why not a hotel? You know, the Carlyle does a great job. Or the Stanhope."

I was prepared for that, at least. "A restaurant's more intimate," I said firmly. "I've been to . . . events at hotels. And a hotel wedding doesn't work for me. It's not romantic."

"Well, I, personally, cannot think of anything more *romantic* than having everything professionally handled at a hotel," Elspeth replied. "By people who have done this hundreds of times before. And when the reception's over, you two lovebirds can just flutter upstairs to your room and *relax*. That, in a nutshell, is romantic."

"Nancy's the one who's getting married," Matt reminded her. He made a protective gesture in the direction of my arm. "To me." He smiled affectionately.

"Thank god!" Elspeth cackled. "Because siblings can't marry in New York State! This isn't Georgia! Sorry, Nancy. I should save these disgusting jokes for the bachelorette party. Are we having one?"

Matt stood up and made his traditional cell-phone gesture. "It's the office. I have to take this." He disappeared with his phone and Elspeth said, "You two are such cellular *citizens*. Matt never takes a business call at the table, and you never take calls at *all*."

I stared at her numbly. When did she find the time to notice this?

"I've made a study of these things," Elspeth added carelessly. "In Matt's case, it's a professional obligation. He's not allowed to discuss deals in public. In your case . . ." She smiled slowly. "Well, I suppose you're a very private person. Maybe you have a good reason to be." She looked up from her menu and cocked her head to one side. "Your cousin Miranda says you've always been a quiet sort."

"I'm not sure what you mean," I said timidly. How has Jason gotten away with leading such a bizarre secret life under the nose of this natural-born snoop? On the other hand, how could he *not* retreat into a biblically inspired fantasy life? I suppose it was a survival tactic for him.

A waiter appeared and offered more bread. "Yes, please!" I breathed, despite the fact that I was starting to fill up. "Maybe you're right," I said politely. "I was never as much of an extrovert as—as you. Or Miranda."

"No." Elspeth said thoughtfully. "I can see that. Anyway, I booked a table for five at Willow—tentative, I know, but some-one's gotta start moving on this," she said cheerfully. "Can Allison and Jasmine make it?" She pulled out her date book. "I already spoke to Miranda! *She's* game."

"You *did?*" I couldn't hide my irritation. "When?"

"Oh, the miracle of e-mail, I can't remember. I wish all your bridesmaids were as easy to find as Miranda! What's better for Allison? Brunch? Or dinner? Why don't you just give me her e-mail address and let *me* arrange it. And what about Jasmine?"

I grabbed a roll and broke off a piece. Jesus. Has Elspeth become Miranda's new best friend? The idea of my future sister-in-law and my unaware cousin chatting it up—perhaps daily—in e-mail is worrying. And how am I going to get Allison to excuse herself from my wedding party without drawing attention to it? There is no way that Jason and Allie can be at this event together. Does Jason realize that the Allison I know from the gym is also the Allison I've picked as a bridesmaid? Is that why he called in sick tonight?

"I'll have to check!" I said wildly. "Maybe I can give them *your* e-mail address?" Matt was sitting down again, and I looked hopefully in his direction. "Have you been talking to Jason about the wedding plans?" I asked him.

"Not much." Matt was perusing the menu. "What's the big deal? He shows up in a suit on the designated day, just like me. Oh, and he carries the ring." Matt winked at me. "This way, if anything goes wrong, it's not our fault."

"Men always think they'll get off scot-free," Elspeth said with an ominous laugh.

Suddenly, I realized how hurt Allison's going to be. When she realizes that this charming stranger, this admirer of hers, is the best man at my wedding—and that *she's* being sacrificed. She'll "understand," but I don't think our friendship can ever be the same. A wedding is "just a formality," she'll say—but I have a feeling in my gut. She'll take it as a snub. And it will hurt her when she realizes that Jason, at the end of the day, is going to be part of this respectable charade that she can't be part of. It suddenly hit me, as I halfheartedly cut into my roasted sea bass, that I did not want to be the one who delivers this sad comment on reality to Allie while she's in the grip of her idealism. Whatever Jasmine might call her—a "sexual socialist," a New Age floozy, a silly bitch, a moral idiot; and all these things have the ring of truth, to be sure—*she's still my friend*. Can this wedding party be saved? How? I wonder.

"So," I ventured, as matter-of-factly as I could, "Jason has no idea who's in the wedding party?"

"He must know about Miranda and me! Just what are you getting at, Nancy?" Elspeth asked in a sharp cheerful voice.

I almost jumped off my chair. "I—nothing," I mumbled. "I was just thinking that . . . that maybe this is not the best time to discuss the wedding plans. Without Jason here." I allowed my voice to trail off as I chewed a piece of buttered roll.

"Matt's right. Jason has a knack for showing up *exactly* when he should—if it's important. Don't worry. We'll just plan everything and the men will appear, like magic." Elspeth glanced at her flashing cell phone and held it to her ear. "Hi," she whispered gruffly. "Do you want me to pick anything up? Of course! Ginger tea? Where would I find *that?*" She closed her phone and said, "Jason's turning New Age on me. Lately he's been drinking herbal teas!" She seemed to find this rather endearing, and I felt, against my will, a stab of sympathy.

"As I was telling Nancy," Elspeth continued. "You're such a Goody Two-shoes about your cell phone, Matt. And it's funny how Nancy has *never once* taken a call on *her* phone in all the time I've known her! Never once, in my presence. But we all know she has one, because we've all called her on it."

"Really?" Matt said playfully. "I have to think about that."

Please don't!

For dessert, Elspeth ordered strawberry salad and balsamic vinegar ice cream—with three spoons. I couldn't wait for the meal to end as I dipped, reluctantly, into our communal dessert.

WEDNESDAY, 5/17/00

Yesterday Jasmine called just as I was leaving the apartment. "Can you do a very fast 'three' at the Waldorf?" she asked. "I had to cancel on him, and I hate to leave him high and dry. He'll give you cab fare on top of the three. And I won't take the full cut," she offered.

"I don't know if I can! Lorenzo's doing my highlights, and then I have to see Milton, and then I have to meet Matt—we've got tickets for *Aida*. I could try and get Milton to come later. But I'm late for my highlights!"

"Well, you'd better go," she said in that serious tone she reserves for all things pertaining to our mutual hairdresser. "I'll try to get someone else. But call me from Lorenzo's, just in case. And tell him I said hello!"

Lorenzo is the only person I've ever heard Jasmine kissing up to. She has innate respect for anyone who has that much power over the way she looks. I sat on the circular couch at Lorenzo's with the other robed customers. Some of us were crowned (temporarily) with foul-smelling pieces of twisted foil. Others were pacing around with toning solution in their hair, chatting on their phones. I put in a call to Milt's office to see if he could come later. A quickie at the Waldorf would be cutting it awfully close, but it would help me exceed my quota this week.

When the phone trilled, I was sitting in a shampoo chair, with my head flung back, hair falling into the sink. I maneuvered the phone to my ear, and the delicate ballet between cell-phone user and shampoo attendant began. She continued rinsing the back of my hair with a gentle motion, and I tried to keep the phone low down on my ear while arching back to make my hair more accessible.

"Yes?" I answered in a hopeful voice. But it wasn't Milt, it was Allie. "I can't talk now. I'll call you back," I said.

"I just found out— I just had a terrible— I can't believe anyone would do this to me!"

"What happened? What are you talking about?"

"I'm talking about Jack! And Jason!"

"Jesus Christ," I muttered. "Another call's coming in. Hold on. Don't go away!"

"Hello?" I said, hoping for Milton.

"Hey, guess what?" Matt said. "My meeting got canceled and I'm getting out early. Why don't we do something before the show? I'll meet you at six, at Chez Josephine."

"At six! I can't possibly."

"Why? What are you doing?"

"I'm at the hairdresser and I won't be out of here in time!"

"It's four o'clock! You won't be done by six?"

"I just got here! And they're running behind schedule."

I was actually near the *end* of my appointment. But I was determined to keep my date with Milt. And, if possible, find a way to fit the Waldorf in on the way home. There is this thing that happens when you lie to a guy—when you give up business to spend time with him *and* you're lying to him. Somehow, it would be okay to have to lie. It would be okay to give up a few dates to keep the relationship on a happy footing. But if you have to deprive yourself of business *and* lie to your boyfriend, you can start to resent him. It's like being taxed twice on the same money! I was determined *not* to start resenting him.

"Why don't I swing by in a cab and pick you up at the hairdresser?" Matt suggested.

"What? No!" My heart leapt into my throat. "For god's sake," I squeaked angrily. "I'm practically breaking my neck trying to talk to you while I get my hair washed and now the phone's getting soaked! I'll see you at the theater!"

When I switched back to Allison, she was gone. As I sat in Lorenzo's pneumatic chair, I ran through the conversation with Matt. Was I too shrill? Did he sound disappointed? Should I apologize? But maybe that will just draw attention to my strange schedule and make him ask more questions. If I cancel the date with Milton and let Matt pick me up—well, I can say I got lucky at the hairdresser, and—

"What's giving you such a headache?" Lorenzo asked, massaging my scalp with his fingertips.

"Boyfriend problems."

"Tell me about it," he sighed, turning up the heat on the dryer. He pulled a round brush through my hair. "Just take it *one boyfriend at a time,*" he added sagely.

Lorenzo doesn't know about my business, of course, but hairdressers are clued in to the ever-changing, temporary nature of happiness. They know there are only good hair *moments*. A good day may consist of many such moments strung together like beads, but this cannot be guaranteed. It can only be experienced. I think this affects their entire view of love, life, and human connection.

I pulled out my phone to cancel my date with Milton. I hate to do this. It gives a bad impression when you cancel on a regular. A client becomes a regular because you're reliable. But maybe this is a sign—*I can't keep thinking like a hooker who's thirty going on twenty-three. I need to prioritize my men here.*

"I'm sorry, but he's left for the day," a secretary informed me.

As I ran out onto the street, my phone trilled and shook in my handbag. Please let this be Milton, and please let's cancel.

"You disconnected me!" Allison said.

"You hung up! And now I'm trying to find a cab!"

A taxi slowed down, and I watched as two struggling shoppers began to emerge with their bags. Tourists! I wanted to grab them and pull them out of the cab with my bare hands!

"Jack accused me of sleeping with Jason!" Allie exclaimed. "I'm so upset!"

The shoppers appeared to be meditating in there!

"How does he know about Jason? What did you tell him?"

"He's been tailing me for at least four weeks," she moaned. "He hired a private detective!"

"I *told* you he was bad news! The man was stalking you! Remember?"

"I know," she said. "I should have listened to you. But I thought I could handle him and I—I kind of liked having a sugar daddy," she confessed. "I've never had one before."

I hopped into the cab and tried to listen to Allie while I gave directions to the driver.

"If the detective's any good, he knows you weren't sleeping with Jason," I said, hoping the driver couldn't hear. "Unless, of course, you were!"

"I was not!" she protested. "Jason came upstairs to help me install some software. Once! But Jack is so narrow-minded— he can't believe a man would come up to my apartment for two hours and not have sex with me! And he said he wouldn't give me the rest of my tuition money unless I stop talking to Jason."

For a minute, I wondered if this would be a good thing—but only in the short term. It would get Jason out of her life, but it would surely get Jack dug in deeper.

"And," she continued, indignantly, "he wants me stop talking to you, too! To everyone and anyone I have ever worked with! And he's starting up again about interior decorating. He says my interest in social work is causing me to spend too much around—around working girls!" She paused, then said, in an outraged wail, "That disrespectful sneak! He's trying to control my life!"

"This is news to you? What did you expect?"

"I thought he really wanted to help me and maybe was a little insecure. I didn't realize he was a—a patriarchal whore-basher with no ability to *evolve!* The things he said—about you, about me, about the girls on the van! I never want to hear from him again!"

"Well, I think you're making the right move here. Establish boundaries," I said, not wanting to overstate my case.

"Boundaries?" Allie said in a bitter voice. "I just want to get paid by the hour from now on. I'll never get involved with a john again."

As I exited the cab, I looked around anxiously. After all this talk of detectives and tailing, I was thinking that if Matt saw me entering my building—when I said I was really at the hair-dresser—I'd be in a bit of a fix. What would I say? As I unlocked my apartment, I heard the business phone. An abbreviated ring told me the call was now in voice mail, and my kitchen clock told me I had no time to start checking messages.

When Milt arrived, I was undressed to the nines and had rehearsed in my mind an efficient routine designed to get him in and out with minimum time wastage. I rewound the video to the raunchiest anal-sex scene I could find, put on a pair of sexy black marabou slippers, and got myself into a strange crotchless item that was neither a teddy nor a merry widow but a sort of hybrid. I know that Milt knows that I know that this over-the-top cos-tume's inappropriate for "a nice call girl like me"—but that's why he likes it.

While Milt sat watching the video screen, I slipped a con-dom on. Then I surprised him by turning around and sitting on his lap—on his cock actually—with the back of my neck facing him. I slid up and down in my heels, concentrating. It's not the easiest position but it's got novelty appeal, and I use it when I'm in a bit of a hurry—because it requires zero effort on the man's part.

After he came, I carefully lifted myself up and gave him a quick kiss on the cheek. We shared a smile of satisfaction.

While Milt showered, I began to check my voice mail. There were two old messages from Allie and a new message from Liane, trying to set up a date for tonight. Then, as I continued through the queue of calls, I heard a female voice invoking the alias I use with men's secretaries and hotel operators.

"This is Elspeth Mackay," said a warm voice. I stopped, confused. I had not heard this voice before—and yet I had—but never on this particular phone. "I'm with the Manhattan district attorney's office and I'm calling for Suzy Rollins. We'd like to know if you'd be willing to talk to us about Etienne L— P_____." Her pronunciation was very accurate for a non-Francophone—she must be saying his name *a lot*. "If," she continued, in the disarmingly friendly voice, "if you'd like to talk to us, please feel free to call me, anytime this week, to make an appointment." And she left a number.

Elspeth. With none of the sharp edges or crackling notes, her girlish voice was almost unrecognizable. If I didn't know who she was or what she's really like—well, she sounds about fifteen years younger, and you'd never guess that she's an assistant prosecutor! In all the time I've known her, I've never heard her so soft, so pleasing to the ear. So this is what she sounds like on the job! And how strange to think that I naively attributed her caustic ways to her *profession*.

I stared in horror at the dial pad as I continued pressing keys. For one mad moment, I thought that Elspeth had accidentally dialed my number and left a message for someone else—a crossed line, a mistake. But, of course, that couldn't be; she'd dialed my *business* number, and she had the name right. I wanted this to be a bad dream.

Shaking, I replaced the receiver and heard the phone ring. I waited for it to go into voice mail, but it wouldn't stop. When I picked it up, I heard Elspeth's message replaying! I had forgotten to exit the system. I slammed the receiver down and unplugged the phone.

"What's wrong?" said Milt. "You look like you've seen a ghost."

I was standing there in my high-heeled slippers, still wearing my Frederick's of Hollywood costume, trying my best to look composed. My mouth felt stiff.

"Suzy? Are you feeling okay? Maybe you'd better sit down."

I fell into an armchair, then leapt up, as if I'd been scorched. Yikes. I never sit with my bare pussy on a chair or a couch unless it's covered with a towel or sheet!

"Oh, my god," I said energetically. "I have tickets for *Aida* tonight. Do you mind if I start getting ready? It's getting late."

"Understood," Milt said, with a curious searching look. "Did you get some bad news?"

"Yes," I admitted. "Very bad news. And," I said briskly, "I do have to start getting ready."

While he dressed, I took off my heels. I knew it would be more professional to undress in the bathroom—why force him to watch this layer of erotic icing being stripped away? But I didn't want to leave him alone to ponder what was wrong with me. That would be *more* unprofessional.

"I'm sorry, I didn't mean to startle you," I said, pulling out a bra from my dresser. "I just got a strange phone call and I—well, I forgot you were here for a minute."

Oops, *what* did I just say? What is wrong with me?

He smiled at the new piece of underwear. "That's pretty. I've never seen that before. Is this what you wear for your boy-friend?"

"Yes. I guess that's right."

"Sorry—did I say something I shouldn't have?"

I looked up and realized that I had been frowning sadly. I had lost my professional bearings and I wanted to grab hold of

Milton's sleeve, cry on his chest. He looked so comforting and solid in his gray suit—Milton never wears any of that business casual stuff that younger guys like to wear—and he was fiddling with his tie. He looks like the kind of man who can take care of someone. Whereas Matt looks like the kind of guy who will certainly try to.

I pulled on a pair of sexy but simple black panties and gazed up at him.

"You look so young without your heels," he said affectionately. "You look adorable *in* your heels, but even younger in bare feet. I'll bet all the guys tell you that."

"No," I laughed. "You're the only guy who ever tells me that." I could feel the blood returning to my limbs, flexibility returning, and I forgot, for a moment, the terrible phone call—forgot the boyfriend I was now dressing for, the sister who was threatening to expose me. Milt and I were alone in our own little world, and Etienne—"If you'd be willing to talk to us about him!"—didn't exist either. I continued pulling clothes out of the closet while Milton combed his bushy eyebrows with one of my hairbrushes. It was a silent, easy moment, and when he slid the money onto my dresser it was the normal amount that he usually gives. Things fell back into place.

When he was gone, I plugged in my phone. I erased my rather bouncy outgoing message—"Hi! So sorry I missed your call!"—and replaced it with the automated voice of the message system. Elspeth did not recognize my voice—I hope—when she called the first time. But if she calls again, she's sure to pick up on some familiar quality. Now, Suzy Rollins will be less real to her, less of a voice and more the anonymous owner of a telephone. Though it's just a matter of time before she starts looking Suzy's number up in the reverse directory—if Suzy doesn't return her calls. And she'll find out that it's not listed under Suzy Rollins—because there is no Suzy Rollins! Depending on how you define *is*, of course.

And what the hell has Etienne gotten himself into here? I haven't heard from him in weeks, and even if he did call, I dare not answer my business phone. Is this the new case Elspeth was so excited about? What can she want from Suzy Rollins? And what is she trying to do to Etienne?

I made my way to the theater feeling very much like a reigning princess whose days are numbered.

But Matt, completely unaware of the crisis, continued to behave like a very confident courtier who has attached himself to a sure thing.

THURSDAY, 5/18/00

Today, in response to my telephonic smoke signals, Jasmine called twice, hung up, then called again. "You're there!" she said when I picked up. "What is this all about? Why aren't you answering your phone? Liane even called me. She says you left a very weird message for her. You shouldn't do that! She's almost eighty and she gets confused, you know."

"I know." I sighed. "But I was desperate to talk to her. Anyway, I've been calling Barry Horowitz. The office says he's 'on trial' in Phoenix. He hasn't called me back, and I was hoping against hope that you would find him for me. Doesn't he have a private cell phone?"

"Maybe." She paused. "Why?"

Jasmine was being cryptic about her access to Barry. She's known him forever—since she was a juvenile offender, a junior ticket scalper. *She MUST have a private hotline to Barry.* "I'd like to know what this is about, before I start trying to hunt him down. You know, he gets a lot of crazy phone calls," she added.

"If I tell you what happened, you'll never believe me. One of the guys, one of my regulars is in trouble. And they're trying to contact *me.*"

"Which guy?" Jasmine said sharply.

"I don't know if you remember him—Etienne?"

"Sure, that good-looking French guy. Isn't he with one of the auction houses?"

"That's the one. I don't know what he did or why they'd want to talk to me."

"Maybe we should warn the other girls. Have you tried to call him?"

"I'm afraid to! He told me about a month ago that he was going to disappear for a while. For a 'knee operation.' I'm afraid to call him from this phone. I'm afraid to use this phone period! I feel . . . trapped."

"I have an idea," Jasmine said. "Can you meet me at D'Agostino's?"

I found her in aisle 6, wheeling around a shopping basket filled with club soda, hydrogen peroxide, and macadamia nuts. "I called Barry," she said in a low voice. "You're not under arrest or anything. This happens to people all the time—so calm down, okay?"

"I'm having the most god-awful time acting like everything's normal in my life. It never occurred to me that one of my clients could get into trouble! I've spent my entire life trying to stay out of trouble myself! You know how it is. You think of these guys as pillars of respectability."

"Everybody has *something* to hide," Jasmine pointed out. "I spoke to Barry on the way over here. He's coming back from Phoenix tonight."

On my way home from D'Agostino's, I stopped at a pay phone and called Liane. I haven't used a coin phone in ages, and I was taken aback by how grubby a phone can get when it's forced to stand on a street corner, month after month.

"Oh, there you are, I was worried about you! What is this about not answering your phone?" Liane asked. "Can you see Roger tomorrow morning?"

"I'm seeing my *lawyer* tomorrow morning. And anyway, I'd be too much of a nervous wreck to see someone new," I told her. "I'm—I think I might have to leave town for a while."

"Leave town? What sort of trouble have you gotten yourself *into?*" Liane said. "Ask your lawyer before you do anything like that! People always think the solution to their troubles is to leave town. Very often the solution is simply to sit still."

"I didn't want to leave this on your machine. But I want to warn you about Etienne L___ P_____. Do you know him?"

"Why yes, of course. Everyone knows him. I've known him for thirty years—and I knew his uncle. What's happened?"

"He's in some sort of trouble. That's all I know. They called me and left a message—they want to ask me some questions."

"They? Who? The police? The IRS? Did you call them back?"

"No! It was someone from the D.A.'s office. I'm going to see my lawyer first."

"Thank goodness for that. Very sensible, dear. And thank you. Maybe this is a good time to take a minivacation if they're bothering Etienne's . . . personal friends. I appreciate the warning." She paused. "I know this is none of my affair, but how are the wedding plans going?"

"How can you talk about my wedding at a time like this?" I pleaded.

"How could I not, dear? The sooner you marry that young man, the better. I don't know what they want from you or what you could possibly tell anyone about Etienne—probably nothing. But you and I both know that it's troubling when official types ask personal questions. They'll want to know how you met him. If you were already married to your fiancé, you'd be in a much safer position—and you'd be less frightened."

"I don't see how—if I were married now—and he found out—"

"A man will protect his wife if she finds herself in trouble. In fact, the trouble may bring them closer together. He may well abandon the same woman if she's his mistress or his girlfriend or his fiancée. It's just another excuse for a man to jump ship. Marry him yesterday!"

Of course Liane doesn't know about Elspeth. Would that put a different light on her theory? Perhaps not.

FRIDAY, 5/19/00

Yesterday, I arrived at Barry's office twenty minutes early. A young Asian-looking guy with a goatee sat at a desk in the waiting room. He picked up the phone the minute I walked in.

"Ms. N. to see you," he remarked quietly. He looked up, nodded toward the armchairs, and said, "Barry will be out shortly. Nice to see you again," then returned to his keyboard.

He recognizes me from last year, but I suppose "How are you" is not a question he likes to ask because he knows that people basically come here when they're already in trouble.

Barry appeared in the doorway and ushered me past two rooms in midrenovation. "Excuse the architectural bullshit," Barry said. "The contractors are favoring exposed plank this week. Welcome to my temporary office."

Barry was wearing a rather foppish red bow tie, irreverent but expensive suspenders, and his signature mustache. He sat at a small conference table that was littered with take-out cups, Patrick O'Brian novels, paper bags. Then he steepled his hands, just below his bow tie, and said, "What seems to be the trouble? And how are you? I see that you're wearing a very nice ring."

"I'm engaged."

"You don't look so thrilled about it."

"Well, the guy I'm engaged to has a sister who's a prosecutor."

And then I told him what I had hesitated to tell Jasmine and Liane about the phone call I'd received.

"*Okay,*" Barry said, "I wasn't prepared for that. And this potential sister-in-law, shall we call her, has no idea that she called *you?*"

"Right. And I can't tell the girls—anyone in the business—that I'm being hunted down by my boyfriend's sister. I would be—I'm sure I'd be seen as a person who's in way too much trouble. Nobody would want to work with me!"

"You may have a point there. But we're not so sure she's hunting you down. Are we? Maybe she's just casting her net to see what she can find out about your client."

"Well, I can't operate on that assumption."

"No, you can't. But we can hope that Mr. L__ P_____ has thousands of numbers in his Rolodex. And he should if he's running the _____ department at _____."

"I think he knew he was in some kind of trouble," I told Barry. "He told me he was going to drop out of sight to get his knee worked on. And he didn't seem to be feeling well when I last saw him."

I paused, wondering if Barry—a guy—would know immediately that Etienne had been having performance problems. But Barry gave me one of his most unreadable looks.

"When was this?"

"A little over a month ago. He was complaining about his boss."

"Aha. And do you remember what he said? What was his complaint?"

"Well, that he seemed to be having in-law problems!"

"So many people are," Barry observed dryly. "I think I've heard about this guy—not your client but his boss. A number of his relatives work at _____, which is a good thing in some ways and bad in other ways. Legally speaking. And your potential sister-in-law? Who is she?"

"Elspeth Mackay."

"Oh, yes. A piece of work." Barry raised his eyebrows. "I know someone who went to law school with her. She's married to a really good-looking guy, can't remember his name, but he's supposed to be quite a decent lawyer. Elspeth's working on some aspect of an auction fraud case."

"How do you know *this?*"

"It's well-known in certain circles—and it's about to become front-page news. There are at least two auction houses involved. And she's trying to see if a third auction house—that would be _____, where Mr. L__ P_____ works—has anything to offer."

"To offer?"

"Well, nobody at _____ has been charged with anything, but there are a lot of subpoenas out there."

"So," I said, with some relief, "Etienne's not in jail or under investigation?"

"He's not in jail, but he is not exactly leading an entirely normal life. I wouldn't call him if I were in your shoes. The phones at _____, at least in his department, are of great interest to the Manhattan D.A.'s office. Did you save Elspeth's message?"

"Yes!" I picked up the phone. "Do you want to hear it?"

After listening for a few moments, Barry hung up.

"Well, she probably got his message records from a secretary. And she thinks you could be one of his art clients. I hate to say this, but . . . normally people in your profession find it useful to have a sort of nom de guerre, only in this case you'd be in the clear if your usual name was linked to this phone call."

He steepled his fingers and looked thoughtful.

"I would?"

"Well, the beauty of being an art client is that you don't have to buy anything. Anybody who expresses an interest in selling or

buying is regarded as a customer, whether or not they actually follow through. Don't you go to gallery openings and art shows?"

"Sometimes. But what do I do now? Call them back? What
happens if I *don't* call them back?"

"You're not under arrest, you haven't been subpoenaed, and
you have no obligation to contact them. But if you don't, they
might get curious. They might also forget you. Etienne L__
P_____ is a bit of an unknown quantity. If they were asking
about his *boss* I would have to say that avoiding Elspeth's call is
provocative. She's definitely going after his brother-in-law. And
she might get more interested in Mr. L__ P_____. We
won't know for another month or so. What's—do you want a
Kleenex? Here, use my hankie. It's clean."

"She—she was going to be my matron of honor!" I cried. "I
just don't know how I'm going to extricate myself from this! I
can't marry this woman's brother! It's insane!"

"Well, when you put it like that," Barry said sympathetically,
"it's hard to disagree."

*

When I got back from Barry's office, I logged on—and began
composing my e-mail to Matt.

> *Dear Matthew,*
> *Circumstances beyond our control have*
> *forced me to rethink our plans.*

Too bureaucratic, ridiculous. He might think it's one of those
joke letters, and we'd have a big misunderstanding about *that*.

> *Matt,*
> *You know I will always love you more than any*
> *other—*

Nobody over sixteen says or believes this. After all, you can't know how much or how little you will love the next guy in your life.

> *Dear Matt,*
> *You are the only man I have ever considered marrying.*

A good beginning.

> *And there are things I have never been able to tell you.*

Oh god. Then why tell him now? Postpone message. No, delete message.

I spotted some new e-mails from Elspeth entitled "Willow, Sunday brunch" and didn't have the heart to open them. I did, however, read an e-mail from Miranda: "Looking forward—even though I really think Elspeth is vulgar and nosy! But I will enjoy seeing Allison again and meeting Jasmine. See you next Sunday. Your cousin xxx." Her frankness was reassuring.

I haven't said anything to Allison or Jasmine about this brunch or about Elspeth's constant requests for their attention. Why? Because I've always sensed, in my heart, that it would be sheer madness to expose my best friends to someone like Elspeth. And now, with this investigation? It would be unprofessional—right off the map—to put them in harm's way.

Liane was right—in her own way—when she told me not to mix these elements of my life. She had other reasons, but what does it matter? The outcome's the same! And how long can Jason be a reliable nonwitness? If things begin to come out, about my other phone, my possible connection to Etienne, Jason might start wondering about my friendship with Allie. He might—as men often do—crack and confess his infatuation with Allison to Elspeth!

This wedding can't happen, and I'll have to—gulp—return the ring. (Unless I can somehow get *him* to break off the engagement. No, that could take months, maybe even an entire year. And how exactly would I do that, anyway?)

LATER

Just got back from doing a quickie with Harry at Jasmine's apartment. But my heart wasn't in it. Jasmine picked up the slack and did most of the dirty talking while I went through the motions of a blow job. Before we knew it, Harry was dressed and out the door, zipping downtown in his black Town Car.

"You need a vacation," Jasmine bluntly told me. "You're not your usual self."

"Do you think he noticed?"

"Of course not. Harry's oblivious. You know, I have *never* known a more self-centered, self-satisfied guy. You'd have to be a man-hating witch for him to notice anything wrong. Harry's found his equilibrium, and he's just going to stay there for the rest of his life," she said. "You, however. You're nowhere close to an equilibrium. Have those prosecutors called you again? What did Barry say?"

"He thinks there's a chance that other girls will get called and—and it all depends on how interesting Etienne becomes to them. His brother-in-law is the real target, but Etienne works very closely with him."

"So," Jasmine said. "What's going on with this wedding? Did you pick out your china pattern? I was thinking the other day that the sooner you get married, the better. When you're married to a guy, he has that evolutionary agenda. He'll *fight* to protect you. But when there's no commitment, he's less invested. And you keep having all these crises. Jason. Allison. Etienne. Maybe it's nature's way of telling you to pair-bond with Matt—make it legal."

"Nature? That last crisis came from the D.A.'s office," I glumly remarked.

"You underestimate Mother Nature," Jasmine told me. "We are always in a state of nature."

MONDAY, 5/22/00

This morning, Matt confronted me over coffee—not his usual style when he's trying to make a breakfast meeting. I was barely awake, but my recent paranoia has been making it impossible for me to sleep when he's awake.

"You've been very distant for the last few days," he announced. "I want to know why. All weekend I feel like you've been *avoiding* me."

"I can't talk to you about my feelings when I'm half asleep," I protested.

"Well, here, have some more coffee, and let's talk."

"Don't you have a meeting to go to?"

He looked at his watch. "I do. But that's my responsibility, not yours. Why are you trying to get rid of me?"

"I'm not!" I said vehemently. "Would you please stop—I don't wake up as quickly as you do! I feel like I'm being tortured!" And there was a lot of truth to that, but for other reasons, of course.

"Okay." He stepped back to avoid my wobbling coffee cup. "Listen. I do have to make this meeting. But I want you to know that I'm committed to making this relationship work and I know how important it is for us to keep *talking*." He sounded very businesslike as he said this, but how else *can* a civic-minded boyfriend sound at seven A.M. when he's trying to fit a listening session in before work?

I spent the morning wondering, Whatever happened to all those insensitive males who don't know how to verbalize? Who fear communication? Where are these guys when you really need them? Maybe I just don't know how to be with a guy like Matt.

LATER

Around one-thirty, after much pacing and contemplation—if you can call paralysis contemplation—I picked up the phone and dialed my fiancé's cell.

"Are you busy?" I asked.

"Well, I'm on my way to a lunch meeting with a client. Why?" He sounded businesslike and gentle, a poignant combination.

"I want to see you."

"When?"

"Now. Soon. I need to talk to you."

"I . . . I can't exactly—" he said, but I could tell that he was flattered by my urgency. "Can we talk tonight?"

"I'm sorry," I answered. "I just—I've been having these conversations with myself for a week and a half."

"I know. I can tell." He dropped his voice. "I love you. Do you think I can't tell when you're unhappy?"

"I love you, too," I said. "But—" My voice was getting weaker. I was sitting on my bedroom carpet, still wearing my pajamas, with my back against the box spring, staring at my left hand. The sunlight through my blinds hit the side of my engagement ring and seemed to follow the ring even as I removed it. "I don't think we should be planning this wedding. I—I just can't go through with this. I'm sorry, Matt."

He was silent for a moment.

"Are you serious?"

"Do you think I would call you at the office and interrupt your day like this if I *weren't?* Just how frivolous do you think I am? Of course I'm serious!"

I reached for a moisturized tissue.

"Please don't cry like that. I've got a meeting with a client in ten minutes. If I were there, I'd—"

"Oh, Matt, don't! It wouldn't make any difference!"

If he held me, I'd feel better for a while, but the facts wouldn't change. My past is what it is, and this was never meant to be.

15 Turn of the Century

This afternoon, as I was leaving the Parker Meridien, my new cell phone started buzzing in my coat pocket. I pulled it out and ducked into the Chase bank on the corner, instinctively looking around for eavesdroppers. Not that I would ever say anything incriminating in a public place—after what I've been through in the last year.

"*Bonjour, petite mignonne,*" said a long-absent voice.

"Ah, bonjour!" I said playfully yet genuinely surprised. "You're back!" And I was glad I had kept the same number.

"Well," Etienne said, with a hint of regret, "I am just back for a visit. But we must see each other while I am here. I really do miss my old neighborhood. And my old—my young friends."

I smiled at this reference to our age difference.

"After my knee operation, the doctor ordered me to leave New York, and now I am running a small gallery in Paris—I live full-time in my former pied-à-terre."

"Oh, dear," I said, knowing full well that Etienne is extremely happy to have escaped with his pied-à-terre intact. "What happened to Sixty-seventh Street?"

"Oh, my son is living there, but he may sell it. This market!" Etienne chuckled. "So when do I have the pleasure? I am staying at the Pierre for four days."

I frowned. "Are you . . . alone?"

"*Bien sûr.* And at liberty during the day for the most part. My son and his wife try to keep me busy in the evening."

We hung up, having made our date, and I called Jasmine. "You won't believe who's in town," I told her. "And he's carrying on about that fake knee operation—as if all that stuff in the newspapers never happened!"

"You're kidding. Well, he's a born survivor. But you know," Jasmine said, "he did the right thing. If he hadn't left the country, you would have been subjected to endless questions. And look what almost happened to Liane. But you just know he didn't do it to save *our* skins—he must have had much bigger people to protect . . ."

When I got to a safe spot—Tiffany's—I went upstairs to the ladies' room and opened Milton's envelope. After all these years, I still count the money—but not in front of him, of course. And it's always correct. My only recourse, if it weren't, would be to never show up at the Parker Meridien again. But counting the money, minutes after we've parted, and getting the right amount reminds me that I can count on Milton. Makes me glow with affection—and a bit of vain pride.

FRIDAY, 2/2/01

At last, a foolproof way to encrypt my diary. Sadly, I'm unable to *de*crypt my entries from the last six months. But if I can't undo them, nobody else can! So I guess my secrets are safe. Up to a point. Are secrets ever safe?

I wondered about that on my way to the Pierre this afternoon. Etienne has a respectable room—not a lavish suite—with a view of the park.

"It is remarkable," he said, "how one goes outside and feels swamped by tourists in this neck of Manhattan. Yet this hotel casts a magic spell and seems to ward off the crowds, without being haughty."

My first attempt to work a New York hotel bar was at sixteen on the ground floor of the Pierre. I remember it well, and the room seems not to have changed much.

"Yes," I said. "It's been my favorite hotel ever since I arrived in the city."

Etienne was sitting patiently on the bed, watching me undress. I affected a casual manner and giggled a bit when my small pink thong was the only thing left.

"How I have missed this delightful pink circumstance!" he said. "Come sit next to me."

He hasn't changed, of course. As I slid onto his lap, he brought his mouth closer to mine—closer and closer while I gracefully fell onto the sheet, evading his kiss.

"As tricky as ever," he said. "What is your excuse today?"

"I'm saving my kisses for my husband," I told him.

"Your husband . . ." He glanced at the rings on my left hand. "Somebody was quite busy during my absence! You *are* a sly child. I cannot leave New York without losing you to some—some *husband*," he said, as if a husband were actually a variety of pirate.

Etienne himself is a husband but suspends a lot of detail when he's flirting.

"Did you have a splendid wedding? Where was it? I did not see your picture in the *Times*. Though of course, I do not read the *Times* with any regularity anymore."

"No," I said, with relief. I'd never wanted it to be in the *Times*—too many nagging fears about certain people perhaps having something on Matt if they were to recognize my name or my picture. "We were married by a judge. We eloped."

"No family? No in-laws? No cake? A *real* elopement?"

"The real thing," I said smugly. "No complications with bridesmaids or best men, either."

"Lucky bride, lucky groom," Etienne said thoughtfully. "Family situations are highly overrated. Especially those concerning in-laws."

"I know," I said, looking right at him. "And if you hadn't left the country, perhaps I wouldn't have married."

He smiled pleasantly—he thought I was just flirting—but it's truer than he realizes.

"Off with your G-string," he said aggressively (for a gentleman over sixty).

I enjoyed the civilized tugging at my thong and lifted my buttocks to help him slip it off. I opened my thighs slowly as he leaned down to lick me.

Will I never tire of being treated like a saucy young girl by a man old enough to be my grandfather? I don't understand how other women can live without this. Now that I'm married, does this make me a sociopath? I like to think I would have been considered quite normal at the turn of the last century. . . . So was I just born at the wrong time?

It's been said that nobody is more a product of his time than the man who thinks he was born in the wrong century.

It's probably true of working girls, too.